FAMOUS LAST WORDS

Also by
KATIE ALENDER

Bad Girls Don't Die

From Bad to Cursed

As Dead as It Gets

Marie Antoinette, Serial Killer

FAMOUS
LAST
WORDS

BY KATIE ALENDER

Point

For Kevin, Jillian, and Robert,
whom I love and admire
for their strength and resilience

Library of Congress Cataloging-in-Publication Data

Alender, Katie, author.
Famous last words / Katie Alender. — First edition.
pages cm
Summary: High-schooler Willa has just moved to California with her mother
and film director stepfather, and she will be attending a private school — but
her real problem is that she keeps seeing things that are not really there, like
a dead body in the swimming pool, and her visions may be connected to a
serial killer that is stalking young girls in Hollywood.
ISBN 978-0-545-63997-2 (jacketed hardcover) 1. Paranormal fiction.
2. Serial murderers — California — Los Angeles — Juvenile fiction.
3. Stepfamilies — Juvenile fiction. 4. High schools — California — Los
Angeles — Juvenile fiction. 5. Detective and mystery stories. 6. Hollywood
(Los Angeles, Calif.) — Juvenile fiction. [1. Mystery and detective stories.
2. Clairvoyance — Fiction. 3. Serial murderers — Fiction. 4. Stepfamilies —
Fiction. 5. High schools — Fiction. 6. Schools — Fiction. 7. Hollywood (Los
Angeles, Calif.) — Fiction.] I. Title.
PZ7.A3747Fam 2014
813.6 — dc23
2014008920

10 9 8 7 6 5 4 3 2 1   14 15 16 17 18

Printed in the U.S.A.   23
First edition, October 2014
Book design by Yaffa Jaskoll

CHAPTER 1

Nothing glittered.

I'd never been to Hollywood before, but like any other person with eyeballs and a television, I'd seen it a thousand times. I expected wide, palm-tree-lined roads and mansions that overflowed with fabulous movie stars.

What I got was a normal city. Except the sky was pale brown, and the freeways went on forever in every direction. The houses crept up the sides of distant mountains like a fungus. Nobody looked particularly fabulous, especially not the roving bands of tourists taking pictures of every street sign, sidewalk, and tree.

I felt a little cheated, to be honest.

"There's Hollywood Boulevard," my new stepfather, Jonathan, said. "That's where you'll find the Walk of Fame and the Chinese Theatre. We should go there tomorrow."

Party foul. "Tomorrow's Monday," I said. "I start school."

"Oh, right." He was quiet for a second. "Well, they're nothing special. Just a bunch of old footprints and handprints. Movie stars had tiny feet."

"Even the men, right?" my mother piped up. "I think I read that somewhere."

I didn't reply. Not speaking when I had nothing to say had become a bit of a habit for me.

"Look, Willa! The Hollywood Sign — right through those buildings!" Mom's nose was practically pressed up against the glass, and her voice had the chirpy cheerfulness of a preschool teacher.

I squinted to see the line of writing on a far-off hillside. "Oh . . . yeah," I said. "Cool."

"Are you all right?" She studied me, concealing her anxiety beneath a thin veneer of calm. "Do you have a headache?"

"Why would she have a headache?" Jonathan asked.

My mother clamped her mouth shut.

"I'm good, Mom," I said.

As exciting as it was to ride from the airport to our new house in a stretch limo, the limitations of this mode of transportation were tragically apparent. I sat on the front bench, facing backward, with Mom and Jonathan on the forward-facing bench looking directly at me. It was like being in a fishbowl. Give me the backseat of our old Camry anytime — at least there was relative privacy.

But there was no more old Camry. No more old anything. My new stepfather was rich, which meant Mom and I were rich, too . . . unless I messed everything up.

No. I'd already destroyed our lives once. It wasn't going to happen again.

If we had to leave, what would we go back to? Joffrey, Connecticut — a town where we no longer belonged. No house, no job, no car. No friends.

This new life in California was the end of the line for us. It was going to work out.

Because, well . . . it had to.

We followed a series of labyrinthine streets to 2121 Sunbird Lane. There was a little hiccup in my heart as our new home came into view.

Jonathan always referred to it as simply "the house," but apparently he had a pretty warped idea of what a house was, because this was obviously a full-on mansion.

It was separated from the road by a tall privacy hedge and a metal-spiked fence. The front yard was huge and perfect, with freshly mowed grass and a fountain in the center.

I stood in the driveway looking around while Jonathan and the chauffeur got our bags out of the car. The house (there, see? I was doing it, too) was an elegant old Spanish-style with crisp white stucco walls and a red-clay-tile roof. Its beauty was simple, unadorned . . . and expensive-looking.

"Willa?" Mom called. "You coming?"

With a start, I realized that they were waiting for me on the front porch.

Jonathan unlocked the dead bolt. "The door's original," he said, sounding proud — as if a plank of wood lasting almost a hundred years was somehow a credit to human ingenuity and not, you know, trees.

Inside, the house was cool and open. Pale sunlight streamed in, reflecting off the cream-colored walls and gleaming hardwood floors. Overhead, a heavy iron chandelier was chained to the wall from three sides, like a wild animal. A set of stairs curved gracefully toward the second story.

My mother spun in a circle, taking in all the details. "It's gorgeous, Jonathan. When was it built?"

"Nineteen thirty-three," he said. "For an actress named Diana Del Mar."

"Really?" Mom said. "We *love* her movies! Willa, remember those old musicals we used to watch at Grandma's house?"

A vague memory bubbled to the back of my mind — kaleidoscopic arrays of dancing girls with fluffy skirts and huge headdresses, armies of bright-eyed young women cheerfully marching around in tap shoes.

"Sure," I said.

"She was big in the thirties, and then she had a string of flops. She got a reputation as box office poison and retired." Jonathan sounded a little apologetic, like he wished he could give us a better movie star.

"Amazing." Mom ran her hand over the banister. "Just think of all these walls have seen and heard."

"People have probably died here," I said.

Mom winced a little, then tried to laugh. "Oh, Willa."

But Jonathan nodded. "I'm pretty sure Diana Del Mar *did* die here. I don't know the exact story of when or how, though."

"We could look it up online," Mom said. Her frantic agreeableness made my brain itch.

"Or we could ask her ghost," Jonathan said, winking at me like we had an inside joke.

I turned away, a chill passing up my spine.

Does he know?

He can't possibly.

My mother wandered a little farther into the foyer, and I wondered if she felt as out of place as I did — or even more so. After all, I still got to be a relatively normal teenager. For her, this house represented a whole new identity, as the glamorous wife of a famous Hollywood film director.

It was hard to reconcile that with the picture I'd always had in my head of her as a decidedly non-glamorous suburban mom. Still, she was slim and pretty — my height, five foot six, with the same dark chocolate-brown hair as me. Our eyes were the same muted blue that edged into gray. I had her high cheekbones, but softer features in general — people had always said I looked more like my dad.

I could almost picture Mom at a movie premiere, walking the red carpet. Jonathan told us he wasn't famous enough for the paparazzi to care about, but his agent had already called him about magazines wanting the inside scoop. *Rich, successful director sweeps small-town widow off her feet. Whirlwind romance leads to Valentine's Day wedding at City Hall.* Apparently there was a Cinderella element to the story that people found irresistible.

Only . . . if my mother was Cinderella, what did that make me? One of the dancing mice? Maybe a pumpkin.

Jonathan led us on a tour of the house. The gourmet kitchen that overlooked the backyard. The dining room, with its massive oak table. The den, with a huge flat-screen TV and oversize leather couch. The formal living room, with a fireplace big enough to park a golf cart in. The powder room. The other powder room. The study, with shelves and shelves of DVDs. The master bedroom, with its soaring beamed ceiling and four-poster bed. There were even a maid's room and a butler's room and a chauffeur's quarters out near the garage — though, as Jonathan pointed out, we had neither a maid nor a butler nor a chauffeur — just a cleaning lady named Rosa who came twice a week.

And that was just the ground floor.

Upstairs were four more bedrooms, each with its own attached bathroom. And at the end of the hall, Jonathan's office, where he and his assistant worked on the days when Jonathan wasn't needed on set or at the studio. I pictured an uptight secretarial type lurking around and decided I might be spending a lot of time in my room.

Jonathan had lived alone since he bought the house a year earlier, but it was furnished for a family of eight or nine people, with enough bathrooms for all of them to go at once. Even with the three of us, it seemed echoing and empty.

The last stop on the tour was my bedroom.

"If you want one of the others, feel free to switch," Jonathan said, pushing the door open. "We put you here because it's the most private."

It was a nice room, with a big window looking down over the backyard. The furniture was heavy wood and clearly expensive — definitely not the kind that came in a box with its own little tools for assembly. The pictures on the walls were of fruit and sailboats. I walked closer to inspect them and found they weren't just prints — each one was an actual painting, with brushstrokes and a signature and everything.

"Take those down, put up whatever you want," Jonathan said. "You guys can go shopping over the weekend."

Shopping — with his credit card, spending his money? No, thanks. I'd rather live with boring still lifes, even if they were as far from my style as you could get. In fact, nothing in the room reflected my style — or the style of any person under thirty.

But it was fine.

Mom cleared her throat. "Maybe Willa wants a little time to get settled. Take a shower or check her email."

Maybe Willa's right here and you don't need to talk about her in the third person.

But I was grateful for the opportunity to be alone. I waved to Mom and Jonathan as they left, then shut and locked the door.

There was something I needed to do, and it had nothing to do with checking email.

My heart began to thud as I set my suitcase on the bed and unzipped it.

You don't have to do this. You can quit. Turn over a new leaf. Start your new life like a normal person instead of a superstitious loser.

I dug through my toiletry bag for a small black suede pouch, out of which I fished a silver ring set with an oily-looking green stone. Tucked inside one of my sneakers, wrapped in tissue paper, was a purple candle and book of matches. I lit the candle and set it on the nightstand.

7

Then I slipped the ring on my finger and sat cross-legged on the bed with my eyes closed, taking a deep, self-conscious breath.

I imagined every corner of the room filling up with a bright white light. (Supposedly the souls in the beyond love white light. They're drawn to it like moths to a flame. Immortal moths.)

No matter how many times I'd done this, I always felt slightly silly. . . . But here's the weird part: After a minute or so, something happens — something I can't explain. My whole body starts to sweat, especially my forehead, around my hairline. And I get a pounding insta-headache.

The book says to wait for a sign that you've made contact — a sweaty headache could be a sign of connection, right? — and then you have to concentrate on your intentions.

Dad.

It's Willa. I'm looking for you. Find me. Please.

I'd been repeating these words for more than a year. Once a day, sometimes twice.

There was no response.

There had never been a response.

I waited a few minutes in silence, then slid the ring off my finger.

Bye, Dad. Talk tomorrow . . . maybe.

I pictured the white light beginning to fade out, like it was on a dimmer switch.

Suddenly, the whole house gave a sudden bone-rattling jolt.

My first earthquake, I realized.

Then another thought dawned on me . . . one that left me with a sour taste in my mouth.

Had it really been an earthquake . . . or was it just in my head?

Stranger things had happened, unfortunately. It wasn't just headaches that struck like a thunderclap. I'd catch swiftly moving blurs of foggy light at the edges of my vision and hear random sounds without any possible source. I'd lose my footing when I walked — like that horrible feeling when you reach the bottom of the stairs and expect another step but there isn't one.

It was all those things. And even more than that, it was this sense I had — almost an instinct — that I couldn't trust myself.

It had begun shortly after my father's death. Mom, a brand-new widow, was understandably concerned that her daughter was suddenly having bizarre episodes. She was convinced I had a tumor and insisted on getting me a slew of medical tests, including an echocardiogram and an MRI. Thankfully, the doctors gave us the all clear, and for the past year or so, things had been calm. In fact, Mom was so sure my problems were in the past that she never bothered to mention any of it to Jonathan.

What she didn't know was that the problems weren't in the past.

I just wasn't telling her about them anymore. I taught myself to live this way, to make things easier for everyone.

Early on, one of the doctors suggested to Mom that the cause might be emotional, and that I should try talking to someone about my father's death. But I refused.

Believe me when I say that I could spend the rest of my life *not* talking about that morning.

There was a panicked knock at the door.

"Willa? Willa?" Mom shook the doorknob. "Are you all right? It's locked! Can you let me in?"

I snapped back to reality and turned to blow out the candle, but the flame was already extinguished, black smoke floating lazily toward the ceiling. I shoved the ring under my pillow and opened the door.

Mom's eyes were wide as she pulled me into a frantic hug. "Did you feel that? Are you okay?"

"Yeah," I said, wriggling free. I did feel okay — my mood was greatly improved by the knowledge that I wasn't the only person who'd felt the jolt. "Is Jonathan okay?"

"Yeah, he's fine." She smiled sheepishly. "He says it hardly even qualified as a quake. Sorry to make a fuss. You know, if there's ever an earthquake and you're not here, you need to call me immediately to tell me you're all right."

"Even if I'm trapped in a pile of rubble?" I asked.

She turned a color I can only describe as "bright gray."

"Mom, it was a joke." *Note to self: no more jokes.* "You're in California now. You have to loosen up a little or they'll send you back to Connecticut."

She gave me another hug. "Oh, look!" she said, peering over my shoulder. "You're already settling in. How great."

I glanced down at the candle.

Which was lit again.

"Really, Willa, I'm so pleased that you're embracing all of this," Mom said. "A lot of people wouldn't."

I smiled and tried to ignore the curious little chill that crawled up my spine.

Mom gave me a gentle pat on the cheek. "We're ordering dinner in. Is Thai okay?"

"Sure," I said.

"But not for a couple of hours. So unpack or read or . . . or maybe rest? Or whatever."

I closed my door again and sat on the bed, then leaned over to blow out the candle. I took the ring out from under my pillow and tucked it back into the little suede bag. Then I opened the nightstand drawer and put the ring inside, careful to tap three times on the wood to drain any pent-up energy from the realm beyond.

Okay, yeah. I realize it all sounds a little over the top. Maybe even ridiculous. But ridiculous or not, I couldn't stop myself. No matter how many times I vowed to quit, every night I found myself with the candle lit, the ring on my finger, trying to get through to my dad.

Because I needed to find him.

I needed to tell him I was sorry I killed him.

CHAPTER 2

"Are you kidding?" Mom's fork hit the side of her plate with a clatter. "A serial killer?"

"It's not an imminent threat," Jonathan said. "I mean, it's not a threat at all."

He'd come to the dinner table tense, the *Los Angeles Times* website pulled up on his iPad, and told us about a recent spate of murders that had been occurring in LA. The killer's latest victim — a young woman — had been discovered earlier in the day. Pinpricks of fear and curiosity shot through me.

Mom was taking the news a little harder than I was. "But it seems like you're warning Willa," she protested, glancing at me with an expression approaching crazy-paranoid googly-eyes.

Jonathan shook his head, reaching for his water glass. "I wanted to tell you both," he explained, "because it's important to be aware. Not because there's a chance that anything might happen."

"Maybe not to us," I said, shrugging. "But for some people there's a chance."

"A specific category of people. Actresses." Jonathan looked over at me, a hint of sardonic amusement in his eyes. "You're not an actress, are you?"

I was about to say no, but Mom interrupted. "She has done some acting."

"Mom," I said. "Seriously."

I could have sworn I saw a wary flash come over Jonathan's features. Like he was momentarily questioning whether my mother had schemed and married him to advance my acting career.

"She played a juror in *Twelve Angry Men*."

"Two years ago," I said, taking a bite of pad Thai. "Freshman year, before I knew better. And the general consensus was that I made a very poor angry man. Mom, it's not about people who happen to have been in a school play."

"How could you know that? Who knows what goes on inside the mind of a killer?"

Jonathan sighed. "I'm sure Willa will take care to avoid *any* circumstance where she could be mistaken for an actress."

"Absolutely," I said.

"Don't tease," Mom said.

Jonathan patted my mother's hand reassuringly. "The last murder was five months ago. Well, until today. There have only been four, total. Even if Willa were an actress, the odds are astronomically small that anything would happen to her."

"But it's cool," I said. "Because I'm not an actress. And I never will be one."

"Promise?" she said, smiling a little.

I held up my right hand, like I was swearing an oath. "I hereby promise that I will never be an actress."

"Very wise," Jonathan said, nodding. "Acting is a hard life, even when you're successful. Maybe especially when you're successful."

"Willa might be a writer," Mom said.

Oh, come on. I stuffed another bite of noodles into my mouth and looked away.

"Really?" Jonathan said. "What do you write?"

"Nothing, actually," I said. "Nothing at all."

"She used to write a lot."

"That's in the past," I said. "Writing is for people who have something to say."

"Oh, honey," Mom said, looking hurt. "You have so much to say. What's inside you is so . . ."

Um, no. I turned to Jonathan, eager to change the subject to something less depressing than my mother's useless hopes for my future. "Hey, let's talk more about the murders."

"Oh, *honestly*, Willa," Mom said, seeing right through my plan.

Jonathan sat up straighter. "Well, they're pretty interesting, actually. Macabre, but interesting. The killer recreates iconic scenes from classic movies. He posed his first victim to mimic the final attack scene from *The Birds*. Then there was the wheelchair falling down the stairs from *Kiss of Death*. . . ."

I shivered, trying to picture it. I hadn't seen either of those movies, but I felt a twinge of morbid curiosity. Maybe that was what made the murderer do such awful things — knowing that people would be so intrigued.

"What do they call the killer?" I asked. "They all have nicknames, right?"

Jonathan looked down at his iPad. "The media's been using the name 'the Hollywood Killer.'"

I stared down at my glass of water. "How about *'the Screamwriter'*?"

"That's actually pretty good," Jonathan said.

"A little over-the-top," I said.

"Yeah, but it's catchy," he said.

"Catchy?" I said. "Or gimmicky?"

"Oh, for heaven's sake, you two," Mom said. "This is not proper dinnertime conversation."

No, I suppose it wasn't. But for the first time in a long time, I'd felt normal for a couple of minutes. Of course, what did it say about me that joking about murders made me feel normal?

After we carried our dinner dishes into the kitchen, Jonathan cleared his throat. "So, Willa. I got you something. A welcome-to-California present."

He set a large, flat box on the kitchen counter. It was wrapped in pearl-white paper with a hot-pink bow.

"You shouldn't have," Mom said.

"Really," I said.

"No, I wanted to." He rested his hands on the granite countertop. "I know this isn't an easy transition for you. And I know that I could never replace your father — and I'm not going to try. But I do hope we can be . . . friends."

I was speechless, in a horrified sort of way. I'd assumed that everything that needed to be said between us would eventually make its way to the surface. But this grand declaration of friendship? Mentioning my dad? Giving me a present? It seemed like such a cheap, obvious move to buy my goodwill.

Anger flared up inside me, and it took all the self-control I had to stamp it out.

"Yes . . . friends," I managed to say. I carefully unwrapped the box, aware that both my mother and Jonathan were watching my reaction with eagle eyes.

"Oh, wow," I said. "Wow."

"What is it?" Mom asked.

It was . . . a monstrosity.

It was a backpack, but instead of being made out of regular backpack material — I don't know, canvas? — it was tan leather, printed with small interlocking *G*'s. It had a huge green-and-red-striped patch down the pocket, and a giant gold *G* logo.

"It's Gucci," Jonathan said, in the same self-satisfied tone of voice he'd used to brag about the door.

"Gucci," I said. "Fancy."

"It's beautiful." My mother reached out and touched it with the tips of her fingers, like it was a prize racehorse.

"There's more." Jonathan grinned at me and wrapped his arm around Mom's waist. "Look inside."

As I drew the zipper pull smoothly along its path (okay, the zipper was excellent quality, I'll give him that), I was already cringing inwardly at the prospect of what I'd find inside. I pictured a hideous blinged-out watch or a designer fedora or something.

But it was a computer. A beautiful, brushed-metal, razor-thin laptop.

"I thought you could use it for school," he said.

"Thank you," I said. "I'm sure it'll be really useful." There was no point acting like this was the greatest gift anyone could have ever given me, because I knew enough about my new stepfather to know that spending fifteen hundred dollars on a computer was no big deal to him.

"Jonathan, you shouldn't have," Mom said. "Willa has a laptop."

"That rickety old one she was using on the plane? The screen's practically falling off."

But my dad gave it to me, I didn't say. My dad, who knew I was desperate for a computer of my own. My dad, who brought his old work laptop home for me when they were upgrading him to a new one. The night he gave it to me there had been joyous squealing and hugs and jumping up and down.

That was nothing like this night.

Jonathan was buying me nice things to keep the peace and make himself feel better about uprooting me. Not that it wasn't a perfectly kind gesture, but make no mistake — this wasn't about what I wanted.

Which was fine, because I didn't want anything.

Nothing money could buy, anyway.

I woke with a start in the middle of the night.

The clock read 3:23, and I had a headache that felt like two sharp electrified sticks were trying to meet in the center of my head. Under my multiple layers of blankets, I was drenched in sweat.

I sat up and pushed off the covers. The room was too bright. I'd forgotten to close my curtains before falling asleep, and the ceiling was awash with rippling moonlight reflected off the surface of the pool outside. But that wasn't it. There was another source of light. . . .

The candle, flickering away on my nightstand.

Don't be ridiculous. The candle can't be lit.

But the candle was totally lit.

I searched for an explanation. Maybe Mom had come in and lit it. . . . You know, the way every safety-obsessed mother lights candles around the house in the middle of the night. Maybe it was one of those novelty candles that relights itself. Except it was the third one from a three-pack, and neither of the others had ever done anything like this. . . .

Or there had been a trace of a spark burning on it all evening, and then it had gradually reignited itself.

That had to be it. Because any other explanation would be crazy.

And I was *so* not going to go crazy right now.

But I was unnerved, and a little wired. I wandered to the window, my head suddenly full of the Hollywood Killer and my lame new backpack and the earthquake and everything strange about my life now. The strangest thing, by far, being that I was here, in *California*. Everything I'd ever known was carrying on without me, three thousand miles away, on a completely different part of the continent.

I realized I was staring longingly down at the pool.

I love to swim. Even after what happened with Dad, I still love it. I feel more like myself in the water. It holds you together in a way that air doesn't.

I found my swimsuit in a box marked SUMMER CLOTHES and grabbed a fluffy towel from the bathroom. I twisted my long hair up into a bun and secured it with two bobby pins.

There was no way Mom and Jonathan would hear me from across the massive house, so I didn't bother to be particularly quiet as I found my way outside through the doors off the living room.

The temperature was about forty-five degrees, and my skin was instantly blanketed with goose bumps. Under my feet, the patio tiles were so cold they practically burned.

The backyard was amazing, truly befitting a Hollywood legend. Tucked throughout were pristine white loungers and comfy-looking chairs surrounding squat clay chimneys. To my right was a charming little cottage — a guesthouse? — with a miniature front porch and a pair of small windows like curious, watchful eyes. The landscape was shady and rambling and lovely.

But I only had eyes for the pool. It was huge and gorgeous, with gentle curving edges and a rock waterfall, and it glowed an otherworldly pale aqua in the moonlight.

A breeze ruffled the leaves in the trees and sent me hurrying for the water. I figured someone like Jonathan — who was so pool-proud he'd given us a mind-numbing tour of the entire chlorine-free filtration system — had to keep his pool heated, even in March. And I was right — instantly, luxuriant warmth shrouded my body. It drew me down the steps like a siren's call.

I ducked under, the water covering me in a second skin. For a few minutes, I floated on my back and stared up into the inky night sky, the cold air on my face and the sound of my own breathing echoing in my ears. Then I flipped over and swam as far across the pool as I could without coming up for air. I felt clarified and cleansed, like the tension had been wrung out of me.

I bobbed up at the deep end, taking a big breath. I prepared to plunge under again and swim back to the shallow end. I could almost imagine that I was Diana Del Mar, a movie star, and this house was all mine — no stepfathers or headaches or new school to worry about — just me, beautiful and adored, gliding like a water nymph through my fabulous swimming pool.

Then something brushed my ankle.

I yelped in surprise and spun around, treading water as I searched for whatever had touched me.

Nothing — there was nothing.

It must have been bubbles, a random current — maybe a sunken palm frond.

But then I felt it again.

This time it took hold and pulled me under.

Fear and adrenaline burst through me in a massive, soul-shaking pulse. My heart slammed around in my chest like it was trying to break out of my rib cage.

Then something grabbed my other foot.

For a moment, I didn't even process it as something that was really happening. Because it couldn't be happening — it wasn't happening —

Only it was.

I tried to kick free, but my legs were held fast.

I managed to flail above the surface of the water and gasp in an enormous breath before being yanked back down toward the blue-tiled bottom of the pool.

My brain was on red alert, acting on pure animal instinct. *THIS IS NOT OKAY.*

I thrashed and groped at my ankles in an attempt to pry off whatever had wrapped around them. But I couldn't free myself. In fact, as far as I could see, there was nothing to free myself *from* — not another person. Not a rope or piece of plastic. Not even a nightmarish monster.

Only the sharp outline of my own body as I flipped and struggled.

I was rapidly running out of air. Panicked, I looked up toward the sky — and saw another person in the water.

For the briefest second I thought it was someone else swimming, and I wondered wildly why they wouldn't help me.

But then it hit me with ironclad certainty — this person wasn't swimming.

They were floating.

And it wasn't a person. . . .

It was a corpse.

CHAPTER 3

I stared in terrified stillness at the body floating overhead like an abandoned ship adrift on a calm sea.

The corpse was female, wearing a knee-length skirt and a gauzy blouse that formed a translucent border around her rib cage, like the body of a jellyfish. She was barefoot, and her hair hovered in a thick halo around her head, silhouetted against the night so that I couldn't tell what color it was, or how long.

I couldn't see her face. . . .

I was *so* glad I couldn't see her face.

Suddenly, whatever had been holding my ankles let go.

My lungs burned. But as badly as I wanted to reach the surface, I didn't want to float upward and collide with a dead body. I fought my way toward the shallow end. In what felt like a year but was probably just five seconds, I was finally able to stand up and gulp in air. My eyes locked on the deep end of the pool . . . which was empty.

Ever so slowly, I forced myself to turn around. Maybe the body had made it across the pool without my knowing it —

floating behind me . . . inches away, about to brush my bare skin with her cold, swollen hands . . .

Suddenly, something was alive and thrashing next to me. Then I was being grabbed and dragged through the water again. I frantically fought to push away.

"Stay calm!" The voice, deep with authority, echoed off the walls of the courtyard. "I've got you, just stay calm!"

Jonathan.

"No! I'm fine — I'm not —" I tried to say, but by then we'd made it to the steps of the pool, and he could see for himself that I was fine.

Well, fine-*ish*. I'd been better, let's put it that way.

"Willa!" Mom came running over and reached out for me. "What on earth are you doing?"

"Nothing," I said, staying clear of her arms. "Nothing."

Jonathan was panting. "We saw you from the window. You were struggling."

I didn't know what to say. If I pretended nothing had been wrong, it would be obvious that I was lying. But I couldn't possibly tell the truth.

"My hair got caught in the filter," I said without thinking. Then I saw my mother's gaze land on the tight bun coiled at the top of my head. "I mean, my necklace."

They both looked at my bare neck.

"I managed to break it, but it got sucked down." I shrugged. "It's okay, though. It wasn't an important necklace."

For a moment, nobody spoke. Then Mom stepped toward me again.

"Come on," she said, wrapping the towel around my shoulders and hustling me toward the house. "It's freezing out here."

"The water's pretty warm, actually," I said. "It's nice."

Except for the dead body.

The tiny, crisp buds of the night-blooming jasmine on the trellises framed the entryway like glow-in-the-dark stars. After Jonathan shut the door, we stood in an awkward triangle of silence, still surrounded by the flowers' dreamy-sweet scent.

I pulled the towel tighter around me. "I'm sorry. I was just trying to clear my head."

"I hope it worked," Jonathan said, the tiniest hint of irritation in his voice.

Yeah, well. Not quite.

"Good night," Mom said, kissing me on the forehead. Then they turned and started down the long hall that went to the master suite, leaving me alone in the darkness.

The next morning, my mother steered Jonathan's SUV into the parent drop-off lot at my new school, Langhorn Academy.

Back in Connecticut, all the local private schools had ivy-covered brick buildings and manicured grounds. Langhorn — one of the fanciest and most exclusive schools in LA — looked like an industrial office park. It was a collection of boxy concrete buildings set between a tattoo shop and a furniture store that sold chairs shaped like hands.

"Want me to come in with you?" Mom asked.

"No, thanks," I said. I mean, I didn't expect to win any

24

popularity contests, but I did have my pride. "The paperwork's taken care of, right?"

She nodded. "Just go to the office and talk to Mrs. Dunkley. She'll get you your schedule."

"Okay. See you later." I nervously smoothed the hem of my green-and-black-plaid pleated skirt. I still couldn't believe I had to wear an actual uniform. I couldn't shake the feeling that I was going to a really stressful costume party.

"Willa," Mom said, "wait."

I waited, even though I wanted to get out of the car quite badly.

Was she going to talk about last night? After hours of fitful, restless sleep, I'd managed to convince myself that the dead body I'd seen had been nothing more than a stress-induced hallucination. I wasn't eager to rehash the incident.

But it wasn't that. Mom reached sheepishly into her purse. "I got you a present, too. It's not as nice as Jonathan's, but . . ."

Not as nice as the monstrosity currently sitting between my feet, mocking me with its grotesque designer logos?

I took the small, flat package from her. Even before I peeled the wrapping paper off, I knew it was a journal. The cover was caramel-colored leather, and the pages were plain white, unlined. It was a perfectly nice journal . . . for a person who needs that kind of thing in their life.

"Oh," I said.

"Listen, I know you don't think you have anything to write about, but I think if you just let yourself try . . . Even if it's just one line every day."

"It's great." I wished I could inject even a hint of sincerity into my words. "Thanks."

"Don't do that." Mom's voice was barely above a whisper. "Don't just say 'great' when things aren't great. I'm your mother, Willa. You can say anything to me."

Anything? Maybe there was a time when I could have told her about trying to communicate with Dad. Maybe I could have told her that the headaches and visions never really went away. Maybe even that I thought I'd seen a corpse. Or that something had held me down in the pool last night.

But now, I wouldn't even know where to begin. Telling her about any of it would mean telling her *all* of it. And I'd been hiding things from my mother for so long that I couldn't get a toehold.

She didn't even know the real reason my ex-boyfriend, Aiden, had broken up with me back home. She thought it was because he'd found another girl, when really it had been — how had he put it? — my "wall of pain." Shutting myself in and shutting him out. My mother considered Aiden the bad guy, when the truth was that *I* was the one who couldn't deal with being close to another person.

Rather than answering, I leaned forward, unzipped the monstrosity, and slid the journal inside.

"I should get going," I said. "See you after school?"

Mom nodded and leaned over to give me a hug and a kiss. Then I got out of the car before she could say anything else.

CHAPTER 4

Lunchtime. Where the lonely and friendless go to be devoured.

I told myself that by the time I made it through the food line, the universe would, in an uncharacteristic fit of benevolence, find a way to show me where I was supposed to sit. Some girl from one of my morning classes would take pity, wave me over, and then BOOM, instant BFFs.

Instead, I found myself holding my tray, staring out over a sea of people who seemed sophisticated, comfortable, and totally not in need of a new friend.

The Langhorn lunchroom looked like the mutant offspring of a regular high school cafeteria and a hip nightclub. The ceiling was vaulted, with real wood beams, and the lights were nice hanging lamps, not cheap fluorescent bulbs. Then there were the couches, two semicircles in the center of the room. (So in case you wondered what thirty thousand dollars a year in tuition buys you — it's the right to eat your lunch without a table.)

As I made my way past the tables of smiling, laughing kids, someone called, "Hey, Connecticut."

A girl beckoned to me from one of the couches.

I froze.

She clucked her tongue at me, like I was a dog, and patted the sofa next to her.

"You look agonizingly lonely." Her voice had that detached flatness I was used to hearing from the kids at my old school who spent too much time in New York City. Only I could tell this girl really meant it, because the boredom went past her voice, into her eyes and the turned-down corners of her mouth.

She wore exactly what the rest of the female students wore: a green-and-black-plaid skirt, white collared shirt, green cardigan, and black tights. But she seemed much older and wiser, like a twenty-five-year-old trapped in the body of a high school junior. Her blunt-cut black hair brushed her shoulders and her glasses were cat-eyed with rhinestones at the corners.

"You're staring, and it's creeping me out," she said. "Just sit, please."

I blinked. And then I sat.

"I'm Marnie Delaine." She nodded at the other kids next to us. "That's Kas, Kinde, Rami, and Alana. And you're Willa, right? Willa from Connecticut. I'm in your French class, second period. How do you like Langhorn?"

I sat primly, my legs crossed at the ankles, lunch tray balanced on my lap. "Seems all right so far."

"Well, it's only your first day. You'll discover the sordid truth soon enough. Go ahead and eat."

My appetite had vanished, but I started picking at my food anyway, because I didn't want Marnie to think I was weird.

"Your father is Jonathan Walters, right?"

I practically spat out a bite of mashed-up sweet potato fry. *"Stepfather."*

"Okay, okay, calm down. Keep your food in your mouth." She seemed amused. "So . . . your stepfather's Jonathan Walters?"

"I guess." Now I was blushing. "I mean, yes. Why do you ask?"

"Because that's what people do when they meet other people. They ask questions about their lives and experiences."

Oh. Right. I guess two years of social isolation hadn't exactly honed my people skills. "Yes, he's Jonathan Walters. What about you? Who are your parents?"

"My dad's a producer, and my mom dabbles in everything. Lately she's been talking about opening a dog rescue. Except she's afraid of dogs." Marnie waved her hand nonchalantly. "But you know — details."

I tried to smile.

"What's your schedule like for the rest of the day?" she asked.

I pulled it up on my phone. "Trig, English Lit, and Chemistry."

"Cool." She leaned back again. "Have you met a lot of people?"

"Um . . ." I said. "You."

Her laugh was loud, like she didn't care who heard her, but it was also pleasantly musical. "Hey, you could do worse. Better no friends than the wrong friends. Take them, for instance."

She pointed to the tables next to the window, where the sunlight made gold halos around a bunch of kids who were obviously popular. Effortless confidence radiated off of them.

"The pretty people," Marnie said, with an exaggerated sigh. "Even I can't deny that they're nice to look at. But talking to them is like being sucked inside a video of a cat playing the piano. Pointless. If you're into discussing what to wear to sorority rush two years in advance, by all means, those are your people."

"I don't think I'm the sorority type," I said.

She nodded approvingly. "All right, let's get the rest out of the way. Over there, the football players — our team is terrible, but they still get treated like minor gods. . . . On the left you have the Ivy League Army, who are just trying to get into a good east coast school so they can leave this California hippie-dippie nonsense in the past. . . . Over by the teachers' table, those are the trust-fund kids. You see a two hundred thousand dollar car in the parking lot, guaranteed it's one of theirs. Like half their parents should technically be in jail for fraud, and I'm not even joking. To our right we find the musicians — obsessed with local bands," Marnie went on, her tone as dry as a desert. "A couple of them play, but they're no good."

I nodded. Once the bell rang and the kids scattered, I knew they'd all look the same to me again. But there was something reassuring in having it all laid out in advance.

"Finally, you have the hackers, the slackers, and the . . . there's just no polite way to say this — the dumb kids."

The so-called dumb kids looked perfectly normal. And they seemed by far like the happiest people in the whole school.

"And who are *you* guys?" If I was only going to have one friend, I might as well know what I was getting into.

"We're the Hollywood kids," Marnie said with a shrug. "Our parents run studios, write million-dollar screenplays before breakfast, and direct blockbuster movies. Hence your belonging with us. I can't promise we're super nice or anything, but at least you'll never have to hear the word *jeggings* come out of our mouths."

"That's a relief," I said. So it was no coincidence that she'd invited me to sit there? I didn't dwell on the thought – there was too much else to think about.

"I know it's a lot to take in," she said. "Feel free to glaze over and ignore me for a while."

My eyes traveled to a table next to the emergency exit, where a guy sat alone with his laptop in front of him and a stack of notebooks out to the side. He had a mop of light brown hair, hipster-y plastic-framed glasses, and a solemn, focused look. I could tell that he didn't belong to any of the groups Marnie had pointed out. He was oblivious to everyone and everything around him.

"Who's that?" I asked.

"Oh," Marnie said, arching a single eyebrow. "Wyatt. Steer clear."

"Why?"

She gave me a wry glance. "Have I given you reason to doubt me? Just stay away from him. You'll thank me later."

I stared at Wyatt a second longer. You couldn't call him "cute" — he was too serious for that. But there was something appealing about his well-defined jaw and the earnestness of his expression.

"All right, twist my arm," Marnie said, leaning closer. "So I assume you've heard of the Hollywood Killer?"

I nodded. "Is it him?"

She laughed, but there was an uneasy note in her laughter. "First semester of junior year, everyone at Langhorn has to do a big project — it's called the PRM, Personal Research Mission. It's, like, Langhorn's 'thing.' They love to brag about it on the website. Anyway, Wyatt did his on the Hollywood Killer."

I glanced over at the bespectacled boy, rethinking his attractiveness. "What *about* the killer?" I asked. "Like, trying to figure out who it is?"

"Honestly, nobody knows what Wyatt's after." Marnie's smile flattened. "The assignment's been over since January, but he won't let it drop. He's not a detective or anything, so what difference could he possibly make? Apparently, he finds the whole thing fascinating, which . . . draw your own conclusions."

"Weird," I said. I mean, yeah, I'd found the killings a little fascinating myself — but I wouldn't do a school project on them.

"*Very* weird. And with yesterday's new victim, it's like Santa Claus came last night." Marnie watched Wyatt warily. "Let's just say he doesn't get invited to a lot of parties these days."

"What's he like?" I asked. "Is he nice at all, or just strange?"

"Complicated question," she said, turning back to her lunch — a tiny bag of pretzels and a container of yogurt. "If you're lucky, you'll never have to find out."

Chemistry was my last class of the day. The teacher, Mr. Hiller, was about ninety years old. He was faultlessly polite, calling all the students "Miss" and "Mister."

"Miss Cresky, you'll need a lab partner," he said, glancing around the room.

There were two empty spots. One was at a table near the front, where a beautifully groomed blond girl — one of the pretty people — sat staring at her notebook. She looked up and gave me a pointedly unwelcoming smile.

"Right there in the back," Mr. Hiller said. "Mr. Sheppard."

Mr. Sheppard?

Ah, yes. That would be Mr. *Wyatt* Sheppard. Of course. Because that's how the universe and I roll these days.

I carried my things to the back of the room and sat down next to him.

He glanced up, and his eyes settled on my Gucci backpack. Then they flashed back down at his laptop like there was nothing we needed to say to one another.

Fine with me.

As Mr. Hiller lectured, I tried to keep my eyes from slipping shut in the sleepy afternoon warmth of the classroom. I couldn't afford to sleep now — I needed to save up my tiredness to counteract the inevitable insomnia awaiting me at night. Especially as relaxing moonlit swims were no longer an option.

I jerked upright after beginning to nod off and looked down at Wyatt's notebook to see if I'd missed anything. But what he was writing wasn't actually notes on chemistry. It was a list of names, written in an impossibly precise print.

Before I could figure out what any of them meant, he saw me looking at the page and pulled the notebook toward himself.

When the final bell rang, I stacked the stuff on my half of the table and slipped it into my bag. I turned to Wyatt, thinking that, since we were stuck together for the rest of the school year, it would be polite to at least say *something*.

"Have a good —"

Wrong.

"Not interested," he said.

He swung his bag over his shoulder and walked away.

CHAPTER 5

Mom picked me up from school, buzzing with questions about my first day. But I didn't feel like talking. Even though it hadn't been a total disaster — I'd made one friend, after all — Wyatt's cold rejection stung me more than I wanted to admit.

He's just a weirdo, I told myself, remembering Marnie's warning. Why should I even care what he thought?

After dropping me off at the house, Mom had to go to a hair appointment at a Beverly Hills salon (Cinderella can't walk around her new castle covered in cinders, after all). I ordered her not to come home blond and went up to my room to start on my homework.

As I sat cross-legged on my bed reading about chemical reagents, my eyelids grew heavy, and the sticky tendrils of a headache slithered around my brain, threatening to take hold. So I shut the textbook and leaned over to slide it back in my bag. As I did, I noticed that there were not one but *two* spiral notebooks inside.

The first was green, crisply new — mine.

The second notebook was red, its edges worn from use. Written on the front, in thick black marker, was: W. SHEPPARD, PLEASE CALL IF FOUND: 323-555-4334

I must have accidentally grabbed it at the end of class.

My first thought was, *Wyatt must be freaking out.*

My next thought was, *Well, I obviously have to look inside.*

I set the notebook on my bed, halfheartedly debating in my head. *You shouldn't,* said one part of me. *It's Wyatt's business. You should text him and tell him you have it.*

What would the text say, though?

Hi, it's Willa, the girl whose head you bit off when I tried to be nice to you in Chemistry. I know you already hate me, but you have to believe it was a TOTAL ACCIDENT that I ended up kidnapping your precious notebook.

Yeah, no.

And then my inner debate basically died because I'd already opened it.

Wyatt's handwriting was so tiny and precise that it looked like it had come out of a printer.

BRIANNA LOGAN, 20 Y.O., TAKEN MAY 17, FOUND MAY 21

FAITH FERNANDES, 19 Y.O., TAKEN JUNE 9, FOUND JUNE 13

LORELEI JULIANO, 21 Y.O., TAKEN OCT 31, FOUND NOV 5

TORI ROSEN, 18 Y.O., TAKEN MARCH 18, FOUND MARCH 22

This was the list of names I'd gotten a glimpse of in class.

I blinked at the perfectly formed letters, a chill spreading through my body.

March 22 — that was yesterday's date.

These had to be the names of the murder victims.

The first two were written in black ink. The third and fourth were in different colored ink — different pens — because they'd happened after Wyatt started his research.

I pulled my new laptop onto the bed and typed in the first name: *Brianna Logan*. About a billion results popped up: MOVIE-THEMED MURDER BAFFLES LOS ANGELES POLICE — YOUNG ACTRESS FOUND MURDERED — STAGE SET FOR MURDER —

Next, I typed in *Faith Fernandes*. "HOLLYWOOD KILLER" STRIKES AGAIN — POLICE BELIEVE MOVIE MURDERS ARE RELATED —

With each new name, the headlines grew more ominous. After Lorelei's murder, the tone of the writing was deadly serious.

LOS ANGELES POLICE DEPARTMENT CALLS IN FBI FOR HELP WITH HOLLYWOOD KILLER — POLICE URGE ACTRESSES TO USE CAUTION —

I found an article from that morning's *Los Angeles Times* that detailed the ways the four killings were similar: The victims had all gone missing days before being found. They were all young, beautiful up-and-coming actresses who lived alone. None of them were famous yet, but all had had bit parts in TV shows or movies. Each one had been found dead in an abandoned or empty house. The girls had all been poisoned, and then their bodies had been arranged in scenes set to mimic famous movies, just like Jonathan had said. The movies that "inspired" the killer were *The Birds*, *Kiss of Death*, *Heathers*, and *Vertigo*. I'd heard of *The Birds* and *Heathers*, and Jonathan had mentioned *Kiss of Death* last night, but I hadn't heard of *Vertigo* before.

Apparently all of the girls had auditions scheduled for the days they disappeared — the problem was that none of their calendars contained any helpful leads, just references to the names of fake talent agencies the killer had made up, a different one for each girl. The police thought he must be using disposable cell phones.

The girls' striking smiles shone from the pictures lined up alongside the article. As I looked at them, the temperature in my room seemed to drop twenty degrees. The reality of the murders hit home. The victims weren't much older than me. Intellectually, I knew I wasn't in danger, but still. . . . It was just so *creepy*.

I went back to Wyatt's notebook. Its pages contained detailed descriptions of the way each girl was found — Brianna sitting back against a door, covered in scratches, with fake birds staged around her; Faith in a wheelchair at the bottom of a set of stairs; Lorelei posed as if she'd crashed through a glass coffee table; and Tori set up like the victim of a fall from a tall bell tower.

The dead girls wore full costumes, wigs, and makeup to look exactly like the characters from the films. The killer took exquisite care to get every detail perfect.

x

Wyatt's notebook also contained the girls' addresses, their heights and weights and clothing sizes, their meager acting credits, the dates and times of the anonymous tips advising the police where to find the bodies, and the names of the responding police officers. It was more information than you could ever get just by reading news articles online.

And yet Wyatt somehow knew all of it.

I sat back, my heart pounding and head throbbing. I shoved the notebook to the floor. I didn't even want it in my room. It felt dirty. It belonged in a bonfire. A shredder. But I didn't dare destroy it, so I put it in my backpack and zipped it closed. Then I shut the backpack in my closet.

The murders were obviously disturbing enough by themselves — but what kind of person would be so obsessed with them? Who would take such detailed notes on the deaths and let thoughts of them consume his every spare minute?

Oh, just my lab partner, that's all.

A flash of light flickered in my peripheral vision. An empty ache grew in the pit of my stomach.

I could feel the walls closing in on me. I had to get out of the house.

My new neighborhood was made up of narrow roads that wound along the hillsides. The houses ranged from sleekly modern to old-Hollywood glam, from cottages to mansions. Some were perfectly kept up, like our house, and some were descending into rot and ruin, smothered by ivy and huge magenta-flowering bushes.

I stayed at the edge of the road, where the asphalt met the curb, and kept my head high to listen for oncoming cars. Thanks to the tall shrubs and blind corners, they seemed to sneak up on me at fifty miles an hour. By the time I completed the looping route that took me back to the house, I was panting from the uphill climb, my feet were aching in my flip-flops, and I was totally jumpy from almost being run over about nine times. But at least the walk served its purpose — it took my mind off the Hollywood Killer and Wyatt's awful notebook.

I couldn't wait to kick off my shoes and drink a tall, cold glass of water. I reached for the handle of the heavy wood gate and pulled.

But the gate was locked.

I didn't bother trying the call box, because I knew no one was home. And even if I had my phone with me, there was no point in bugging my mother at the salon.

The skin on my cheeks felt like it was cooking in the brutal sunlight. My throat was parched. It was so dry here — as Jonathan pointed out once, with his usual misplaced pride, *the city of Los Angeles is an actual desert.*

I tried typing numbers into the keypad — 1-2-3-4. 0-7-2-0, Mom's birthday. 0-2-1-4, Mom and Jonathan's anniversary. I knew they wouldn't work, but it was all I could think to do, and I had to do *something.* Then I just started randomly punching the buttons.

Finally, I stepped back to assess whether I could climb over the fence. Not a chance. It was eight feet tall, with metal spikes at the top. It went all the way around the property, and the backyard was bordered by a steep ravine that was full of cactuses and probably snakes.

I was on the verge of crying, but before I could muster a sniffle of self-pity, the gate swung open.

"Excuse me." The guy standing there was a couple of years older than me, with messy-on-purpose dark hair and piercing green eyes. "What do you think you're doing?"

I had no idea who he was.

"Trying to get in?" I said.

He stared me down. "Did it ever occur to you that maybe you shouldn't be 'trying to get in' to someone else's private property?"

"I'm sorry," I said, mortified. "I just moved here and . . . I must be at the wrong house. I thought I was locked out. I'm sorry."

Loser, loser, loser.

I was about to turn away to find the right house when his green eyes brightened with understanding.

"Hang on — what's your name?" he asked.

"Willa."

"Willa?" he repeated. "You're *Willa*? Oh, no. I'm so sorry. Come in, come in."

He held the gate open, and I hesitated, still unsure as to who he was or what he was doing at the house.

He gave me a friendly, slightly crooked smile. "I'm Jonathan's assistant, Reed."

This was Jonathan's assistant? I guess in Hollywood even secretaries look like they could be on TV.

"I just got a call from the alarm company saying somebody was punching a bunch of random codes into the gate," Reed explained. "How long have you been stuck out here?"

Heat and frustration were under my skin like a coating of grit, and I was a little afraid I'd burst out crying if I tried to talk. So I shrugged without making eye contact, and we walked in silence across the front yard.

"Come on." He opened the door, and clean, cool air came billowing out of the house. "Let's get you some water."

I followed him to the kitchen, where he filled a glass from the filter next to the sink. After a few gulps, I felt a little more stable. Brave enough to look at him again.

Holy crab shacks, was he cute.

"Your name is Reed?" I said. "I'm Willa . . . but you knew that."

He gave a little bow. "Reed Thornton, at your service."

The old Willa might have said something flirtatious. Bold. And maybe it would have made me blush, but I would have done it, because I used to do things that were unknown and even a little scary just for the thrill of it.

But not anymore. I didn't feel thrilled about anything these days. Not even being in the presence of someone so unbelievably handsome.

"Thanks," I said. "Sorry for inconveniencing you."

He shook his head, smiling. "I'm an assistant. It's all part of the job."

I tried to smile back, but I was pretty sure that my attempt came out as a weird grimace. So I drained the rest of my water glass and darted out of the kitchen.

Back in my room, I got my bookbag out of the closet, vowing not to let some stupid rude boy's stupid notebook scare me.

I'd just sat down on the foot of my bed and pulled my chemistry book out again, when there was a knock on my door.

As I swung it open, I said, "You'd better not be blond."

"I'm not," Reed said.

I gasped, then felt my cheeks grow warm. "Sorry, I — I thought you were my mother."

"Yeah, I get that a lot." He grinned, and it felt like someone had opened a window and flooded the room with sunshine.

"Um . . . what's up?" I asked.

"Well, I . . ." He frowned slightly and scratched the back of his neck. "I thought I'd say good-bye, because I'm leaving, only . . . it seems way weirder now than I imagined it."

"Oh," I said. "That's because I make everything weird."

He laughed. "I thought I was the only one."

I searched for something semi-intelligent to say. "Do you come to the house every day?"

"No," he said. "Mostly I work at Jonathan's office at the studio. But sometimes there's random stuff that needs handling, so I come by here."

I nodded. "Are you going to be a director, too?"

He shrugged, his modest, crooked smile returning. "That's the dream."

"Did you go to film school?"

"Not yet. I'm taking a couple of years off before college to get experience and make some money. I figure working for Jonathan will get me into any film school I want."

"Is he that big of a deal?" I thought back to how Marnie had described the other Hollywood kids — as if their parents were the industry elite — and how it was unspoken that I fit right in.

"He's good at what he does," Reed said. "That's more important than being a big deal."

I hadn't seen a single Jonathan Walters movie until he and Mom started dating and she'd made me watch them all with her. Actually, I liked them a lot. They were exciting without being mindlessly action-packed and thought-provoking without being boring or preachy.

Then again, I didn't know enough about movies to know if that made someone a good director or not. I guessed I'd have to take Reed's word for it.

"Right." I felt weird about wasting his time and figured he must be eager to go. But he didn't act like he was in a hurry.

He leaned against the doorway and slid his hands into the pockets of his jeans. "You started at Langhorn today, right? How'd you like it?"

"It's okay. I haven't met many people yet."

He nodded. "They can be a bit closed off, until they get to know you."

"How do you know so much about them?"

"I'm a proud fighting Rattler. Graduated two years ago." He smiled. "Ebony and emerald forever, right? *'Rattle, rattle! is the cry of our battle!'*"

"Yeah . . . guess I don't quite have the rattle in my heart yet." I thought of Wyatt's icy rejection. "And 'closed off' might be putting it mildly."

Reed sighed. "Yeah, I've been there. I was on scholarship, and my parents were nobodies. I had no connections. No famous friends. A lot of doors never opened for me."

"I'm extremely nobody," I said. "That doesn't bode well, door-wise."

"No, it'll be different for you," he said. "You're Jonathan Walters's stepdaughter. Even if I weren't obligated by the terms of my employment to say that counts for something, I'd say it counts for something."

"And you work for Jonathan," I shot back. "So you're connected, too. See how it all worked out?"

Reed laughed again. I felt a twinge of happiness, realizing that I could make him laugh. I wanted him to like me — not necessarily *like me* like me, but to want to be my friend. Being in his presence was like being on a walk in a peaceful forest. The longer it went on, the calmer and more grounded I felt.

He gestured to the floor next to the bed. "Gucci isn't your style, is it?"

He'd noticed the backpack.

If you don't have anything nice to say, don't say anything at all.

I smiled.

The sunlight danced in Reed's eyes. "It's okay. I'm the one who picked it out. Now that I know you, I would have picked something completely different. I just figured, east coast . . . probably uptight . . . I was wrong, obviously."

The thought of Reed buying a gift for me — even if it wasn't technically *from* him — sent a tiny electric charge through my body. Instantly, I liked the bag about five times more.

"It's all right," I said, picking it up. "It's growing on me. The zipper's, like, unbelievable."

"You're a good sport." Reed glanced out into the hall. "Well, I guess I should get going. . . ."

Was I crazy, or did he actually sound a little reluctant to leave?

Trying not to smile too brightly, I stood up to say good-bye. Just as I got to my feet, I felt a tremendous head rush.

A blinding white light flashed in front of my eyes.

*I*t suits you," says the voice — friendly and soft, amused. He reaches down and gently touches the delicate chain he's fastened around my neck. Tests the weight of the rose charm in his fingers.

I turn my head away. I don't want to look at him. I know it will make him angry, but I can't help it. If I look at him, I'll throw up.

"Fine. Be that way." He withdraws his hand, stands, and walks a few feet away. "You're all the same, you know that? So self-involved. You only think about me, me, me."

The room is cool and dark, with a low ceiling. A lightbulb hangs down over a table in the corner. He's leaning over something on the table, a large box. When he turns back, he's holding up a pea-green dress.

"You're going to change into this," he says. "And you're not going to try anything stupid. I'm going to be right here, do you understand?"

I nod, and he reaches down to free my ankles. Then he extends his hand. I'm supposed to take it, to let him help me to my feet. But I can't — I can't bring myself to touch him.

I manage to get up on my own. He gives me the dress.

"What if it doesn't fit?" I choke the words out.

"It's your size," he says.

47

This is my chance to run — to scream, to fight back — it's what I've been waiting for since I woke up. How long ago was that? Hours?

No. That's wishful thinking. It's been days.

But the world swims around me. The air feels thick and heavy. My legs are like the trunks of trees, useless, numb. I can't run.

I can't do anything.

"Right over there," he says. "In the bathroom."

I can feel a lump in my throat — hopelessness threatens to overwhelm me. I want to collapse to the floor and sob.

"Brianna." Now there's a warning in his voice. "Do you remember our talk?"

I sniffle and nod.

"There's an easy way, and a hard way. I prefer the easy way — and I can't help but think you will, too." His voice hardens. "So do as I say before we have to change our tack here."

I can feel tears biting at my eyes.

"Don't cry!" he snaps. "How many times have I told you not to cry?"

I blink and stare at the ceiling to keep my eyes dry, and then I slowly walk toward the open bathroom door.

As I pass the box, I look down and gasp.

There's a head in there.

A millisecond later, I realize that it's not a head. It's just a blond wig on a faceless Styrofoam form. But somehow that's almost as bad as a head. And what surrounds it is even worse —

Shiny black feathers.

Birds. Dead, or stuffed, or just realistic-looking fakes, I don't know. Dozens and dozens of birds.

"It's going to be great," he says. "Just like we rehearsed. Your star-making performance."

CHAPTER 6

I gasped and raised my hands to my face, pressing them over my mouth.

"Willa?"

I shook my head, unable to speak.

"Hey — Willa?"

Maybe the only thing in the entire universe that could have snapped me out of my shock was the feather-light touch of Reed's hand on my cheek.

I blinked and turned to look at him.

"What happened?" he asked. "What's wrong?"

I shook my head and managed to say, "Nothing."

He wasn't convinced.

"I . . . I just remembered I have a huge test tomorrow, that's all," I said. "I should start studying."

Reed's eyes searched my face for a few moments, then he relaxed slightly. "I remember that feeling. It's the worst. And Langhorn takes academics pretty seriously."

I nodded, wondering if I'd be able to hold it together for the amount of time it took him to leave.

Thankfully, he reached into his pocket and pulled out his vibrating phone. "It's Jonathan. I need to take it. Good luck on your test."

I nodded mutely.

"Hey, Jonathan," I heard Reed say. "Yeah, I'm at the house. Just finished up. On my way out right now, in fact."

As soon as he was gone, I closed the door and sat on my bed, shaking.

What just happened? What *was* that?

It felt like a dream — like the most realistic dream I'd ever had. I could still picture the box on the table, with the wig and the dead birds in it. I could feel the leaden heaviness of my legs. And I could hear the voice. Low, gravelly. Distorted in a dreamlike way, just like the rest of it had been — the room I was in, the dress, the strange square outline of light in the distance.

It had to be a dream.

Except, of course, I wasn't asleep.

For a moment, I was tempted to reach into my bag for the red notebook, but I didn't need to look. I already understood the full meaning of the name I'd heard.

"Brianna," the gravelly voice had called me.

But the voice wasn't talking to me —

It was talking to Brianna Logan, the first victim of the Hollywood Killer.

My mother was blond.

When she poked her head into my room and saw me sitting

dazed on my bed, she cried, "Don't be mad, Willa! Francisco said it suited my skin tone."

I stared at her. She didn't look like herself, but she didn't look like a stranger. More like a long-lost cousin from Norway.

"He said dark hair was too severe at my age," Mom went on, her voice oddly pleading. "Do you hate it?"

I shook my head. How could I focus on my mother's hair minutes after having a full-on serial-killer hallucination?

"Oh, no, you hate it," Mom said. "You look horrified. Is it that bad?"

I *had* to tell her. This was as clear an opening as I was ever going to get. I should tell her about the corpse in the pool, and the terrifying vision — and even if it meant I was totally crazy, at least then . . .

I shied away from letting myself think *at least then everything will be better.*

Because the fact is, everything would be worse. Immediately. Much, much worse.

"Joanna! Willa!" I heard Jonathan calling from downstairs. "Dinner! I picked up sushi."

I swallowed back anything I planned to say and followed my newly blond mother downstairs.

As the three of us sat down at the dining room table, Jonathan cleared his throat. "So, Willa, I think this is a good time for us to talk about last night — about the pool, I mean."

I glanced up. "Excuse me?"

Mom was making such an effort to seem nonchalant that I thought she might bust a blood vessel. "Jonathan and I were thinking that you should probably stay out of the water unless someone else is around. Just to make sure we don't have any more incidents —"

"Accidents," Jonathan said, giving me a magnanimous look. Like his not assuming that I was a juvenile delinquent was one more generous gift. "Obviously, it was an accident."

"Of course," Mom said. "It's only for your safety, honey."

Inside me, a little volcano of rage began to spew ashes and fire. I stared at my plate for a second, studying the neat line of sushi rolls.

Get a hold of yourself, Willa.

So my mother and Jonathan clearly thought I was unreliable, maybe even unstable. Thank God I hadn't actually told Mom the truth. What would they say if they knew what was *really* going on in my head?

"Okay," I finally said, the words as cool as stone.

Jonathan nodded neatly and picked up his water glass. "You met Reed today?"

I looked at him, not wanting to talk but determined not to show them how upset I was. "Yes," I said.

"He's so handsome," Mom said. "Don't get any ideas, Willa."

She was teasing, but I wasn't in the mood to be teased.

"He's too old for me," I said, fighting not to blush.

"He's only nineteen," Jonathan said. Mom must have shot him a meaningful glare, because then he added, "Too old. You're right."

I went the rest of dinner without speaking another word. Then I stood, carried my dish to the dishwasher, and walked up to my room without even saying good night.

I sat on my bed, staring down at the journal. *Just one line every day,* Mom had said.

How hard could that be? I used to write long articles for the school newspaper. I wrote a story that won second place in the entire state of Connecticut. Words used to come to me so easily.

But now, staring down at the clean white expanse of space, I felt like I was locked up in a cell, and anything I could possibly think to say was on the other side of a six-inch-thick steel wall.

It was so horribly hopeless that I almost laughed.

Just one line? It might as well have been a hundred pages.

I flipped the empty journal shut and put it away.

"It's about to boil," Wyatt said.

I glanced at the beaker suspended above our Bunsen burner. "Nah, it's okay."

It was the end of my first week at Langhorn. We had a lab project to do, so Wyatt Sheppard was finally forced to talk to me. And every word he spoke implied that I was a complete moron.

He let out a frustrated sigh. "If it boils, it'll ruin the experiment," he explained. "You may not care if we fail, but I have an academic standard to maintain."

I tried not to roll my eyes. Wyatt was apparently just as obsessed with his GPA as he was with the Hollywood Killer.

But I wasn't in the mood for micromanagement. I'd spent a week of sleepless nights tossing and turning, and the days between the nights obsessing over the fact that I seemed to be losing my mind.

"If you stop it too early, it won't be hot enough," I snapped, my patience expired. "I'll handle the beaker, you write the lab report. If it gets ruined, you can tell Mr. Hiller it was all my fault."

A moment later, when I saw a bubble appear, I reached over and turned the burner down.

"Are you happy now?" I asked.

"Ecstatic." He scowled down at the lab report.

We argued our way through the rest of the experiment. Then, after demonstrating our results for Mr. Hiller, we sat back down, facing away from each other.

Wyatt had been in a terrible mood all week, and I was pretty sure I knew why.

Because he couldn't find his notebook.

My initial plan had been to give it back to him as soon as I saw him Tuesday morning outside the school. But that was before he greeted me with a glare, and Marnie pulled me away by the elbow, trying to do me a favor by keeping me out of his path.

And when I'd walked to our table in Chem that day, and spent a second studying him, to gauge if the moment was right, he looked at me and snapped, *"What?"*

"Nothing," I'd said, turning away. "Never mind." And I hadn't tried to bring up the subject for the rest of the week.

Did I feel bad about hanging on to someone else's personal property, when he was clearly desperate for its return? Well, yeah. Did I find the notebook disturbing and want it away from me as soon as possible? A million times *yeah*.

But why couldn't Wyatt show even the smallest hint of compassion or empathy toward me — a new student who'd just had her life turned upside down and been paired with the most hostile lab partner in the history of high school chemistry?

I'd done absolutely nothing (well, nothing he was aware of) to deserve that kind of treatment. So I decided to let him freak out about his stupid notebook for a while.

First thing Monday morning, I'd turn it in to the lost and found. But until then, he could just suffer.

CHAPTER 7

That night, Jonathan and Mom made plans to go out to dinner and a movie. My mother was clearly worried about leaving me home alone, but I convinced her I'd be okay.

What I said was, "Of course I'll be fine. I'll call if I need anything." What I didn't say was, *OMG! A whole night where I don't have to worry about doing or saying the wrong thing in front of Jonathan? Sign me up yesterday.*

That just seemed impolitic.

A tiny piece of me was kind of skittish about being in the house alone, but that was nothing I was willing to share with Mom anyway.

My big plans for the night included lounging on the big comfy couch in the den, neutralizing my general sense of anxiety with trashy TV shows. First, I went upstairs to put on my pajamas. As I moved my schoolbag from the bed to the floor, Wyatt's red notebook caught my eye.

Ignore it, I told myself. *Don't waste a single second thinking about him.*

But I couldn't suppress a mental slideshow of images of

someone carrying dead girls around, posing them like dolls, taking care to get every detail correct. . . .

Worst of all, I couldn't shake the awful, hopeless feeling of actually *being* Brianna, scared and alone. Even though I knew the vision I'd had on Monday hadn't been real, it had *felt* so real. I'd been dodging miserable memories of it all week.

My room wasn't cold, but I shivered as I changed into my pajamas. Then, without thinking, I reached for the ring and candle — but just as my fingers brushed the suede bag, I stopped. I'd wasted, what, ten minutes a day? For almost two years? All in a desperate attempt to reach someone who probably didn't even want to hear what I had to say — and that's if there even *was* such a thing as ghosts, or spirits, or whatever you want to call them.

Why did I even bother — because one stupid book I'd found at a used bookstore said it would work?

Forcing myself to leave the ring untouched in the drawer, I walked to the sink in the bathroom to splash water on my face. My thoughts raced. *What if I'm quitting one day too soon? What if this would have been the night Dad found me?*

But I knew I could do this. I could sweat it out. I just needed to think about something more relaxing, that's all. Something more pleasant.

The image that came into my mind when I closed my eyes was Reed's face. His crooked smile and his clear green eyes, calm and confident. We'd had a couple of chance encounters during the week. I was finding that the hope of spending a few minutes talking to him was one of the things that got me through the days and the long, torturous nights.

Then, out of nowhere, I heard a voice.

"This is . . ."

I didn't want to hear the words, but it was like when you get some random idea in your head, and you can't get it out. The harder you try not to think about it, the more it haunts you.

"This is the kind of . . ."

The words came together like leaves tumbling around in the wind, meaningless sounds until they coalesced for a brief moment, long enough to fill the room with the whispered phrase — and then broke apart again.

I fought and pushed and shook my head, like I could dislodge the sound from my brain.

But the voice grew louder.

"THIS IS THE KIND OF —"

Stop, stop, stop.

"THIS IS THE KIND OF DREAM —"

I tried to grab on to thoughts of something else, anything else — school, Mom, Reed. Even my painful memories of Aiden. It didn't work.

Then the whole thing came whooshing toward me, ringing in my ears like a bell.

"THIS IS THE KIND OF DREAM YOU DON'T WAKE UP FROM, HENRY."

I had no idea who Henry was. Or whose voice I was hearing. Or why this particular message was being delivered to me.

The back of my neck prickled and my head ached. In desperation, I threw open my nightstand drawer. But instead of grabbing the ring, I yanked my journal out and flung it onto the bed.

Just one line, huh? For once, I was too frustrated to agonize over whether I had anything worth saying. In huge, blocky letters, I filled a whole page with one sentence:

I WOULD JUST LIKE FOR THINGS TO BE EASY FOR A LITTLE WHILE.

Then I slammed the journal shut and shoved it back in the drawer, my chest heaving.

I went downstairs, determined to distract myself for at least a few hours. But when I turned on the TV, the opening credits of a movie were playing.

I kid you not, the movie was *The Birds*.

So I did what any crazy person would do . . . I sat down and watched it.

It was ten past midnight. I was in bed and — surprise, surprise — I wasn't even close to sleeping. Watching a horror movie about homicidal birds definitely hadn't helped.

I flopped back onto my pillow and caught two flashes out of the corners of my eyes — the kind that usually mean a huge headache is about to sink its claws into my skull.

The wind picked up. Whenever a particularly strong gust blew, the branches of the huge walnut tree outside my room hit the windows with a smattering of sharp sounds. If you closed your eyes and blurred your brain just right, you could imagine a raging horde of birds clawing at the glass, desperate to get inside.

Don't be silly. They'd just break the glass.

In the movie, they'd pecked through a roof, for heaven's sake.

So then I pictured teeny tiny birds — baby birds. Gnashing their needle-size beaks and banging against the glass with all the force they could muster. Before long, one of them would hit hard enough to crack it, and then they'd come flying in like a horde of vampire bats — or how I imagined vampire bats when I was a kid, swarming around me and drinking my blood, like they'd done to Tippi Hedren, leaving her catatonic in the attic —

Okay, nope. Not helping.

After a few minutes, the wind died down, and the scratching subsided, leaving a sudden silence.

In the quiet, I became aware of another noise — a soft, steady sound, so persistent in its rhythm that soon I couldn't believe I hadn't heard it before:

Drip . . . drip . . . drip . . .

I told myself to ignore it. I mean, there were like twelve bathrooms in the house — one of them was bound to spring a leak at some point, right?

I buried my face in my pillow.

Drip . . . drip . . . drip . . .

It was the type of sound that could drive a person bonkers.

Finally, I got up and checked the bathroom that adjoined my room. All the faucets were off. I opened my bedroom door and looked down the silent, empty hall stretching before me, its polished floorboards lustrous in the moonlight.

I took a deep breath. Then I ducked into each of the upstairs bathrooms, inspecting all the faucets, but found nothing that could have caused the dripping noise.

Finally, I stood at the far end of the hall and stared at the door to the only room I hadn't checked yet: Jonathan's office.

I should really, really go back to bed.

But as I hesitated . . .

Drip.

Let's be clear — simply being in Jonathan's house seemed like more than enough of an imposition. I wasn't exactly dying to bust into my stepfather's office uninvited — *but* —

Drip.

— it wasn't like I was going to go sit at his desk and mess with his stuff. I just wanted to tighten a faucet handle and get out. No rational person would get upset about that. Even thinking that Jonathan *might* get upset made me feel irrational.

Drip.

I opened the office door and paused to look around. The room felt like a time warp, a glimpse at life back in the golden age of movies. The walls, covered in luxe dark green wallpaper, were decorated with posters from classic movies like *Casablanca* and *Sunset Boulevard*, as well as posters of Jonathan's own movies, signed by some of the biggest stars in the world: Brad Pitt, Jennifer Lawrence, Gwyneth Paltrow, Denzel Washington. Jonathan's laptop sat on the desk, the single modern-looking element.

The dripping was louder in here.

I opened the bathroom door and hit the light switch, but no light came on. Maybe the bulb had gone out. In the shadowy darkness, I walked over to the old-fashioned claw-foot bathtub.

When I saw it, I froze.

The tub was full of water.

When I say full, I mean filled up 100 percent. Its upper brim was a perfectly flat and motionless layer of water. And on the side closest to me, water crept over the edge and dripped to the floor, one slow drop at a time.

Drip . . . drip . . . drip . . .

The echoes of the plinking water were like something from a scary movie about a creature dwelling in a subterranean cave.

I stood over the tub, holding my breath and studying my dim, distorted reflection. Every time a drop slipped over the edge, it sent a tiny shudder through my face.

If I reached in to pull out the drain stopper, it would send a gush of water over the side. I'd have to bail some out first. I found an empty glass on the counter and dipped it into the tub, a stream of droplets spilling over and splashing my feet. I repeated the process about ten times, filling the glass and dumping it in the sink, until the water level had gone down an inch.

I rolled up my sleeve and returned the glass to its spot next to the sink.

Then I turned back to the tub.

The water was perfectly level with the top again.

Okay, no.

I stepped closer and peered down into the bathtub.

A face peered back at me — pale, with dark circles under the eyes. A slack, sullen mouth. A halo of short curls.

Not my face —

That is not my face.

I jumped back, slamming into the wall behind me — and the light switch — flooding the room with bright light. For a second, I searched my reflection in the mirror, praying I'd see dark circles, lips sullenly parted, a hint of curl in my hair. Anything to convince me that the face I'd just seen had been my own . . . and not the face of a stranger.

It didn't work.

Forget this. You're beyond tired. You're completely lacking any sense of judgment.

I started to back out of the bathroom. I should never — *never ever ever* — have come in here. And I never ever ever planned to do so again.

I pulled the office door open.

A shadow blocked the doorway.

I shrieked and stumbled backward, losing my balance and crashing to the floor, nearly taking a table lamp with me.

When I looked up, the shadow was directly over me, like a monster about to destroy its cornered victim.

"Willa?"

The voice did not belong to a monster. It belonged to Jonathan.

He flipped on the lamp and stood watching me, his expression wary. My mother hurried to his side. "Willa? What's going on? We heard someone walking around."

I shielded my eyes from the sudden brightness. "I heard something dripping."

Jonathan had his arms crossed, waiting for me to get to the part about why I was in his office.

I sat up and dusted my hands off on my pajama pants. "I checked all of the other bathrooms first — but I could tell it had to be coming from in here."

"How could you tell that?" Jonathan asked.

"With my ears." I hadn't meant it to sound disrespectful, but judging by the way Jonathan's brow furrowed in annoyance, I knew it had come out that way.

"Did you find anything?" Mom asked.

"Yeah," I said. "And it's weird."

I thought it would be easier if they just looked for themselves, so I pointed to the bathroom. They filed in, Jonathan first.

I got to my feet and listened for their exclamations of surprise.

But there was silence.

"Willa?" Mom asked. "What is it? What did you find?"

Some part of me knew, as I came around the corner and peered through the doorway, that something was wrong.

The bathtub was perfectly empty and dry.

Words probably needed to be said, but none presented themselves. I felt like I had a mouthful of dirt.

"Where's the leak?" Jonathan's dark eyes flashed. He wasn't much taller than me, but he carried himself with so much authority that he seemed to loom above me like the monster I'd mistaken him for.

For the second time in a week, I found myself scrambling to cover my tracks.

"That's it," I said. "I found . . . nothing. And that's weird, because I *definitely* heard something."

"You heard something," Jonathan said. "Here. In my office bathroom."

I nodded.

"Behind the closed door," he said. "From all the way across the house."

"Yes," I said. "I swear."

My mother inhaled. I waited for the exhale, but it started to seem like she was going to hold her breath forever.

I decided to break the silence. "How was the movie?"

"Not bad," Mom said.

"Terrible," Jonathan said. "Painfully derivative."

"Ah," I said. "Well . . . I guess I'll go back to bed."

I led the way back to the hall, and they followed behind me, like my own private security detail.

"Good night," I said, starting to duck into my room.

"Hold on," Jonathan said. "Please."

I turned around. They stood at the top of the stairs, shrouded in shadows.

"In the future," he said, "I'd appreciate it if you wouldn't go in my office without permission. There are sensitive papers in there. Confidential."

"Right." My voice came out as a puff of air. "Sorry."

"No harm done." His voice sounded easy and relaxed, but his body language was rigid. "We'll call a plumber tomorrow to check things out."

I nodded and watched as he and Mom went downstairs together. Mom clutched his arm like she could hold on to him and keep him from bolting out of our lives.

I went into my room and lay in bed, staring at the ceiling, for hours.

And the house was silent the whole time.

CHAPTER 8

Saturday afternoon, my phone buzzed with a text from Marnie: *Hey Connecticut. Hangsies today? 2ish? Your house?*

I'd spent the morning hiding out in my room, avoiding Mom and Jonathan. In spite of my resolution to swear off, um, hangsies and live a miserable, isolated existence for the good of everyone around me, the boredom was already getting old.

So I replied, *Sure*.

A half hour later, Marnie steered a pale blue convertible BMW into the driveway. The top was automatically closing itself over her head as I came out to meet her.

I was curious to see what she'd wear outside of school. Based on what little I knew of her, I'd imagined her to be an all-black-and-combat-boots type. But she was wearing skinny jeans and a ruffly white tank top with flip-flops. Her sunglasses were sparkly blue. I was a little disappointed, to be honest — I'd expected something more dramatic.

She checked out my outfit, too, which had to be a huge bummer for her. I had on an olive-green long-sleeved T-shirt and a pair of overalls my mom had owned since the early '90s.

My hair was in a low, sloppy bun. My feet were bare, but during my time alone that morning, I'd painted my toenails bubble-gum pink.

So I had that going for me, I guess.

Marnie hugged me, then stood back. "You look like a boy," she said. "Not in a bad way. A cute boy."

My mother, whose plans for the day consisted of making some crazy-elaborate dinner, was in the kitchen when we went inside. Mom seemed to like Marnie, but she also seemed a little thrown by her cynical vibe. Mostly, my mother seemed relieved I'd made a friend — that I wasn't doomed to life as a shut-in chasing around imaginary dripping sounds in the night.

Jonathan, thankfully, was off scouting a location for a movie, so I didn't have to deal with *that* potentially awkward interaction. I gave Marnie a quick tour of the house — she didn't seem impressed, though she did say that the pool was "decent, if you're into that kind of thing."

I actually found it comforting, the way Marnie scoffed at things. It was like she knew the world was messed up, so what was the use of trying to pretend it wasn't?

We hung out in my room for a while and Marnie filled me in on all the major Langhorn gossip, starting back in eighth grade. She was happy just to have an audience, and I was happy just to listen. She didn't ask any hard questions about my life in Connecticut or how I was adjusting to California. It was so much easier than having to conceal what I was really thinking.

For a moment, I actually considered confiding in her. I could start by casually mentioning that the house was a little spooky, and I heard strange-ish sounds sometimes — I even thought I'd seen something in the pool. But where could I go from there? Would I really tell her about the visions and voices? It was such a small, slippery slope from strange-ish to crazy. And Marnie was my only friend.

So I kept my mouth shut.

After examining the nautical-themed paintings on my walls and proclaiming them "droll," Marnie suggested we go for a drive, on the condition that I change out of the overalls, which I happily did. When we presented the plan to Mom, she was pretty reluctant — especially as the car in question was a convertible, and therefore not reinforced with giant bars of steel and airbags popping out from every angle. But eventually she must have remembered that it had literally been *years* since any of my peers had invited me to do anything at all, and she agreed to let me go.

Marnie cranked up the radio, and I swallowed the urge to ask her to ease off the accelerator as we zoomed through the neighborhood. When we made it out to Laurel Canyon Boulevard, the traffic forced her to slow down, and I relaxed a little, tilting my head back to stare at the ribbon of sky above us.

"Laurel," as Marnie called it, was a narrow road that curved through the hills between Hollywood and the Valley, which I knew nothing about except that Jonathan seemed to resent ever having to drive there.

The canyon felt like its own little world, a stripe of coziness tucked away from the sprawling city. Houses clustered tightly together, their front doors only a few feet from the road. Their backyards were steep hillsides covered in pale green grass and thickly flowering desert shrubs. In some places there was nothing but exposed rock, washed bare by mudslides.

Power, telephone, and cable lines crisscrossed overhead like party streamers, dripping with tendrils of ivy. In some places, the trees and shrubs grew so close to the road that I could have reached out and grabbed them. On every corner was a sign that read NO SMOKING IN THE CANYON. A hawk circled lazily overhead.

You could totally see why the hippies flocked here in the '60s and '70s. With its sharp turns and slabs of uneven concrete, it was a little dangerous feeling. And dirty.

Basically magical.

We drove all the way to the Valley, which, contrary to my expectations, looked like a pretty regular place. We stopped at an old-school diner called Du-par's for coffee and doughnuts with sprinkles, like two normal teenagers. *Normal.* It was a beautiful word . . . a beautiful feeling. Spending time with a friend, talking about school and TV shows. There were no voices in my head, no hallucinations. I felt an intense, almost wistful gratitude. . . .

Probably because I knew it would never last.

It was closing in on dinnertime, so we got in the car and made our way back into the hills. Marnie sang along to a country song about a guy who'd been waiting for his wife to come home from the grocery store for ten years. The breeze was cool, and the air smelled clean, like pine trees.

When we reached the house, Marnie parked in the driveway, then turned to me. "Watch out, Willa," she said, an impish little grin on her face. "You're starting to lose your deer-in-the-headlights look. Are you actually *enjoying* yourself?"

I laughed. "Maybe miracles do happen."

"Want to come over?" she asked. "I was thinking about watching *Kiss of Death*. Apparently it's super twisted."

I tried to think of a gracious way to say *no way on earth*, but before I could speak, the world went white.

*T*he light comes on suddenly, blinding me. I close my eyes and turn my head away. I don't need to look. I know he's there.

Then I hear his footsteps. He walks toward me and stops with an abruptness that makes me flinch.

"You smudged your makeup." His voice is edged with jagged steel.

I would apologize — I would say anything to keep him from being angry with me — but there's a piece of tape over my mouth.

"You promised me," he says, kneeling down. He wipes my cheeks with a paper towel so roughly that I start to cry again. "You promised you would try your best."

I feel like I've been punched. I am trying. I'm trying so hard. Can't he see that? For days I've been trying to do as he says, to be good enough.

"Faith, when we started rehearsals, I told you that if you got the scene right, I would let you go."

I nod. I try to plead without words. I try to convey how frightened I am. Maybe he'll take pity on me. Maybe he'll give me more time.

He takes my hand in his. His voice is soft with compassion. "I'm so sorry. It's just not working out."

I'm paralyzed by the words. He makes a regretful clucking sound and reaches forward. I flinch until I realize that he's not trying to touch me — he's playing with the necklace that hangs around my neck, moving the rose charm back and forth on the chain. "I understand if this is upsetting. I'm sorry I was short with you earlier. I know that's not the way to bring out your best work. You might as well go ahead and cry. I'm going to have to fix your makeup anyway."

The tears break free in a flood.

He walks back to the door, pausing to move a wheelchair out of his way, and turns to look at me. "We'll do the final performance tonight. I have a few things to take care of first."

Then he shuts off the light and leaves me alone with the echoes of his footsteps climbing the stairs.

CHAPTER 9

I drew in a huge gasping breath, like I'd been released from an airless room.

I stared at Marnie for a moment, then looked around, trying to make sense of my surroundings. We were still in her car, parked in the driveway in front of the house. The sky was blue, the grass was green, the late-afternoon light was turning soft and pink.

Not a single indication that it was anything other than a normal March afternoon.

"What? Why are you looking at me like that? Is there a spider on me?" Marnie swiped at her hair. "I had a spider fall on me once from a tree. It was huge. Horrible things. I hate them."

Even if I could have found my voice, I wouldn't have known what to say.

Her smile disappeared. "Are you okay, Willa? Seriously?"

"Um . . . yeah . . . I'm okay." *Except for being totally not okay.* "I should get inside, though."

She groaned. "Sorry. I'm a terrible driver. I should have asked you if you get carsick."

"It's all right," I said, trying not to wince from the headache that pounded on the inside of my skull.

The thought fell through me with a thud:

It happened again.

Any hope I'd held on to that my first vision-dream-episode thing — I didn't even know what to call it — had been a fluke . . . was now gone. This time it had been Faith, the second murder victim, whose thoughts had filled my head as if they were my own.

What is happening to me?

Marnie bit her lip and started to turn off the car. "Do you want me to go get your mom?"

The very idea gave me a shot of strength, enough to unbuckle my seat belt. "No. My mom is crazy overprotective. She'd freak."

Marnie stared out the windshield. "Must be nice. My parents are too busy managing their social media presences to overprotect me."

"It's okay," I said. "I'm fine."

"You don't look fine," Marnie said, but she could tell it was time to drop the subject. "Text me later, all right?"

"Yeah," I said, managing to smile as I got out of the car. After she drove off, I stumbled up to the front door. I was vaguely touched by her concern, but all I could concentrate on was the . . . dream? — *No, not a dream, it wasn't a dream* — it was more of a . . . *waking* dream.

But in the moment, it all *seemed* so horribly real.

As I opened the door, I was surprised to feel a rush of relief — the feeling of coming home.

"Willa?" Mom called. She met me in the foyer, looking a little harried.

"Mom," I said, still dazed. "Do you have a minute?"

She didn't hear me. "You left your phone!"

"Oh . . . Did you try to call?"

"Yes." Her smile was odd, and she spoke more deliberately than usual, enunciating like an actor in a play. "You have a visitor."

A visitor? I rounded the corner and came in view of the den.

Then I realized what was off about my mother's voice. It was the tone she'd used two and a half years ago, back when Aiden first started calling the house to ask for me. It was her *oho! there's a boy somewhere in a hundred-foot radius* voice.

Wyatt Sheppard was sitting on the couch. He got to his feet when I came in.

"I'll leave you two alone," Mom said. "My pork chops need me."

I turned to flash her a *no please don't* look, but she was already headed for the kitchen.

I had no choice but to face Wyatt. It was a bit of a shock to see him out of his school uniform, in jeans, boat shoes, and a moss-green sweater. He looked way preppier than a standoffish, murder-obsessed jerk had any right to look.

And way cuter, I thought, and then I mentally smacked myself for thinking it.

"Sorry to just show up." He wasn't smiling, and he didn't look sorry. "I didn't have your phone number."

And yet he somehow knew my address?

"I live three blocks away," he said, as if he'd read my mind. "And I knew where Jonathan Walters's house was because my mom memorizes all the celebrities in the neighborhood to impress our out-of-town guests. Trust me, great-aunts love to hear about Diana Del Mar."

I nodded, circling around the back of the couch, to put something solid between us.

Did he know about the notebook? He couldn't. He had to be here to discuss chemistry or something. Maybe even to apologize for being so rude all week.

"I'm here because I can't find a notebook that's really important to me," he said. "It's been missing since Monday. I'm extremely concerned about it. I've looked everywhere and asked everyone, with zero luck. The last time I definitely remember seeing it was in chemistry class. I just wondered if maybe you noticed it at some point."

I blinked, paralyzed.

He cleared his throat. "So . . . did you?"

"No," I said. "Sorry. What does it look like? I mean, I guess I might have seen it. What color is it?"

"Red," he said.

"Oh. Then no."

"Did you see a notebook that *wasn't* red?" He tilted his head questioningly, his eyes never leaving my face.

I shook my head. "Nope. No, no notebooks. Except my own. Which is green."

I was totally kicking myself for not just saying I'd found it on the floor and picked it up to give back to him later. Now I was caught in a web of lies.

76

I cleared my throat and tried to act normal. "So . . . what was in it?" A normal person would ask that, right?

He shrugged. "A project I've been working on. It wasn't for school. It was . . . personal."

Personal how? Personal like, "I'm a serial killer and that's my personal notebook about serial killing"?

"Sorry," I said. "Sounds important. I hope you find it."

He shook his head. "I'm such an idiot. I should have backed it all up."

I was afraid to speak, afraid anything I said would give me away.

"I'll go." He turned and walked with rounded shoulders toward the hallway, looking so dejected that I racked my brain for a way to spring it on him — *Hang on, did you say a RED notebook? Wait, yes. I do have a red notebook.* Maybe his relief at getting it back would be so great that he would forget to ask me why I'd lied about it.

But the moment passed, and he was all the way to the foyer.

Just the thought of his leaving calmed my nerves a little. Except, after he opened the door, he swung back and stared at me.

"You're positive," he said. "Totally positive you didn't see it anywhere?"

"Nope." His eyes brightened, and for a moment, I was almost overcome by panic. "I mean, yes. I'm positive. I didn't."

As he stared at me, I realized what it was about him that was so strange — he was so incredibly *honest.* You could tell just by having a short conversation with him that everything he said was the complete truth.

Which is why the next words out of his mouth almost made me pass out.

"I think you're lying," he said calmly.

It was like being blasted by a stun gun. My voice caught in my throat. "What?"

"You're lying." He didn't sound angry, which just made it worse. "I think you know where it is. You might even have it. You can't even look me in the eye."

I raised my hand and combed it through my hair.

"And that — touching your hair. Fidgeting. That's a sign, too."

I couldn't stand to look into his wide brown eyes, so I angled my body away from him. "I'd like you to leave, please."

To my dismay, he moved even closer. "If you have it, just give it to me. It's nothing to you. Why would you need to keep it? Or did you —" Fear flickered in his eyes. "Do you not have it? Did you do something to it?"

"No!" I said, turning away. "Please leave me alone!"

"I've watched you at school," he said. "It's not just this. You lie about everything. You're *always* lying."

For a beat, we stared at each other. He was infuriatingly placid. I was petrified.

"Hey, Willa?"

Wyatt and I both turned to see Reed walking toward the house from the garage.

My burning-hot cheeks grew one shade warmer. "Um . . . hi," I said to Reed, folding my arms in front of me. "What's up?"

"Just took Jonathan's Porsche out to get it washed." Reed's hand lightly touched my sleeve as he looked from me to Wyatt, and I thanked God that Marnie had made me change out of the overalls. "I don't mean to interrupt, but I wanted to check with you about something."

"Great timing," I said. "Wyatt was just leaving."

Wyatt gave me a meaningful stare and then walked away. I waited until I heard the *clunk* of the lock catching on the gate, then sighed and looked at Reed. "What do you need?"

He shook his head, his eyes wide and serious. "Nothing, actually. You looked uncomfortable. I thought I'd give you an out."

I could have hugged him, but I managed to restrain myself. "Solid," I said. "Thank you."

"Who was that? Was he bothering you?"

"Just a guy from school." I tried to downplay my uneasiness.

Reed glanced toward the gate. "He seemed a little intense."

"A lot intense," I said.

A lock of dark hair had fallen down over his forehead. Without thinking, I reached up and swept it back into place. Then we stood in silence for a second. My heart was pounding, for an entirely different reason than it had pounded when I was talking to Wyatt.

"I should go," Reed said, giving me a quick smile and heading back to the garage.

As soon as I was alone again, the glow of talking to Reed faded, and the horror of Wyatt's words returned.

If I could have been sucked into a hole in the ground, I would have. Crushed by a falling boulder? Fine. Awesome.

Anything but having to go to school Monday with my secrets exposed. On display. The shell I'd spent two years building up around me completely obliterated.

I don't know why Wyatt thought it would be okay to strip a broken person of her last defenses.

I don't know how he knew that everything about me was a lie.

But I did know he was right.

CHAPTER 10

For the rest of the weekend, I couldn't get Wyatt's accusations out of my mind. I was hurt and insulted and so . . . so . . .

Sad, I told myself.

You know, the kind of sad that makes you want to punch someone in the stomach.

I couldn't even manage to get worked up about the vision I'd had in Marnie's car. What was the point? My life was a surreal sham anyway. Might as well throw in some trippy delusions, too. Keep things interesting.

Sunday evening, Mom roasted a chicken, and I helped her set the table with cloth napkins and fancy silverware from the sideboard in the dining room. (But first I had to ask her what a sideboard was and be told that it was the low cabinet-thingy. So, to be less pretentious about it: I set the table with cloth napkins and fancy silverware from the low cabinet-thingy.)

We sat down to eat, with Jonathan at the head of the table.

"Could you get me a carving knife, Willa?" he asked. "They're in the sideboard, in a long, flat box."

Mom gave me a secret smile, like we'd accomplished something great by learning the names of all the furniture in time to anticipate my stepfather's whims. In the middle drawer, I found a long, flat box containing a narrow, curved knife and an oversize two-pronged fork.

"Joanna, this is gorgeous," Jonathan told Mom, carving away. "And so was last night's dinner. But, honey, we can hire a cook. Or have Rosa come in more often and handle the kitchen cleanup."

Mom blushed. "I don't mind. I like cooking. I even enjoy doing the dishes."

I hadn't thought anything could distract me from my self-pity party, but Mom's words hit me like a freight train.

Until my mother had somehow captivated Jonathan with her suburban-mom wiles the previous summer, she'd been the Media Relations Coordinator for Joffrey, Connecticut. She got to interact with film crews who wanted to shoot in our town (hence aforementioned captivation of Hollywood director). She even had a weekly radio show, chatting with cantankerous Joffreyites about their grievances — *Talk of the Town with Joanna Cresky*. She was good at her job. She loved it.

Now she loved doing the *dishes*?

Since the wedding, all she seemed to care about was making sure things were convenient for Jonathan — that we weren't too intrusive; that we were on our best behavior, always.

"We'll talk about it later," Jonathan said.

My mother smiled a non-smile. And my stepfather, who had apparently married her without knowing any of the important things about her, smiled back.

I studied my fork for a few seconds, then looked up at Mom, who was carefully spooning roasted carrots onto Jonathan's plate.

On the wall behind her, in jagged letters about a foot tall, were the words:

THIS IS THE KIND OF DREAM YOU DON'T WAKE UP FROM, HENRY

The letters were black and gooey-looking, like fresh paint or tar or oil. And as I stared, more writing appeared, underneath the sentence:

818

I blinked and closed my eyes and shook my head.

"Would you like carrots, Willa?" Mom asked. Her voice buzzed in my head. "There are also dinner rolls."

I tried not to look at the letters and numbers, but I couldn't stop myself. The words were still there, circling all four walls of the room. And then the numbers began appearing again and again — *818 818 818 818 818 818* — in fast, reckless strokes.

It's a hallucination, I told myself. *Just another stupid hallucination.*

"Willa?" Mom leaned across the table and reached out as if to touch my arm.

I dropped my fork with a clatter and jumped away from her. I don't know why. I suppose part of me was afraid that if she touched me, she would be able to tell that something was wrong.

"Honey, what's going *on*?" Mom asked.

I waited for her to add, *Where did those numbers come from?*

But instead, she said, "Why are you acting so . . . so frightened?"

I shouldn't have been surprised, but I was. I guess when something seems so incredibly real, no matter how improbable, your brain fights to believe you're not crazy. That it's really happening.

But Mom and Jonathan didn't see the writing.

So I *was* crazy.

"I'm fine," I said. I forced a cough. "I swallowed something wrong, that's all. Had to wait for it to go down."

"Goodness, you scared me," Mom said.

"Jo, she's fine," Jonathan said. "Let's all eat."

So we ate. I mindlessly chewed and swallowed carrots and chicken and a dinner roll while trying to ignore the fact that the walls were covered in words and numbers that only I could see.

By the time the meal was over, the writing had faded to a few pale gray streaks.

I started to carry my dishes to the kitchen, but my mother took them from me. "You go upstairs and rest," she said. "You don't look like you feel well."

I had a headache like a bass drum. "Mom, I'm totally fine."

But she sent me upstairs anyway, so I went.

"Feel better," Jonathan called after me.

Wyatt was right. I was a huge liar. But what was I going to do — tell them the truth?

The body in the pool. The force that held me down. The waking dreams. The voices. The overflowing tub.

How long was I going to ignore the writing on the wall?

Especially now that there was *literally* writing on the wall?

I guess you could call me a fool for taking so long to connect the various incidents to each other. Although, in fact, nothing actually did connect them. What could a dead body in the pool have to do with the name "Henry"? How did the number 818 fit together with an overflowing bathtub?

I had a list of unexplainable events. What I didn't have was the tiniest hint of a suspicion about their origins.

Well . . . I might have had the *tiniest* hint.

Jonathan had said that the movie star Diana Del Mar died in this house.

No, Willa. Don't even go there.

The food I'd forced myself to eat was churning in my stomach, and my headache was making my vision fuzzy. I stumbled and knocked into the corner of my desk, sending a stack of papers and binders to the floor.

Kneeling to clean up the mess, I noticed that one of the notebooks had fallen open. Wyatt's notebook.

I glanced at the page just before I closed it, and in that millisecond, the words burned into my eyes. I gasped and then pawed through the pages, looking for what I'd seen — not even totally sure I'd really seen anything. Maybe I was hallucinating again. Maybe I misread.

But then I found the list, written in Wyatt's impeccable, unmistakable print:

WATER (BATHTUB/POOL)
ROSES
NECKLACE (ALSO ROSE)
HENRY

CHAPTER 11

Wyatt didn't notice me waiting by his locker until he was only a few feet away. By then I was holding the notebook in front of me, cradled against my chest.

"You were right," I said. "I've had it for a week. I tried to give it back right away, but you were such a jerk that I changed my mind."

His mouth hung open slightly.

Full speed ahead. "I have some questions for you. About something you wrote."

Wyatt adjusted his glasses. "I don't want to discuss it in public."

"Why?" I said. "Because you're the murderer?"

His face twisted in disbelief. I half expected him to snatch the notebook out of my hands. Instead, he just glared at me, his eyebrows furrowed, and said "Seriously?" in a supremely annoyed voice.

"If you're not the murderer," I said, "why do you have so much information about the killings?"

He glanced around, but we were the only people in a thirty-foot radius. "Are you kidding? You think I'm the Hollywood Killer?"

"No," I said quickly, biting my lip. Backpedaling. "Of course not."

"You're lying again," Wyatt said.

A frustration bomb went off in my head. I gripped the notebook so hard that the metal spiral dug into my skin.

"Why do you say things like that?" I said. "Don't you realize how uncomfortable it makes people? I mean, really, no wonder you don't have any friends."

He snorted. "*I* make people uncomfortable? You just accused me of being a murderer!"

Okay, well. Maybe that was a fair point.

"Look, I'm sorry," I said. "But this —" I held the notebook out again, and this time he took it.

"Not here," he said quietly. "We should talk someplace more private."

"I don't understand."

He gave me a level, appraising look. "You haven't made a lot of friends yet, have you?"

There was no point in lying just to save my wounded pride, so I shook my head.

"Well," he said, "if you ever *want* to make friends at Langhorn, you should try not to be seen with me."

I didn't have the energy to protest. "All right. Where can we talk?"

"The library," he said. "After Chemistry."

"Fine."

He nodded briskly. "See you then."

I found Wyatt in the far back corner of the library, well clear of the circulation desk and the handful of students studying at the tables near the door. He was already leaned over, absorbed in his notebook. When he noticed me, he sat up and closed it automatically. I dropped my backpack and sank to the floor beside him.

"Okay," Wyatt said. "What did you want to talk about?"

First things first. "Why are you still investigating the murders?" I asked. "Your project's been done for months. Don't you think the police can solve them?"

He sat back, looking offended. "I didn't come here to defend myself."

"I'm not attacking you," I said. "I'm just trying to figure out what kind of person is so completely obsessed with someone else's crimes."

He looked up, his brown eyes walking the line between insulted and amused. "Me," he said. "My kind. Now, did you have real questions or are you just trying to psychoanalyze me?"

I held out my hand. "Can I see the notebook?"

He hesitated for a second before handing it over. I began looking for the page I'd seen last night.

"If you're worried about the killer," Wyatt said, "I think you should know that you're not his type."

I let the pages slip between my fingers and looked up at him. "Excuse me?"

"In the first place, you're not an actress, are you?"

"Not remotely."

"Then you're off his radar. He exclusively targets young female actresses with a specific body type, an isolated home life —"

"Thanks for your concern," I said, "but I'm not worried about myself. What I want to know about is this."

I held up the page so he could read it:

WATER (BATHTUB/POOL)

ROSES

NECKLACE (ALSO ROSE)

HENRY

"What does this mean?" I asked. "How do these things tie into the murders?"

He stared at the writing and seemed to choose his words carefully. "They don't."

"Obviously they do," I said, "or they wouldn't be in here. Don't tell me this is a shopping list."

"It's information," Wyatt said, frowning and pulling the notebook from my hands, "but not real information. Yes, it's connected to the investigation of the murders, but it's just speculation from a highly unreliable source."

"What source?" I asked.

He flipped back a page. "Leyta Fitzgeorge," he read out loud, a sarcastic flourish in his voice. "Psychic to the Stars."

I stared at the page he was looking at. He had actually written out *Psychic to the Stars* under her name.

"Leyta Fitzgeorge submitted those words to the police with a suggestion that they would help solve the murders," he explained. "But they're meaningless."

They had meaning for me. And for a second, I thought about telling him as much — relaying my stories about the pool, the writing on the wall, the name "Henry." But then I remembered that this was Wyatt Sheppard I was dealing with. I wasn't eager to draw any more of his scorn.

Finally, I asked, "What does the number eight-one-eight mean?"

"It's one of the LA area codes. For the Valley." Wyatt watched me intently. "It seems like there's some major thing you're not sharing."

"Do you know anything about Diana Del Mar," I asked, "aside from where her house is?"

Wyatt sat back, thinking. "She starred in movie musicals, right? Did she date Howard Hughes? No, that was what's-her-face. Why? What about her?"

An idea popped into my head. "The movies the serial killers used to pose his victims — were any of them Diana Del Mar movies?"

He shook his head. "Nope. She was long dead by the time any of them were released."

Another question occurred to me. "What did you mean before, when you said I shouldn't be seen talking to you if I want to make friends?"

He glanced down. "Nothing specific."

"Now *you're* lying," I said.

"I'm not lying," he said. "I'm just not going to provide you with the sordid level of detail you seem to be craving. If you want stories, you can get them from Marnie."

"Marnie has stories about you?" I asked.

He ran a hand through his hair and looked up at me, his brown eyes a little distant and sad. Then he blinked the mood away. "No doubt she does. Are we done? Because —"

"Almost," I said. "Can I ask a question that's not about the murders? Or Marnie?"

He nodded, a little wary.

"What did you mean at my house when you said I lie about everything?"

He shook his head. "That was out of line. I apologize."

"But you were right," I said, feeling a sudden heat in my chest. "How could you tell?"

He took a second to study me before answering. "Your body language is closed off. See how you lean back, cross your arms? You never maintain eye contact. And the touching, like I said — your face and neck. Covering your mouth."

I nodded, letting it all sink in.

"I didn't mean you tell actual lies." His voice was lower, almost gentle. "More like omissions — like you're shut off from people on some fundamental level."

Ah, yes. Where had I heard that before? A memory of my last talk with Aiden flashed painfully through my mind. "And you're not?" I said.

"Is this about me now? I am who I am. People can take me or leave me. I have nothing to hide." He wrote something in his notebook, and then tore off the sheet and handed it to me. "If you need to talk — I mean, if you have more questions — you can text me. Here's my number."

I pocketed the piece of paper. "One more thing?"

He narrowed his eyes. "If I can ask you something, too."

"Fine," I said. "What are you after? What's your endgame? At what point are you going to say you've done enough — when they catch him?"

"Maybe," Wyatt said. "Or maybe it's more like . . . Have you ever walked into a room, and you know something's different? Like your little brother's been messing with your stuff and tried to cover it up but you can tell?"

I shook my head. "I'm an only child."

Wyatt gave me a look. "I am, too. It was a metaphor. Do you ever get the feeling that you're missing something you shouldn't be missing?"

"I don't know," I said. "Maybe I feel that way all the time."

"That's how I feel about these murders. Like we're all missing something. There's some piece of the puzzle we haven't found yet. So I don't know if it's catching the killer I'm after . . . or just figuring out what's off. Making it easier for someone else to catch him."

"Fair enough," I said.

"My turn, right?"

I looked at the carpet and waited.

"What is it?" he asked. "What you're afraid of? The thing you hide." His voice was low and had a note of compassion in it that made me want to shove him.

Tears sprang to my eyes, and I reached up to swipe them away. "I don't think that's a fair use of your question."

"It's being angry, isn't it?"

I stared at him in shock. I didn't need to answer, because the look on my face was all the confirmation a person could ask for.

"I can tell. . . . I mean, I make people angry on a pretty regular basis," he said, giving me a self-conscious smile. "Apparently I come across as a little abrasive sometimes. But with you, I've said things that make you mad on some caveman level, but it's like . . . the emotion dies inside you. Without ever coming out."

I hardly dared speak, for fear of how my voice would sound. "And what's wrong with that?"

"I don't know." He shrugged. "It can't be healthy."

"Lots of things aren't healthy," I snapped. "We do them anyway. Like devoting our lives to studying a serial killer. I have to go."

I stood up and grabbed my backpack, then turned to leave.

Wyatt's soft voice stopped me. "But why? What's the worst that could happen if you let yourself get angry?"

I turned around and stared into his eyes. *You want eye contact, Wyatt? Here's your eye contact.* "The worst that could happen is that someone else could die."

CHAPTER 12

When I got home, Reed was sitting in Jonathan's office with the door open. He looked up and waved as I walked to my room.

I got the feeling that he wanted me to go in and talk to him, but I needed a few minutes to myself. I'd spent the drive home deflecting a barrage of Mom-questions, and I hadn't had a chance to process my conversation with Wyatt, especially the things he'd said at the end — things he had no right to even think about, much less say to me.

Instead I focused on the reason we'd talked in the first place: the list of items that he insisted were worthless, because they came from an "unreliable source." But that list was proof that my experiences weren't just the results of my overtaxed mind finally breaking down completely. Someone else knew, somehow, that those things fit together.

And that someone just happened to be a woman who billed herself as the Psychic to the Stars. I sat down with my laptop and Googled the name Leyta Fitzgeorge. A cookie-cutter website popped up.

Her number was listed, but I stopped short of calling her. Reaching out to Leyta Fitzgeorge might seem like the next logical step, but my most pressing goal was to clear away the drama in my life, and getting in touch with a psychic was a pretty obvious move in the opposite direction. So I set my phone on my desk. Maybe I'd call her later.

I changed from my uniform into slim-fitting jeans and a teal V-neck T-shirt that brought out the blue in my eyes, telling myself that this extra bit of care with my appearance had absolutely nothing to do with Reed's presence at the house. It didn't matter anyway, because when I went into the hall, there was no sign of him in Jonathan's office.

As I went downstairs, I could hear him talking to Mom in the kitchen.

"And anything that could be considered office supplies — printer ink or pens or stationery — I can arrange to have delivered from the studio. Just drop me a text or an email the day before you need them, and I'll take care of everything."

When I entered the kitchen, my mother looked up at me. "Oh, hi, Willa."

"Hi," I said, more to Reed than to her.

Mom cleared her throat a little awkwardly. "Thanks, Reed. We'll definitely let you know if you can help."

"Absolutely," Reed said. "Anytime."

He gave me a little eyebrow raise on his way out, and I had to fight to keep the corners of my mouth from turning up as I went to the sink to get a glass of water.

"He's very nice," Mom said, after he'd been gone for a minute.

"Yeah," I said.

"I'm going to have to talk to Jonathan, though," she said slowly. "I'm just not sure how I feel about having him in the house all the time."

I set my glass down with a louder clatter than I'd intended. "What do you mean? He's not here all the time."

"You know what I'm saying." She shrugged. "This is our home. Having a stranger here doesn't seem like —"

"He's not a stranger," I said. "He works for Jonathan. He's just trying to save money for college. You don't have to kick him out. Where will he go?"

"Oh, Willa, don't be so dramatic," Mom said. "He can work at Jonathan's office."

"But there's stuff that needs to be done here," I said. "He doesn't just do work on the movies. He handles a lot of random stuff around the house, too." I fought to keep my voice light and unemotional, when really, I was flipping out at the thought of not getting to see Reed on a regular basis. It wasn't that I had a crush on him — *I mean, maybe I do, but so what?* — but he was the only person in California who seemed to see me as the person I wanted to be.

My mother stood up to her full height (which was the same as my full height and therefore not terribly intimidating). "Anything that needs to be done here can be done by me."

"Why?" I asked. "Because you're suddenly some little wifey? What is this, 1950?"

She frowned, her eyes searching my face. "What on earth has gotten into you?"

Her question hit me someplace deep and raw. I looked down quickly, embarrassed.

Mom put the back of her hand against my forehead. "Are you feeling all right? Is it a headache?"

For once, it wasn't a headache, but I nodded anyway. "A little one."

"You're not getting them a lot, are you?"

I backed away from her gentle touch, shaking my head. "No, I'm fine. Forget it."

Her eyes flashed, a little wounded. "If you have something to say to me, then we should talk about it. But I feel like what you're trying to say doesn't have anything to do with Reed anymore."

I swallowed. Mom was always good at getting to the heart of things. But I wouldn't even know where to begin now.

"Willa?"

I shook my head. "I'm not trying to say anything. I just wanted a glass of water."

Mom's cell rang, and it was Jonathan, so she excused herself and went out the sliding door into the backyard. I let out a breath, put my glass in the dishwasher, turned to leave — and saw Reed standing in the kitchen doorway.

He was hovering, like he didn't know what to do with himself.

"Oh . . . hey." My words felt all stumbly and loose. "How much of that did you hear?"

"How much of what?" Seeing the skeptical look on my face,

he gave me a sheepish smile. "All of it. Sorry I didn't say anything. I didn't want to embarrass your mother."

"She doesn't mean any offense," I said.

"Of course not. I didn't take any. She's totally right. This is your house now. Jonathan has to change his bachelor ways." His lips twitched mischievously. "He might even have to take the Porsche to the car wash himself now."

The subversive little glint in his eye was gone as fast as it had appeared — but I'd seen it. And I was pretty sure he knew I'd seen it.

It kind of made me want to grab him and kiss him.

Reed tilted his head. "So that's what your real smile looks like."

My breath caught in my throat. "What?"

"Nothing." His fingers traveled absently up the side of the doorframe. "It was cool of you to defend me. But I don't want to cause any strife between you and your mother."

"Oh, don't worry about that," I said. "There's never any real strife."

He was less than two feet away. I could smell the boy smell of his perfectly rumpled jacket.

I looked up into his eyes. And he looked down into mine.

"Willa," he said, "you're . . ."

I held my breath.

The room was silent — for a few seconds, anyway. Then I heard:

Drip . . .

"Are you kidding me?" I said, looking up at the ceiling.

Reed took a jerking step back. "I'd better get back to work."

I stared at him, watching for any reaction to the sound.

Drip . . .

Nothing. He didn't hear it.

"Yeah," I said. "And I have some homework. Not a ton, but enough that I should . . . do it. I mean, get busy. I mean . . ." *I mean, ugh, SHUT UP, Willa.*

Then we both started for the stairs at the same time, which was incredibly awkward. But what was the alternative, him standing at the bottom watching me go up? Or me watching him?

"I think I'll get a — another glass of water," I said, ducking back into the kitchen as he went up toward Jonathan's office.

But I wasn't thirsty, so I simply stood in the kitchen, waiting.

And listening to the last sound I wanted to hear in all the world.

Drip . . . drip . . . drip . . .

That night, I sat in my room, my homework done, staring at the clock. It was only nine, and going to sleep so early felt like committing myself to nine solid hours of staring despairingly at the ceiling. I'd convinced myself that calling Leyta Fitzgeorge would be a fool's errand. It would waste her time and my own. Worst of all, Wyatt would be proved right.

Drip . . . drip . . . drip . . .

The sound had followed me around the house through dinnertime, until I wanted to pull my ears off and throw them out the window.

My fingers itched to take some concrete action. But what action can you take when your problems are the furthest thing from concrete?

When your problems are caused by a . . .

You know what it is, said some tiny, traitorous voice from someplace in the back of my mind.

In a fit of frantic, frustrated energy, I dug my fingernails into my palms, trying to suppress the thought — but it was too late. The word was in my head, and there would be no getting rid of it.

I grabbed the journal out of the drawer next to my bed and flipped it open. I took the pen, determined to let everything inside me come out on the page.

But despite how complicated my feelings seemed, it all came down to one simple thought:

GHOST, I wrote.

IT'S A GHOST.

And just like that . . . the dripping stopped.

I set down the pen and picked up my phone.

CHAPTER 13

Willa?" Wyatt was winded, his cheeks pink and a lock of sweaty golden-brown hair stuck to his forehead.

I pulled my French textbook from my locker and then shut the door, turning to face him. "Yes?"

He looked like he'd run all the way from the parking lot. "I have to ask you a question."

"Go ahead," I said.

"No." He glanced around at the almost deserted hall. "Not here."

"Wyatt, I'm not going to run and hide in the library every time we have four words to speak to each other. First bell's going to ring in like three minutes. If you need something, now's your chance."

He didn't look happy about it, but he conceded. "About yesterday — about that woman —"

"Leyta Fitzgeorge," I said.

"I just wanted to ask you not to call her."

"Too late. I called her last night." I almost said *sorry*, but I stopped myself. Because I wasn't.

For a moment, Wyatt seemed too dismayed to speak. "What did you ask her?"

"If I could go see her today."

He was so jittery that it almost made *me* nervous. "What? Why? What did she say?"

"She said yes," I said.

"But that's —" He stood up straight. "You need to cancel."

I let out a surprised laugh. "Um, no. You weren't willing to help me, so I'm helping myself. And now you don't even want me doing that?"

"You're not supposed to have that information." He stepped closer and lowered his voice. "*I'm* not supposed to have that information. If she complains to the police about you getting in touch . . ."

I waited for the second half of that "if," thinking he might reveal something about his source. But he clammed up.

"Why would she go back to the police?" I asked. "According to you, they ignored her before."

He huffed unhappily.

"Don't worry," I said. "I won't tell her where I got her name. Although she's a psychic, so . . ."

"You'll be wasting your time." There was a hint of presumptuous authority in his voice. "She's a crook."

I felt oddly protective of Leyta Fitzgeorge all of a sudden. "Why would you say that? You don't even know her."

"It's obviously true," he said. "Psychic abilities? More like made-up nonsense."

I shrugged. "I guess I'll find out for myself."

"So . . . wait. You actually think she could be right about something? All that stuff about water and the roses and . . ."

"Henry?" I said.

"Right, Henry." He rolled his eyes. "You know what she said? She said she got a 'feeling' about the name, but she couldn't be sure if it was a first name or a last name or even a middle name. Hey! Maybe it's the killer's dog's name! Ridiculous."

"It's a first name," I said.

For a beat, Wyatt was surprised into silence, which I found extremely rewarding.

Then he squinted at me. "How would you possibly know?"

"I know because I've . . . seen it. And heard it."

Wyatt adjusted his glasses. "What are you saying?"

"That Leyta Fitzgeorge might be right."

He shook his head and laughed nervously. "So you believe in psychics?"

Be careful, Willa. Where you're going, you can't come back from. "Well . . . I don't know, actually," I said. "But I do believe in ghosts."

He spluttered. Like, *"Spluh!"* Only he didn't say the word aloud. You could just see it coming out of his brain.

I hadn't quite meant to break it to him that way. On the other hand, it was a bit of a relief to have part of my secret out in the open. Even if I was telling it to someone who assumed everything I said was a lie.

"Excuse me?" he said.

"I said, I believe in ghosts," I pressed on. It felt like riding a bicycle down a steep hill — I couldn't stop even if I wanted to,

 104

but there was something exhilarating about it. "Specifically, I believe in a ghost who's living in my house and refuses to leave me alone."

A blend of emotions swept across Wyatt's face: disappointment, curiosity, and stubbornness. But his voice was utterly blank when he said, "A ghost . . . in your house."

"A *ghost*," I repeated. "In my house. Want me to say it again?"

"No. Thanks." He started to turn away. "Good luck with that."

"Wait," I said, grabbing the strap of his backpack. "You're seriously walking away from me right now?"

"Yeah, I'm seriously walking away." He looked flustered and upset. "I have no idea what you're doing. For all I know, this is all some bizarre prank that Marnie put you up to . . . And I'm not playing along anymore."

"It's not," I said. "Marnie wouldn't —"

"Oh," he said, and he laughed, a single bleak *ha*. "Oh, I can assure you, Marnie would."

"She didn't!" I said. "Nobody put me up to this — unless you count the stupid ghost who's giving me horrible visions about the murders and leaving me messages and trying to drown me —"

"A ghost tried to drown you?" he repeated, incredulous.

"In the pool," I said. "The night I moved in. I went swimming and I couldn't surface and —"

His eyes went mockingly wide. "Are you sure you actually know how to swim?"

I glared at him, and he shrank back a little. "I'm an *excellent* swimmer," I said. "My dad and I used to swim every morning.

I know the difference between not knowing how to swim and not being *able* to swim. Something held me under the water. And I saw —"

He was listening raptly, but I cut myself off. I wasn't sharing any more with him until he stopped being a jerk, which basically meant never.

"What?" he asked, interested in spite of himself. "What did you see?"

"Never mind," I said. "I was starting to think maybe you would listen to what I had to say without judging me. But I guess I was wrong."

"I'm not judging you," he said. "I just don't believe you."

"Fine." I could feel nervous, angry sweat beading at my hairline.

"Look, I get it," Wyatt said, startling me — he sounded almost understanding. "You move to a strange new city, into an old, drafty house with a lot of history. You're feeling uncomfortable in your new family situation, and —"

"What are you doing?" I snapped.

He looked a little hurt. "Trying to talk to you."

"You're trying to talk me down from believing in ghosts?" I said.

He seemed vaguely confused about it himself. "I don't know. I guess."

"Tell me this — if the psychic is a fraud and I'm hallucinating, why do the things that are happening to me appear on her list?"

"What? Really?" He looked genuinely surprised. "Well . . . it must be a statistically improbable set of correlations. I can see why you'd find it curious, though — if you're telling the truth."

"*If* I'm telling the truth?" Flabbergasted, I tried to muster what remained of my dignity. "You know what? Forget it. This has been a total waste of energy."

I was done being insulted and second-guessed. Just when I'd managed to convince myself I might not be insane, now Wyatt was actively trying to persuade me that I was. I wished I hadn't told him anything.

"Wait," he said, and the smirk disappeared from his face. Regret flashed through his brown eyes.

I held up my hand to stop him from saying more, and turned to head to class.

But then the world went white.

It must be almost morning. He blindfolded me but I've managed to get the blindfold down past the corner of my eye, and I can see a dim, blurry slit of my surroundings.

This is a different place. Not the place where we've been rehearsing. The table is set. I can see the roses. They've begun to wilt, just the faintest lack of crispness at the edges of the petals. He's so obsessed with detail, I wonder whether he'll replace them — and then, my heart drops into a dark, echoless chamber inside me.

He won't replace them. He doesn't need to.

Today will be the day.

I'm sure of it on some level I don't even understand.

He keeps telling me that if I behave, if I do well, he'll let me go, but that's a lie. He's a pretty good actor, but when it comes to outright lies, I can read him like a book. I know I've done a great job. Every cue, every mark, every line, I've delivered beyond his expectations. I can see it in his eyes, in the way he gets lost in the scene. I've been better than good enough.

I've been great.

And still, he'll never, ever let me go.

I know he'll be back soon, because he never stays away long. He comes and goes, bringing water and food and letting me use the restroom. He's perfectly hospitable.

I hate him.

What's more, he hates me. I can tell. I'm not like he thought I was. I'm not quiet and obedient — that was an act to earn his trust. But once I figured out he was lying, something inside me changed. Call it my foolish pride. I couldn't grovel to someone who was just waiting for the right moment to turn me into another trophy in his case.

Today is the day. I know it in my soul. And part of me is terrified — how could I not be? Every time he comes near me or speaks, something in me turns into a lost, frightened little girl.

I have a plan, though. It's not an escape plan —

I know better than that. I'm going to die here.

But I'm going to do it on my terms, not his. I've already broken his stupid necklace. He hasn't noticed. I stuffed it in the pocket of the skirt he makes me wear, my costume. Maybe when the police find me — afterward — they'll find it, and make some kind of connection.

Maybe they'll catch him, and keep him from doing this to anyone else, and it'll be because of something I did.

He's made me sit here at this table, my ankles and wrists bound so I can't run away, dressed in an old-fashioned skirt and scratchy blouse, with my hair pinned so tightly my scalp feels bruised, and talk about love and Namur and old ladies and apple carts. He's been in control. It's all been on his terms.

But tonight is on my terms.

He can take away my ability to run, but not my will to resist.

He can kill me . . . but he can't kill my spirit.

CHAPTER 14

I slumped back, hoping I'd run into a wall to lean against, but there wasn't one.

Wyatt grabbed me a split second before I could tumble to the floor.

"Hey!" he said. "What's going on? Willa?"

"Stop yelling," I said, because I didn't want him attracting attention. "Please. I'm fine."

Then we were faced with the fact of my being in his arms — a twelve out of ten on the awkwardness scale. I tried to straighten up and pull away, and he held on too long, and *thank God* nobody was watching.

I fought to steady myself, wanting to be as far from Wyatt as I could get, as soon as I could possibly get there.

"What just happened to you?" he asked. "Was that a seizure?"

"No," I said, though I'd never actually considered that possibility. "I mean . . . I don't think so. I don't want to talk about it."

He wasn't going to let it drop. "You froze up completely," he said. "It looked like a petit mal seizure —"

"They're not seizures," I said, careful to keep my voice cool and calm but betrayed by the drop of sweat trailing down the side of my face. "They might be hallucinations, but they're not seizures."

In spite of my desire to cut and run, I wasn't going anywhere until the heavy, dizzy feeling passed. Wyatt seemed to sense that, and — much more gracefully this time — he put his hand on my arm and gently eased me down onto a bench behind us.

He watched me anxiously. "What do you mean *'they'* — this has happened more than once?"

"Yes," I said, too dazed to lie. "That one makes three times."

"What is it that actually happens?" he asked.

I tried to find a way to explain it. "It's like a dream, except I'm actually there."

"Where?" His eyes searched me, taking in every detail of my appearance, the way he always took in every detail of everything. It made me feel prickly and self-conscious.

"Wherever the Hollywood Killer kept his victims."

"You're there . . . *with* the victims." The disbelief in his voice sent an angry chill through my body.

"Not *with* them," I said, bristling. "It's like I *am* them."

That shut him down long enough that I could continue.

"Like the one from *The Birds*," I said, "Brianna. And Faith, with the wheelchair. And then this one, with the dinner table and the roses. But I didn't hear the girl's name this time. I guess it was probably Lorelei."

Wyatt stared at me.

"It's like . . . a vision, or a trance or something. I feel what they felt. I can even see the necklace he makes them all wear — the *rose* necklace. I can't see the killer's face, and I can't really hear his voice . . . I don't know how to explain it, only — I'm there."

"Willa." Wyatt frowned. "I'm sorry. There's got to be some other explanation."

"Why?" My voice was hollow and brittle. Maybe because he really did sound apologetic.

"Because there hasn't been a murder with a dinner table or roses," he said. "And there are no necklaces. You must be imagining all of it."

No table. No roses. No necklace.

Could I really be making it all up? The headaches, the visions, the flashes of light — could there be a tumor pressing on my brain, convincing me that all these crazy things were real? I thought of the dead body that wasn't in the pool and the water that wasn't in the tub and the writing that wasn't on the walls.

But the name Henry. Water. A necklace. The stuff the psychic said . . .

"Is there anything I can do or say," Wyatt said, "to talk you out of going to see this Fitzgeorge woman?"

I took a shaky breath and straightened my cardigan, trying to think up a reply.

"Right," Wyatt said. "I didn't think so. Then can you do me a favor?"

I glanced down at the floor, my resolve slipping away.

And then he said, "Let me come with you."

The parking lot was deserted — Wyatt insisted we wait until everybody else had gone home, so there was no risk of our being seen together.

I was halfway to his silver Prius before a couple of thoughts tumbled into my head at once. Firstly, that maybe Wyatt was the murderer and here I was, hopping into his car. Secondly, I was still supposed to be mad at him. In fact, since the moment we met, I'd never *not* been mad at him.

I stopped walking and turned to him. "Just to be clear . . . you're not the killer, right? If you are, you have to tell me. Murderer's honor."

He raised a single eyebrow and unlocked the car doors. "You coming or not?"

"Yes, coming." I opened the door and climbed in, tossing my backpack into the backseat. When I was all buckled in, I looked over at him as he plugged Leyta's address into his GPS. "So tell me again why you offered to go with me?"

He glanced at me before pulling out of the parking lot. "I had a feeling you'd try to take a bus or something —"

"A cab, probably," I said. "If I tried to take a bus, I'd end up in Kansas."

"Anyway, I thought it would be better if I drove you."

"But you don't believe in psychics."

"No," he said. "I don't."

"And you don't even want me to go."

"No," he said again. "I don't."

We stared at each other for a second before he pulled his eyes away to look at the road.

"Then you haven't answered me at all. Why are you doing this?" I asked. "You clearly think I'm crazy."

"I never said you were crazy. I said you must be imagining things. But in retrospect, maybe that was a little dismissive."

"*Harsh* might be a better word. *Insensitive* . . ."

He gave his head a frustrated shake. "You can't be angry with me for not believing in something I have no experience with, okay?"

We turned down Hollywood Boulevard, which was thick with sightseers. There were costumed characters everywhere — Spider-Man, Superman, Catwoman, Elmo, the Statue of Liberty, a guy in metallic paint pretending to be a robot. . . . They looked weird and fake even from a distance, but people were still lining up to get their pictures taken with them.

"There's the Chinese Theatre," Wyatt said as we drove by a building that looked like a pagoda. "It's pretty famous. Have you been yet?"

"No. I heard it's not much to see. Movie stars have tiny feet."

He snorted. "All of them?"

"Well, let's see, Wyatt. Let me consult my list of famous people's shoe sizes right here and —"

"Why are you reacting that way?" he asked.

"Why do *you* have to pick everything apart?" I shot back.

He sighed and checked the mirror as he changed lanes. "Okay, forget it. I was only trying to make conversation, but I guess I shouldn't bother."

I glanced over at him. He looked a little hurt. "I'm sorry," I said. "It was nice of you to try. But talking to you is so . . . complicated."

"What does 'complicated' mean to you?"

"In your case?" I said. "It means you don't know when to let things go."

He adjusted his air vent so it blew away from him. "Yeah, I can see that."

I gazed out the window as the navigation voice instructed us to turn left in two hundred feet. We'd passed from the crowded, garish boulevard into a residential neighborhood where the tiny houses were small and crumbling. Each one was unique, but they all shared the qualities of age and neglect: chipping paint, cracked windows, limp curtains, drooping chain-link fences.

"I don't like letting go of things," Wyatt said in a thoughtful voice. I realized he'd been thinking of my words this whole time. "Not until I understand them."

I wasn't sure how to respond.

"What's the number on that duplex?" he suddenly asked.

I craned my neck to see it. "Fifteen-oh-one."

"Then we're here," he said, pulling into a spot in front of a decrepit building. "Let's go find out what the future holds."

CHAPTER 15

Leyta Fitzgeorge was about thirty, tall, and wispy thin, with long waves of mouse-brown hair. She wore a forest green polo shirt that said GAME WORLD with a pair of khaki pants.

"Sorry about the shirt," she said. "I know it detracts from the mystique and all. I have to leave for work pretty soon."

"It's fine," I said. "I'm Willa, and this is my . . . classmate, Wyatt."

"You work at Game World?" Wyatt asked.

She nodded. "I can match any customer with their perfect game. I've never had a return."

Wyatt scoffed.

She took out her phone. "Want to call my manager and ask?"

"No," he said, looking a little shocked by the suggestion.

Leyta's teeny apartment was clean and pleasant. The carpet was old and worn in places but free of stains. The pictures on the walls were posters of paintings in cheap plastic frames. The only one I recognized was Van Gogh's *Starry Night*. The air was scented with traces of cinnamon.

"Sit, please," she said, pointing us toward a blue velour recliner in front of a small table. On the other side were two folding chairs. Those four pieces of furniture pretty much filled the living room.

"Thanks for meeting with me," I said, sitting on one of the folding chairs.

"That's fine," she said. "You need it, I can tell."

"You can tell?" Wyatt said, his voice painted with skepticism. "Really? How?"

I turned to him. "Do you mind? This is my appointment."

"It's okay." Leyta waved a hand in his direction. "Let him talk. That's his flow. His journey."

"Yes, Willa," Wyatt said, leaning back and folding his arms. "Let me flow on my journey, please."

I gave him a dirty look and then turned my attention back to the psychic.

"So," she said. "You said you have questions about the future . . . but that's not completely true, is it?"

"You don't have to be a psychic to deduce that," Wyatt said. "She's a terrible liar."

"Wyatt, buddy," Leyta said, "shut your flow for a minute. Okay, Willa. You don't want to talk future. You want to talk past. Things that are done that can't be undone."

"Right," I said. "I need to know about the murders."

She sat back and frowned at me. Like, big-time frowned. "Honey, what are you into?"

"Nothing," I said. "I just have questions —"

She held up her hand and clucked her tongue. "You don't have questions. You may not realize it, but what you have is answers. And that's not all you have."

"What does that mean?" I asked.

She shook her head. "We're getting ahead of ourselves. What about the murders? Why come to me?"

"Because you talked to the police," Wyatt said.

Leyta ignored him and kept her gaze on me. "Why don't you tell me what you know?"

"The necklace," I said. "I know there was one. I've seen it in my . . . my visions. And I know about Henry. And water."

Her expression didn't change, but there was a shift in her energy. All of a sudden, she was very interested. "Is there a smell? Acrid, like somebody spilled a whole bottle of vinegar?"

"No," I said. "Sorry. I never noticed that."

"And what about Henry?" she asked.

"There's a phrase." I glanced at Wyatt. I hadn't told him this part. "It goes, *'This is the kind of dream you don't wake up from, Henry.'* Does that mean anything to you?"

"No," she said, closing her eyes. "Not specifically. I feel that it's right, but I don't know what it means."

"It's not from any of the movie scenes the killer used," Wyatt said. His words were know-it-all, but his tone was subdued — for the moment.

Leyta folded her hands in her lap. "So what are you hoping I'll do for you?"

"Help me make it stop," I said. "It's driving me crazy."

She looked at me with an expression I didn't care for. Too sympathetic. Like she had bad news. "I can imagine."

"Why me?" I asked. "What does it have to do with me?"

"Sounds like somebody's trying to tell you something," she said. "Trying hard."

"But I don't want to hear it." There was a break in my voice, and I realized I was leaning far forward. I forced myself to sit back and take a long breath. "I don't care what it means — I just want it to stop."

"Things come to us in life." Leyta waved her hands around in what was supposed to be an illustration of the flow, I guess. "Good things, bad things. Sometimes we get what we want, sometimes we don't. The important thing about being alive is, what do you do when you can't have what you want? *That's* what determines what kind of person you are."

Wait, so . . . was she a psychic or a guidance counselor?

"But what do I *do*? Can you help? I'll pay you whatever you ask. You could come to my house and —"

"Willa," she said, shaking her head slowly, "just keep listening."

"That's it?" Wyatt sounded like he was trying to keep from losing his temper. "You let her come all the way here to give her a bunch of mysterious, vague non-advice? And then you tell her you can't even help? Some psychic."

She replied sharply, without removing her eyes from mine. "As Willa well knows," she said, "spirits are capable of many things. But there are also many things they're not capable of.

These visions you have — you feel what the girls felt, but you can't see a face, correct?"

When I nodded, she went on. "What you have to understand is that a spirit presence doesn't operate like you or me. We're a mess of thoughts and feelings. A spirit is more like . . . an instinct. Its whole purpose is to drive at something, to convey an idea or a concept."

"Like who the killer is?" I asked.

She sat back and raised her eyebrows. "Perhaps. We can only guess."

"How do I get the . . . the spirit to tell me what it wants?" I asked.

"Let me put it this way," Leyta said. "Tell me what it feels like to be in love."

I swallowed hard. First I thought of Aiden, then I thought of Reed. I glanced at Wyatt and felt myself blushing. He was blushing, too.

Leyta rolled her eyes. "Okay, nix that. I forgot you're a teenager. Tell me what it feels like to be angry. Really try."

I glanced at Wyatt again, and noticed how careful he was not to look at me. "You feel something heavy," I said. "Pushing down on you. Pushing you toward the edge of something. Helpless and . . . hot and . . ."

I ran out of words.

"Exactly," she said. "Now think of trying to convey that idea to someone who doesn't speak your language, who can't even see you. What would you do, if you were a ghost?"

"Hold someone down in the pool so they can't breathe?" I asked. "But the spirit can write. It *writes* on the walls. So why won't it just write down its story?"

"Well, you didn't tell a story just now, did you?" She shrugged. "You didn't say to me, 'Wyatt said this and it ticked me off and then I said this . . . and it made me so *angry*.'"

Her point was beginning to sink in, even though it still felt a little soupy around the edges.

"If I thought I could help, I'd go to your house right now. But nothing's gonna show itself to me. These messages are for *you*, Willa. The ghost itself might not even understand what's going on. It's driven by a need to convey something. And you're the one it's telling it to. Not me. Not your parents. You."

I buried my face in my hands.

Wyatt's voice came faintly from my right. "Lucky you."

"Do you mind if I speak to Willa for a moment?" Leyta asked. "Alone?"

"It's up to Willa," Wyatt replied.

Even though Wyatt could be a total pain, there was something reassuring about having him there. Weirdly, I felt I could trust him. "It's all right," I said. "He can stay."

Leyta nodded, then leaned forward and took my hands in hers. "How long ago did you start messing with stuff you shouldn't have been messing with?"

Her question seemed to vibrate through the air. Wyatt tensed in his chair, and I felt my shoulders slump.

I swallowed hard. "Two years in May."

"What are you talking about?" Wyatt asked. "Drugs?"

Leyta's scrawny fingers, wrapped around mine, were surprisingly strong. Her pale brown eyes didn't waver from my face. "You tried it once, and then you kept doing it, right? You kept pushing and searching."

"I had to," I whispered.

The hardness left her face. She sighed. "I know."

"But I quit," I said. "Last week."

It was as if I hadn't spoken at all.

"Headaches, yes?" she asked.

I tried to ignore Wyatt's eyes boring into me and said, "Yes."

"They're bad, right? You get them every day? What about flashes — do you see flashes? Like light, but hazy?"

I nodded.

"There are voices? Whispers?"

"Maybe," I said.

"And it all started when you first tried to make contact, right?" She sighed and sat back, shaking her head. "Who taught you how to do it?"

"A book," I said. "By Walter . . . somebody."

"Sawamura," she said. "Walter Sawamura. Which book? He's written dozens."

I wanted desperately to pretend I didn't know, but I said, *"Contact with the Spirit Realm."*

She nodded, tapping her fingers on the armrests. "That book was published in 1983. Do you know what was published in 1984?"

I shook my head.

"A letter from Walter Sawamura to everyone who'd bought that book, begging them to send their copies back to him. Some things don't belong in the hands of those who aren't strong enough to control them. He refunded the money out of his own pocket, because he knew he'd made a huge mistake. He lost thousands of dollars. But a few copies slipped through. And I guess you found one."

I nodded.

"Listen to me," Leyta said. "Go home, take that book, and — you have a moldavite ring, I suppose?"

"Yes," I whispered, thinking of the green-stoned ring in the black suede pouch.

"Put the ring in a ziplock baggie full of salt. Put that bag and the book in a shoe box. Put something made of real silver in the box. Duct-tape it shut and bury it. Twelve inches deep at least. Don't ever dig it up."

"Um . . . okay," I said. "And that'll get rid of the ghost?"

Her face fell. "No. But it'll close the door on the energies and spirit forces that are hitchhiking on your aura. It should take care of most of the headaches, the dizzy spells, the flashes. . . ."

Those were all things I'd brought on myself? I couldn't believe I hadn't connected them with my lame, hopeless efforts to contact Dad.

I dropped my head, feeling like the dumbest person on the planet.

"I know it was an accident," Leyta said, patting my hands gently. "But, honey, every ghost in a ten-mile radius came running every time you called, and one of them finally got its hooks in you. Now it's on you to figure out why, otherwise you'll never be free of it. You've created a portal and you draw energy to you, like a magnet. You probably feel like you've been going crazy. Your aura is like . . . like a thunderstorm."

"Excuse me." Wyatt cleared his throat but managed to keep his voice muted, respectful. "If she's been doing this for two years, why did a ghost just now, uh . . . latch on?"

"Because," Leyta said, staring directly into my eyes, "all that stuff before, those were first dates. *This* entity, whatever it is, felt connected enough to get you. And now . . . you're *got*."

"Awesome," I said gloomily. "How do I get un-got?"

"There are no shortcuts in the flow," Leyta said, "no clicking your heels three times and *poof*! This is your journey. You gotta go with it."

I nodded.

She sat back and clapped her hands lightly on her knees. "That's it, kids. Show's over. Can't be late; my manager's in a terrible mood today."

I stood up and reached for my purse. "How much do I owe you?"

"Your money's no good here," she said. "Just take care of yourself."

"Out of curiosity," Wyatt said, "what does my aura look like?"

"Ha," Leyta said. "You, I charge for that information."

She walked us to the door. As soon as Wyatt opened it and stepped outside, Leyta put her hand on my shoulder, leaned forward, and quickly pulled the door closed.

We were alone in her apartment, the two of us.

"May sixteenth," she said in a rush. "Two years ago. I woke up and Paul was here."

Paul Cresky? My father?

May sixteenth. I went numb.

"He said to tell you to be good. And that he loves you." She hesitated. "Was he religious? Because he said to tell you to look for a shepherd."

I didn't trust myself to speak, so I shook my head.

"Listen, you're not going to find your dad, sweetie, and you never were. He's moved through. He's good. He doesn't need to forgive you. *You* need to forgive you, that's all."

I nodded, which was basically the only thing I was capable of doing.

"Anyway, you'd better go," she added softly. "Your friend probably thinks I'm performing voodoo ceremonies on you. He's a bit much, but he cares about you. And don't tell him I told you, but his aura's green. He's a healer."

She opened the door and I stumbled out, crashing into Wyatt a millisecond before I would have fallen down the steps.

"What did she say?" he asked. "Are you okay?"

"Yeah," I said, a pathetic lie.

But he was kind enough not to call me on it.

As we walked toward the car, I couldn't stop thinking about my dad . . . and then it hit me.

Look for a shepherd . . .

Could he have meant *Wyatt* Sheppard?

CHAPTER 16

My mother was in her bedroom, folding laundry, when I knocked on the door.

She looked up at me, a bright smile on her face. "How was studying?"

Oh, right, my cover story — studying at Marnie's house. "Good," I said. "Do you have an extra shoe box somewhere?"

"An empty one?"

I sat down on the bed. "If I didn't want an empty shoe box, I would have asked if you had *shoes*."

"Ha-ha, smartypants," she said. "I'll go check my closet. Here, make yourself useful."

She dumped a bunch of socks next to me, and I set to work matching them. It was weird touching anything Jonathan wore, even if it was on his feet.

A few seconds later, Mom came out, holding a pink box out to me. "Here you go."

"Thanks." I got up to leave.

"Hang on, Wil," she said. "Do you think you could stay at Marnie's the last weekend in April?"

"Sure," I said. "Why? What's going on?" I'd been sitting with Marnie and the other Hollywood kids every day at lunch, and she was the closest thing I had to a friend, but we still didn't feel remotely close. Still, I figured she would be cool with me sleeping over at her house.

A sunny smile bloomed on Mom's lips. "Jonathan and I are going on a little trip to Palm Springs. If you're not comfortable with my leaving, I don't have to go, but since we didn't get a honeymoon . . ."

"Of course you should go," I said. "I'm a big girl."

"Thanks, sweetie. Jonathan had to move a bunch of meetings around to make it work, but he says it's no big deal."

"Mom," I said, rolling the matched socks across the bed to her, "he *married* you. Stop acting like you're auditioning for something."

"Oh, Willa," she said. "It's not like that."

"It kind of seems like it is," I said, studying the intricate hand-embroidered design on their white bedspread.

"I'm sorry if that's the impression I've given you," she said quietly. "But I'm very happy. So is Jonathan. And our greatest wish is that you'll be happy here, too."

"I'm fine," I said. *Unless you count the fact that I've opened a portal to the spirit world, I'm being stalked by a ghost, and my aura is the color of dirty rainwater. Other than that, things are awesome.*

"'Fine' isn't the same as happy," Mom said.

Maybe not. But sometimes it's the best you can hope for.

Back in my room, I put the ring — submerged in a plastic baggie full of salt — into the shoe box. Then I dug through the rest of my boxes until I found the Walter Sawamura book, still feeling conflicted. Why should I get rid of the book if that wouldn't solve my ghost problem? What if I needed it? For that matter, why should I believe Leyta in the first place? Sure, she knew my dad's name and the date of his death, but big deal — she could have spent the whole day Googling me.

But she knew things you can't find online, I thought, feeling a nervous flutter in my stomach. Like the flashes and the head-aches and the voices.

I studied the cover of the Walter Sawamura book. It looked way too innocent to have caused so much trouble. But a lot of things that look normal on the outside contain more than their share of drama — I should know.

I dropped the book in the shoe box.

Then I tucked the box behind the laundry hamper in my closet.

Some things I wasn't ready to let go of yet.

For the rest of the week, Wyatt and I maintained a wary but respectful silence on all topics having to do with ghosts, mur-ders, and psychics. During our weekly lab project, we even managed to be almost friendly to one another.

Things were calm at home, too. Once, sitting at the dinner table, I heard a dripping sound, but it turned out that the cleaning lady had accidentally left one of the powder room fau-cets on.

I found myself hoping that my visit to Leyta Fitzgeorge had shaken something free. Maybe the ghost had finished conveying whatever message it was trying to convey, and now it was gone.

Friday after school, I was sitting on my bed, conjugating French verbs, when there was a knock at the door.

"Come in," I called.

The door opened a fraction of an inch. "Willa?"

"Reed?" I hopped up and went to the door, smoothing my hair as subtly as I could.

"I've been working in Jonathan's office, and my eyes are tired from staring at the screen all day." He smiled that crooked smile that made my cheeks heat up. "I thought I might go for a short walk — would you like to come?"

In what dark, ridiculous corner of the universe would someone say no to that question?

We made our way around the neighborhood, weaving from one side of the street to the other to stay visible to cars that might be zooming around the corners. I remembered the first walk I took in LA — when everything seemed totally foreign and weird. Now it felt almost natural to drift back and forth across the road.

"Are you all right?" Reed asked. "You seem quiet."

"Sure," I said. "All good."

"You know what sets you apart from most girls in LA?" Reed asked.

I glanced up at him. I hadn't realized that anything set me apart from anyone — except maybe my craziness.

"You don't always make it about yourself," he said. "You think more than you speak."

Was it supposed to be the kind of compliment that sends you reeling? Because it did. My stomach felt like a pinwheel spinning in my body.

"Well," I said, "maybe I'm thinking about myself the whole time."

"Maybe." Reed laughed quietly. "But I doubt it. You're an outsider, like me."

"I thought you were born in Los Angeles," I said.

"I was. But I still don't fit in. I don't care about cars, or clothes, or money. I only care about the quality of my work." He shrugged. "You'd be surprised how many girls lose interest in a guy when he doesn't drive an expensive car."

"I don't get the car thing," I said. "Who cares what somebody drives? I mean, say a person has the fanciest car in the world. What if he's a jerk? I'd rather be in a falling-apart minivan with somebody cool."

Then I wondered if my little speech made it too obvious that "somebody cool" in my eyes was . . . well, Reed. I felt a warm flush creep up my cheeks and clamped my mouth shut.

But Reed only grinned at me. "I completely agree," he said. "Hey, how's Langhorn treating you? Make a lot of friends yet?"

I shrugged. "More like *friend*. But she's pretty nice. And then there's one guy who . . . I mean, I don't know if you'd consider us friends. We're more like allies."

"Sounds like a very meaningful relationship," Reed said, his eyes crinkling in amusement.

"The bizarre thing is that it kind of is," I said. "I didn't realize that you can appreciate someone's company without actually getting along with them . . . at all."

He laughed softly. "I'm not sure I follow."

I'm not sure I do, either. "Anyway, let's talk about something else."

"Like what?"

I searched for a topic. "Um . . . movies?"

"Movies," he said. "That's something you never hear about in Hollywood."

I gave his arm a little swat. "So what are your favorites?"

"That's a tough question," he said. "I'm a fan of the old classics, of course — like everybody else. All of the Lord of the Rings films, obviously . . . *The Dinner Party* . . . *Little Miss Sunshine* . . . *Wall-E* . . ."

"Seriously?" I said. *"Little Miss Sunshine* and *Wall-E*? That's so cute."

"Cute, huh?" He grinned and reddened slightly. "I also love *Kill Bill*, does that buy me any street cred?"

"Sure," I said. "It takes you from a two out of ten to a three and a half."

"What movies do you like?"

"I'm more of a book person," I said. "I probably shouldn't admit this, but I've never seen the Lord of the Rings movies. . . . I read *The Hobbit*, though."

"Willa," he said, in mock disapproval. "This is a problem. We have to remedy this at some point in the near future."

Watching movies with Reed? Um, yes, please.

"My favorite movie of all time is *The Princess Bride*," I said. "Mom used to let me watch it when I was home sick from school."

"Sophisticated cinema, there," Reed teased, and I blushed, feeling like a little kid. A few seconds later, he stopped walking and shook his head. "I'm sorry. I shouldn't have said that. I'm in a weird mood today."

"Weird moods are fine by me," I said. "Weirdness in general is kind of my specialty."

He smiled, and his eyes met mine. "You're not weird. You're . . . nice."

You're nice. The words were so simple, but they sent a shiver of happiness up my spine.

Back at the house, we stood on the front porch.

"Everyone wants you to fit into their mold, don't they?" he asked. "But you don't fit. Who cares? I never fit any molds, either."

I held my breath.

"Willa, I —" He hesitated. "What if I told you — No, I shouldn't."

I wanted to grab him by the collar and shake him and yell *SAY IT,* but I didn't.

"Willa . . ." His voice trailed off.

I didn't need any more words — it was enough to hear him say my name like that. It seemed as if we were in a little bubble with our own air. My heart felt like it was being pulled out of my chest, toward Reed.

We took a step closer to each other. His hands moved gently up to my face.

And then we were kissing.

It happened so fast that it took me a second to understand what was going on, which cost me about two seconds of enjoying the kiss, which let me tell you was a very sad loss of two seconds.

The kiss went on and on . . . like we were under a spell, neither of us willing to break it by stepping away. His lips were as warm and irresistible as the rest of him.

After a minute, we pulled apart and stared at each other, stunned.

"I — I can't believe that just happened," Reed said.

Boldness flared up in me like a torch. "I can," I said.

He stepped back. His voice trembled. "No, Willa, you don't understand. Jonathan's your stepfather. And he's my boss. He can never find out."

"He doesn't have to find out," I said, relishing the defiant sound of my own voice. "Why should he?"

He wrapped his gentle fingers around mine, his eyes cast down. "I'm not going to ask you to lie for me."

His thumb made a circle on my palm and left me breathless.

"You don't have to ask me," I whispered.

He reached up and touched my hair, smoothing it gently against my cheek. "Have a good weekend," he said quietly.

The look in his eyes said he wished he could say more.

But we both knew he wouldn't.

CHAPTER 17

Monday at lunch, I was still half lost in thoughts of Reed and our kiss. The past week had been so blissfully ghost-free that I'd hardly even thought about the murders. An unprecedented sense of normalcy was slipping over me. I was even getting night after night of uninterrupted sleep. It was a little eerie.

"Earth to Willa," Marnie said, interrupting my reverie. "I said, do you have plans Friday night?"

"Who, me?" I asked. "I never have plans."

Marnie laughed, filling the air with music. "My dad got me tickets to the premiere of the new Kurt Conrath movie. Want to come? But there's a catch — you have to help me kidnap Kurt and take him home and lock him in my closet forever and ever amen."

"Um," I said. "Okay. I'll need to ask Mom, but . . . What should I wear?"

"All black," she said. "Ski mask. You don't happen to have a kidnap van, do you?"

I tried to laugh, but even joking about kidnapping stirred up unwelcome thoughts of the visions.

"Wear something trendy," Marnie said. "A dress."

I had no desire to be part of a huge, chaotic Hollywood function, but the alternative was sitting at home daydreaming about Reed and still waiting, slightly on edge, for more ghostly messages.

"I have a dress," I said. "But I don't think it's trendy."

"Don't," she said, pointing a finger at me. "*Do not* show up in a dress you wore to some auntie's wedding, please."

Oh. "Then I don't have anything."

"No worries. Just come home with me Friday." She patted my head. "Mama Marnie'll fix you right up."

After school on Friday, I found myself feeling almost enthusiastic as I rode with Marnie to Hancock Park, where the streets were lined with old-school mansions. Her house was light brown with a pointy roof and colorful flowers everywhere. It looked like Hansel and Gretel's cottage — if Hansel and Gretel had been millionaires.

Marnie's bedroom was much pinker than I would have expected, with fuchsia walls and a huge white fairy-tale bed. A makeup vanity with a big round mirror was pushed up against one wall, and the chandelier above the bed dripped with teardrop-shaped crystals. The carpet (what you could see of it, anyway, between piles of clothes, books, and papers) was plush and white.

I set my overnight bag in the corner. This was going to be kind of a dress rehearsal for Mom and Jonathan's Palm Springs trip.

"I like your room," I said, to be polite.

"I hate it," Marnie replied, heading to her closet. "My mom did it during her interior-decorator phase. They shipped me off to summer camp in Oregon, and when I came back, I was living inside a Barbie Dreamhouse. Only it's more like a nightmare house. I swear, the color literally burns my retinas."

"They won't let you change it?"

She shrugged. "It gives me leverage when I want something from Mom." She went into her walk-in closet and pulled out a gold-sequined minidress. "What do you think? It's vintage. Mary Quant."

"Um," I said, trying to conceal my horror.

Her face fell. "You don't like it? I was going to wear it with my white go-go boots."

"Ohhhh," I said. "It's for you? In that case, I love it. It's great."

"Willa, you wear overalls on purpose. You think I would break the laws of time and space by putting you in *sequins*?" She tossed the vintage dress onto her bed, as if it were a T-shirt she'd picked up on clearance from Target. Then she ducked back into the closet.

When she came out holding a slim-fitting cherry-red dress with three-quarter sleeves, I could have hugged her. She handed the dress to me. The fabric was slinky and soft, and the design was simple — a plain high neckline, two pieces of red fabric forming a flattened X at the waist, and delicate gathers at the ends of the sleeves.

"Willa like?" she asked.

"Yes," I said. "Willa like very much."

"That's vintage, too," she said. "It was my great-grandma's, in the forties."

"It's beautiful," I said.

She gave me an approving smile. "It beats overalls, anyway."

Marnie had an array of powders, creams, and blushes that she kept in a case like a professional makeup artist. I was surprised to realize that I remembered how to apply it all — two years of not caring what I looked like hadn't erased the muscle memory of blending eye shadow and making the fish-mouth mascara face.

After we both finished our makeup, Marnie ran her hands through my hair and made an unhappy chirping sound. "What about your hair? How retro are you willing to go? I'm thinking maybe an updo. Keep the '40s vibe going."

"I don't know how to do anything like that," I said, feeling embarrassed.

"Oh, I do," she said, dragging her desk chair into the bathroom. "Sit and prepare to be beautified."

I was a little surprised, to be honest. Marnie seemed so low-maintenance. Only when I saw her vast array of hair-styling implements did I realize how much effort she must have put into looking low-maintenance. Twenty minutes later, after a lot of tugging and twisting and stabbing me in the scalp with bobby pins, she gave me permission to turn around.

"You," she said, "look *legit*. I should get an award for this. Maybe I should be a stylist for a living. Dad produced a movie last summer about a model who's also a spy — *Runway*, did you see it? Never mind, nobody saw it, it was a huge bomb — and the stylists gave me lessons."

Her chatter melted into a hum in my ears while I stared at myself.

Marnie had made me into something . . . someone . . . from another era. My hair was pulled back to the nape of my neck in a low, thick bun that shined like it was made of pure silk. With the cat-eye makeup and the red lips, I looked like . . . a movie star.

"Stare much?" Marnie teased. "Okay, go get dressed. I have to transform my own raven locks, such as they are."

She curled the ends of her hair in a perfect gravity-defying flip. Her lips were frosty pink and her eye makeup behind her glasses was thick and black, with tons of mascara. Then she slipped into the sequined dress while I put on my red dress, and we stood looking at the full-length mirror. Suddenly, I was enthusiastic, for real. The world of psychics and visions and ghosts and murders seemed far away — and getting further every minute.

Marnie went into the closet and reappeared carrying a pair of white knee-high boots for herself and bronze-colored thick-heeled pumps for me. "Ready, Willa? Let's go gift the world a little awesome."

CHAPTER 18

A whole block of Hollywood Boulevard was closed off for the premiere. The traffic nearby was basically standing still. So the driver of our hired sedan had to drop us off three blocks away.

It was hard to feel fancy walking down a normal sidewalk, passing tourists and ice cream stores and falafel restaurants and souvenir shops. But after a few minutes, we heard smatterings of applause and cheering, and a booming voice on a loudspeaker. And when we rounded the corner, we were greeted by an overwhelming circus of people and cameras and signs.

The red carpet stretched before us. It was bordered on one side by a wall that had the Paramount Pictures logo printed on it over and over, and on the other side by hundreds of reporters and photographers.

Behind the photographers, held back by metal barricades, were throngs of fans. Because there were no movie stars present at the moment, the crowd was relatively subdued, chattering excitedly instead of screaming. A lot of them held signs saying things like KURT I LOVE YOU! or MARRY ME, EMMA! One guy held up a sign that said READ MY SCREENPLAY, OSCAR GUARANTEED!

There were balloons, banners, and movie posters set up all over. Groups of people wearing suits and fancy dresses stood on the red carpet, talking and laughing. They weren't famous, but they looked like they belonged there.

We showed our IDs at the check-in table, and they handed us little passes with our names and seat numbers on them. We flashed those to a pair of ginormous security guys wearing ginormous suits, and they opened a velvet rope and let us through . . .

Onto the red carpet.

I paused for a moment, taking it all in.

"Do we have to walk in front of all the photographers?" I asked Marnie.

"Of course," she said. "What, you want to skulk around in the shadows?"

I shrugged, and she looped her elbow through mine. "No," she said. "We're here, and we're going to work it. Even if we're not famous . . . *they* don't know that."

Then she started walking down the carpet. I expected to be ignored, but the photographers noticed us. Some of them took a few pictures. One shouted "Who are you?" as though we might actually be *somebodies*, which was pretty flattering.

Then we heard a commotion behind us, and screams rose up from the crowd. We turned to see a wave of people making their way onto the carpet.

"Those are studio publicists," Marnie said, squeezing my arm so hard it went numb. "See? They all have earpieces.

Someone huge just arrived. Oh my God — it's him. It's Kurt. He's here. Hand me my smelling salts."

The crowd of publicists parted, and a man walked through . . . a man you could only describe as a movie star. You could tell from forty feet away that he had a magnetic, unforgettable quality.

He's still not as cute as Reed, I thought.

The fans began to shriek like a bunch of teenage girls, even though a lot of them were my mom's age or even older. And the photographers went crazy, shouting "KURT! KURT! LOOK HERE! OVER HERE!"

"They want eye contact in their pictures," Marnie said. "See how he's moving his head a little? He's trying to give all of them at least one good smile. God, I have to *marry* him."

I couldn't tell if she was joking or not. We stayed in our spot, trying to look nonchalant, as Kurt and his entourage slowly made their way toward us and then through the lobby doors.

"Should we go in now?" I asked. It was getting cold, and my shoes were a smidge too small. Standing in one place made my feet ache.

Marnie shook her head. "Just a few more minutes. I don't want people to think we're stalking him."

One of the reporters looked at me and cocked his head to the side.

"Are you from that new Disney Channel show?" he asked, raising his camera.

I opened my mouth to say no, but Marnie cut me off.

"Yes, she is!" she said, smiling brightly. "This is Bernadette Middleton. She's also Kate Middleton's cousin!"

Before I could say a word, three dozen flashbulbs exploded in my face. And the air was filled with photographers shouting, "Bernadette! Bernadette, over here! Look right here!"

"Put your hand on your hip," Marnie whispered in my ear. "Turn your body at an angle . . . and *smile!*"

We finally went inside. Marnie giggled maniacally as we got in line for our free popcorn and sodas, on the lookout for more celebrities. "*Bernadette*, I can't wait to watch your show on Disney Channel. When is it on again? Oh, WAIT."

Part of me was a little embarrassed, but I had to admit that I was enjoying myself. Finally, I was feeling the glitter. I could see what all the fuss was about — why people worshipped Hollywood and wanted to be movie stars (or be their friends). It was exciting.

"Can you imagine actually being one of those people?" I asked. "Having the paparazzi go crazy over the fact that you, like, got out of a car?"

"Ugh." Marnie stuck her tongue out. "No. I hate actors. They're so needy. *Look at me! Admire me!* Some of the people my dad deals with are positively *dismal*. . . . No, thank you."

We wandered around, munching popcorn and trying to eavesdrop on Kurt Conrath and his publicists.

"So who's my celebrity alter ego going to be?" Marnie asked, patting the flip in her hair. "How about . . . Ramona

Claiborne? That's a good name, right? I was born in Australia, but I disguise my accent flawlessly. I just landed a new show on HBO. You do realize it's not cool for someone as edgy as myself to be seen with a Disney Channel starlet, don't you?"

"You're so generous." I grinned.

"I know. I'm a genuinely awesome human being. Or Ramona Claiborne is, anyway. Let's go back to the red carpet," she said, her eyes sparkling. "You can tell the photographers you talked me into admitting my true identity as Ramona."

I laughed.

Then I realized she was serious.

"Marnie," I said, "the movie's about to start."

It was true. Everyone was beginning to file into the theater.

"These things always start late," she said. "Come on, it'll be fun. We can say we met through our acting coaches, and —"

"Marn," I said. "I think we should go in."

For a brief moment, there was something in her eyes that made me wish I'd gone along with it. We might have looked ridiculous, but it would have kept me from wondering if she resented me for having my own moment in the spotlight.

But I hadn't asked her to lie to the paparazzi for me — she'd just done it.

I was being paranoid. Oversensitive. Marnie was only playing around. We were practically wearing costumes, for heaven's sake. So she wanted to pretend to be famous for a couple of minutes — what was the harm in that? Wasn't it weird and selfish of me to refuse?

But we'd missed our chance. We were already being swept toward the theater doors, and then we were ushered to our seats. The director of the movie got up and thanked us all for coming, and then the movie started.

It was a mindless romantic comedy, which I thoroughly enjoyed, and even Marnie was too lovestruck by Kurt to mock the happy ending.

Afterward, as we were leaving the theater, a lone photographer called out to us.

"Who are you lovely ladies?" he asked

I waited for Marnie to tell him we were none other than Ramona Claiborne, edgy actress extraordinaire, and Bernadette Middleton, teen celebrity darling and cousin of genuine royalty.

But she gave him her bored smile and said, "Just a couple of fans."

Have you ever noticed that nothing in the entire universe is more comfortable than putting on pajamas after you've been wearing fancy clothes? The soft cotton felt like heaven on my skin, and my feet floated on clouds of happiness after being released from the too-small pumps.

Marnie and I brushed out our hair and flopped down on her king-size bed. We were still too pumped up from the premiere to sleep, so we stayed up and talked, rehashing the details of the evening and laughing. I realized it had been two years since I'd spent time like this with a friend.

"So Kurt didn't propose," Marnie sighed. "He must not have seen me."

"Totally," I said.

"That's okay," she said, leaning back against her pillow. "Love is for suckers."

I didn't answer.

"Did you have a boyfriend?" she asked. "Back in Connecticut?"

I hesitated for a moment, and then told her about Aiden. How we'd met the first day of freshman year, when he beaned me with a kickball in gym class. How we'd spent practically every waking moment together after that.

"Did your parents like him?" Marnie asked.

"Mom did," I said, staring down at the bedspread. "But . . . we grew apart. And eventually we broke up."

"It's never 'we,'" she said. "Who did the actual dumping?"

"He did," I said, remembering the crestfallen look on his face as he told me how he couldn't bear being shut out any longer. "He did it on the anniversary of my dad's death."

"No," Marnie said, sitting up. "Are you kidding? What a horrible person!"

I felt a guilty little pang, because I knew it wasn't that black-and-white. Aiden hadn't meant to hurt me. He just couldn't stand how much our dysfunctional relationship was hurting *him*. He was losing weight, losing sleep, losing control. It was so hard, for both of us. And in the end, he was the one who was strong enough to do something about it.

But I have to confess, it was kind of nice to have Marnie take my side.

"What about you?" I asked. "Have you had a boyfriend?"

Marnie pulled a pillow into her lap. She sighed and looked down at her hands. "Kind of. I wouldn't call it a boyfriend, per se. It's complicated."

Marnie was the queen of taking simple situations — like being at a movie premiere — and turning them into complex puzzles — like pretending to be a pair of TV stars. For her to call something complicated was saying a lot. I was definitely intrigued. "What do you mean?"

She looked up at me, her cat-eye liner and dark mascara making her eyes seem giant and mysterious. "Remember how I told you to stay away from Wyatt Sheppard?"

My heart began to beat faster. Wyatt . . . and *Marnie*? Was that why Wyatt had warned me about her? Had they gone out? I assumed that Wyatt was too low on the social scale for her. Though when I thought about him now, with his dark eyes and square jaw, I admitted to myself that he was definitely sort of cute, in a hunky nerd way. And he was super smart. I could see how he could be Marnie's type.

I nodded, dying to hear more.

Marnie leaned in closer. "Wyatt and I actually used to get along. We were . . . friends. Our parents knew each other, and they would hang out most weekends, so it seemed natural. We did your basic friend stuff — movies, going out to eat, wandering around. I don't even know what we did, honestly. How do people not die of boredom before they can drive?"

I waited for her to get to the part where they dated.

"But as the year went on, I started to feel awkward about it. Like maybe he was a little more into the whole thing than I was. He started getting annoyed if I wanted to hang out with other people. Once he even accused me of flirting with someone else, and he was *angry* about it! I mean, how messed up is that? I can flirt with whoever I want."

I held my breath.

"So finally, it sort of . . . imploded. He was supposed to come over and watch a movie, and I had a really busy day, and I tried to cancel but it was too late, and he showed up and he had brought a bunch of balloons. And he came in and was like, 'Happy anniversary.' And I was like, 'Excuse me?' And he was like, 'It's been six months since we started going out.' And I was like, 'Hold up, cowboy, I think you have the wrong idea.'"

"I don't understand," I said.

"Right? It was so weird. I guess I . . . went along with it, in a way? I mean, I tried to downplay it and laugh, like it was a joke. We watched the movie and hung out, and then he left, and I was relieved that he was gone. After that, I decided to spend less time around him. But he had this way of . . . showing up, you know? It was kind of odd."

I nodded. "Kind of odd" was a fair way to describe Wyatt. Maybe even a little generous.

"So whatever, fine. I'm like, I can be nice to this guy, we're friends, our parents are friends, yada yada. But then the next week, he comes over totally raging. Going on about how selfish I am and how I only think of myself . . ."

"Seriously?" I asked.

"Seriously. I was pretty freaked out. And at the end of it all, he *broke up with me*." She let out a helpless laugh. "I mean, we'd never even been of a status where we could break up. But he dumped me. And I was like, okay, at least now he'll leave me alone. But then . . ." She plucked at the pillowcase and shook her head. "He started texting me, and calling me, and stopping by my locker. There was this blog thing with pictures of me, with, like, *our names.* . . . And then I realized he had my email password."

My heart had begun to thud like a drum. I felt sweat beading around my hairline, but this time I knew it wasn't because of any ghost.

"I thought about it and realized that every time he'd shown up someplace unexpectedly, it was a meeting I'd talked about in an email. Went to lunch with my aunt at Spago? He was there. Went to a secret sale at Nordstrom? He was there. It started to feel like he was . . . everywhere."

"So what did you do?" I asked.

Her huge owl eyes blinked at me. "I told him straight out that he was a stalker and I was going to call the police if he didn't stop."

"And he stopped?"

She shrugged. "I guess. I stopped noticing it as much, anyway. And then he found his murder mystery to obsess over and I got out of jail free . . . so far."

I didn't know what to say. Yes, Wyatt could be argumentative and inconsistent. But something about Marnie's story didn't totally jibe with the guy I'd been spending time with. *Almost like there are two Wyatts*, I thought.

I certainly wasn't going to tell Marnie that Wyatt and I had been hanging out, visiting local psychics, or that we regularly held perfectly pleasant conversations during chemistry class. So I said, "Wow. I'm sorry you went through all that."

"Oh, it's no big deal. I mean, I wasn't a trembling victim in a corner. I started to get weirded out, that's all. My instincts told me it was time to put a stop to it. And I have excellent instincts." She smiled at me. "I picked you out of the crowd, didn't I?"

CHAPTER 19

The next night, I was home, asleep in my own bed, when a sudden noise woke me up.

I lay there, adrenaline zapping through me like lightning bolts, unsure if the sound had been real or if I'd dreamed it.

Then I heard it again. . . .

Knock. Knock. Knock.

My whole body tensed.

In a moment of desperate, naive hope, I thought, *Who would be knocking at the front door in the middle of the night?*

Reed? With some urgent middle-of-the-night news?

But it wasn't the sound of a person knocking on a door. Not a normal person, anyway. It was more like someone was sending a coded message, each knock separate and deliberate.

Knock. Knock. Knock.

It was coming from my bedroom door.

When I heard the next knock, I forced myself to sit up straight and called, "Hello?"

Maybe it was Jonathan. A lot of what he did was kind of

formal and stilted. In theory, he could knock like that. It almost suited him.

But Jonathan didn't answer me.

No one did.

The three knocks finished, but the sound seemed to hang in the air.

I went down the short, terrible list of suspects: an intruder — a robber, maybe, or a serial killer. Or a ghost.

Only . . . the alarm was on, so that ruled out a human.

It's not a ghost, I told myself, *because I am done with ghosts.*

But even as I thought the words, I felt my so-called "normal" life slipping out of existence. I'd been fooling myself. Ignorance may be bliss, but at the end of the day it's still ignorance.

And my ghost had decided it didn't want to be ignored any longer.

I made myself step one foot out of bed. Then the other foot. And I forced my legs, one in front of the other, to walk to the door just as the sound came again:

Knock. Knock. Knock.

As quietly as I could, I dropped to the floor, pressed my cheek against the polished wood, and peered through the narrow opening.

I was fully prepared to see a pair of ghastly, rotted feet. Maybe even shriveled undead fingers worming their way under the door toward me . . .

But what I saw was red. Not blood — it was solid; it had form. But I couldn't tell what it was. Maybe a red carpet? I thought of walking the red carpet the night before with Marnie. Maybe this was a dream.

I sat back and stared at the door until almost a minute had passed since the last set of knocks.

Okay, Willa. Listen up.

You are a reasonably intelligent human. You have some emotional issues to work through, sure, but you'll probably be okay eventually. You'll finish high school, go to a decent college, get a degree in something, and then enter the world as an adult. You have many choices and opportunities ahead of you. You can do anything you want to do with your life.

Except for one thing . . .

You are NOT opening that door.

Go back to bed. Go back to bed this instant.

In slow motion, I rose to my feet and turned away from the door, away from the foolish temptation to prove to myself that I wasn't going crazy. Everything I'd done so far to prove to myself that I wasn't crazy just ended up making me feel even crazier.

I began to walk back to the bed, taking care not to make the merest hint of a sound as I went.

Behind me, the door opened by itself.

Don't turn around. Don't turn around.

How exactly, I wondered, does a corpse stand? Would she be leaning on the wall? Would she be held up, dangling in midair, by some supernatural energy? Maybe she lacked the strength to stand, and had dragged herself down the hall . . . so when I turned to look at her, she'd be lying on the floor, reaching her arms toward me hungrily.

Maybe she was already following me into the room.

Maybe she was right behind me.

At last, the horror of not knowing became greater than the horror of knowing, and I turned around.

But the room was empty.

The door was open.

There was no one there.

Only a trail of rose petals, red and plush. A solid blanket of them, a foot wide, leading away down the hall and disappearing in the inky darkness.

I could go wake up Mom and Jonathan, but I knew from the bathtub incident that there was a very decent chance the hall would be perfectly clean when I brought them back upstairs. I could take a photo, or scoop an armful of flowers, but what would that prove? The obvious assumption would be that I had done this myself. For attention, or as a weird prank, or whatever. Face it — "crazy ghost" is never going to be people's go-to explanation. Not when there's a teenager in the house to take the blame.

Leyta's advice ran through my head:

You just have to work through it.

I walked alongside the trail of roses, keeping one hand on the wall, because I needed to feel connected to something solid, something I could be sure actually existed.

I decided that if the trail led to Jonathan's office, I wouldn't follow it inside.

But it didn't lead there. It led to the third bedroom, the one directly across from the top of the stairs.

I stopped about a foot from the door.

Then I took a step back.

From the other side of that door came a soft:

Knock. Knock. Knock.

Before I could take another step back, it came again — a little faster, a little harder:

Knock-knock-knock!

I hardly had time to catch my breath before the sound turned furious:

KNOCK-KNOCK-KNOCK!!!

Every corner of my consciousness was scared — scared of whatever was doing this, scared that Mom and Jonathan would wake up — and absolutely terrified of what was waiting for me, beckoning me inside.

But if I turned back, I would never get up the nerve to come this far again.

Get through it. That's all you can do. There are no shortcuts in the flow.

This is your journey.

I opened the door.

CHAPTER 20

This room was a mirror image of my own. The bed was to my right, and the bathroom was to my left. I got the feeling that I'd warped into an alternate universe.

The trail of petals stopped just inside the door.

As I crossed the threshold, a headache pierced cleanly through my temples, as if I'd been shot with a poisoned arrow. I pressed my fingers against my eyes, trying to ward it off.

Then I heard:

Drip . . . drip . . . drip . . .

I flipped the light switch and the overhead light came to life — but only after hesitating for a second. Like some force was deciding whether I got to have a light on or not, and it finally took mercy on me.

I followed the dripping sound to the bathroom, knowing what I would find: the bathtub full to overflowing. A serene surface. And reflected in that surface, the face of the ghost that had wrapped its fate around mine like a boa constrictor.

So I went in, mainly because I was beginning to realize that I had no choice.

The light in the bathroom wouldn't turn on. But all right, no big deal. The window over the bathtub let in pale moonlight, and the light from the bedroom spilled through the door. It wasn't ideal, but I could still see — enough to glance around and be sure that there wasn't a corpse, or a murderer.

Just a ghost.

I walked over to the tub and looked down at the surface of the water.

Perfectly smooth and serene, like I'd known it would be.

"I would really appreciate, at this point," I said out loud, "some guidance as to why you've brought me here."

Drip.

"Awesome," I said. "Wow, thank you, that is so incredibly useful."

Now that I'd found my voice, I couldn't stop talking. Getting the words out slowed the chaotic whirring in my brain.

"What we have before us is a bathtub full of water. And I can only imagine that you intend to do another *abracadabra* thing where I look away and the water's gone or overflowing or . . . I don't know, turned to vanilla pudding, maybe?" I closed my eyes and turned around. "So why don't you do your little trick and we can get on with things?"

I counted to five, then spun around.

The bathtub was *not* dry.

But it wasn't just full of water anymore.

The water was thick with rose petals. Thousands of them. In fact, it was more like someone had filled the tub with rose petals first and then filled the tiny spaces between them with water.

"This . . . sucks," I whispered. Then I raised my voice slightly. "Hey, newsflash: I am not putting any part of my body into that water."

There was, unsurprisingly, no answer. I stayed a good four feet away, staring at the water in a state of highly uneasy expectancy.

"Never," I said. "No body parts. No hands, no feet . . . I'm not going to duck my head underwater and look for your corpse. So if that's what you're hoping for, let it go."

Suddenly, the rose petals began to move.

Something was in the tub.

And whatever it was, it was coming to the surface.

I staggered back and ran into the counter, gripping it to keep myself from passing out. Behind me, the bathroom door slammed, shutting me in and eliminating about 80 percent of the light.

And in the sudden darkness, the water trembled.

I couldn't tear my eyes away, anticipating the moment that a hand dripping with decayed flesh would push free of the petals.

Finally, the petals parted. But what came up between them wasn't any kind of hand. . . .

It was a piece of paper.

I looked around for something I could use to fish it out — a toilet brush or a plunger. But the bathroom was devoid of anything remotely useful.

I had to know what was on that paper. I knew in my gut that I needed to see it. I also had a feeling that, no matter how hard I tried, the bathroom door wouldn't open for me unless I followed these ghostly instructions.

I stepped closer. The page was crumpled, and a corner of it floated up out of the water. If I was careful, I could grab it by that corner and pull it out without even touching a single flower petal.

The room was dark, but the tub was lit in a slanted rectangle of moonlight. My heart had taken over my whole body, beating so hard I swayed on my feet.

Slowly, slowly, slowly, I reached my hand down toward the piece of paper.

I was a foot away. Then ten inches. Eight. Six.

Four.

My fingers hovered over my target. The roses in the tub drifted in a slow circle, stirred by some supernatural current.

I grabbed the exposed corner of the paper and yanked it up so fast that I splashed myself full in the face with water.

But I got it. And not so much as a single body part had I submerged in the evil haunted bathtub. I'd given the spirit what it wanted. . . .

Now the door would open and let me out.

Feeling a thin silver lining of triumph, I sighed and turned to walk out of the bathroom.

 164

That's when it hit me. Not a physical thing, but a force, like a powerful burst of wind — my own private tornado. The impact slammed against my torso and propelled me backward, until I lost my footing.

As my feet came out from under me, the backs of my legs struck something hard and smooth, and before I had time to take a breath deep enough to scream, I plunged backward into the bathtub.

CHAPTER 21

The rose petals were so soft. It felt as if thousands of gentle fingers were touching my hands and arms and face and throat and feet, and the parts of my back and stomach that were exposed when my pajama top floated around me in the water. My screaming/breathing reflex showed up just late enough that I opened my lips and nearly choked on a mouthful of wet roses. I sprang out of the tub, about four feet straight into the air, miraculously not landing face-first against the corner of the bathroom counter.

Catching a glimpse of myself in the mirror, I thought for a second that I was seeing another terrible specter: a girl with matted dark hair, white skin glowing in the dark room, hideous black bruises all over her body like spots of decay.

But nope, it was just me. Soaking wet and covered in rose petals.

The door opened without being touched, which was not a comfort. I fought the urge to scream and race down the stairs to Mom's room, and wake her and Jonathan with my story of what had happened.

Instead, I forced myself to walk slowly — not *calmly*, but slowly — toward my open bedroom door. I didn't bother to avoid the rose petals this time. I shuffled right through them. They clung to my wet skin and covered my feet like moist, flaking socks.

They seemed as real as anything else you could touch and smell and see. But when I had passed back into my own room, I knew without having to look that they would be gone when I did turn around.

All that remained to prove anything had happened was the sopping-wet hot mess that was me — and the soggy piece of paper clutched in my right hand.

Under the bright lights of my bathroom vanity, I managed to uncrumple the page and gently stretch it back to its normal dimensions.

I'd never seen a screenplay before, but I knew that's what I was looking at. There were character names and lines of description and action.

It started in the middle of a scene in which two people were eating dinner.

One of them was a woman. Her name was Charice.

And one of them was a man.

His name was Henry.

And the last thing on the page was a line of dialogue.

                    CHARICE
        This is the kind of dream you don't
        wake up from, Henry.

CHAPTER 22

I managed to hold off until seven o'clock in the morning before texting Wyatt. I figured someone as OCD as he was had to be the early-bird-gets-the-worm type — even on a Sunday.

I typed *Are you up?* and leaned against the headboard to watch my phone for his reply. Ironically, that was when the sleep I'd waited all night for decided to sneak up on me. My heavy lids slipped shut as I stared at the darkened screen.

Then the phone vibrated, startling me back to full awareness.

Yes. Everything okay?

I replied: *Ha ha ha ha NO.*

Need to talk?

Yeah, I typed. *Where can we meet? Not my house.*

There was a pause, and then his reply came through: *Mine?*

I must admit that I was dying of curiosity about the home life that would produce a specimen like Wyatt. Were his parents studiously brilliant, obsessed with research and The Truth? Tinfoil-hat conspiracy theorists? Lifelong paint-chip eaters?

I was about to reply *Yes*, but I guess I took a little too long, because another pair of messages popped up from Wyatt:

Promise I'm still not the killer.

Murderer's honor.

At eight o'clock, I slipped on a pair of flip-flops, grabbed my house key, phone, and the monstrosity of a backpack, and set out for Wyatt's house. I left a note for Mom explaining that I was meeting Marnie, which I knew she'd believe since (as far as she knew) I'd never gone anywhere else.

The Sheppards' house was only about a five-minute walk away, and Wyatt was out front when I rounded the corner.

"What happened?" His eyes darkened with concern when he saw me. "You look like you've seen a ghost."

"Is that supposed to be a joke?" I asked.

He looked startled for a second, then realized what he'd said. "Oh," he said. "No. Sorry. Nice overalls, by the way."

I was wearing my softest long-sleeved black T-shirt and Mom's overalls, with a chunky blue scarf wrapped around my neck — the fashion equivalent of comfort food. Wyatt wore jeans and a red plaid flannel shirt, untucked. His feet were bare. The effect was kind of mountain-mannish, if mountain men wore horn-rimmed glasses.

Inside, Wyatt's house was starkly modern, a two-story rectangle made of glass and wood. The whole back wall was made of floor-to-ceiling windows looking out over trees, at precisely the right height so you couldn't tell you were in a city at all. It felt like being in a tree house, or a cabin somewhere out in the wilderness.

"This place is cool," I said. "What do your parents do?"

"My mom's an artist," he said. "My dad's a . . . consultant. Are you okay going up to my room?"

I nodded, and followed him up a set of stairs that didn't even have a handrail. You could have fallen right off. When we reached the second floor, I found myself facing a wall that was covered in dozens of black-and-white photos of Wyatt at different ages.

"Wow," I said.

"For the record, I've asked them to change this," he said. "But they're kind of attached to it."

His bedroom was straight ahead, and I almost hesitated before crossing through the door. But Wyatt went straight toward a leather sofa in the corner of the room and gestured for me to sit. Then he pulled over a bright orange plastic chair for himself.

I sat cross-legged on the sofa and rested my chin in my hands, staring at the floor. "It's in my house," I whispered. "It won't leave me alone. I think it's trying to kill me —"

"Whoa, whoa," he said. "Slow down. Take a breath. Start at the beginning."

I took two deep breaths, but they were that weird jerky kind of breath that happens right before you bust out in epic sobs. Somehow I managed to hold all that in and describe everything that had happened the night before, starting with the knocking and ending with the screenplay.

"So it *is* a line from a script." Wyatt sat back and looked out the windows at the trees.

"It's a scene where they're eating dinner," I said. "Just like in my vision. It can't be a coincidence. It has to be another murder."

"Okay, yes, that's what it sounds like." Wyatt shook his head. "But there are no unsolved murders fitting that profile anywhere in southern California. I checked after we met with Leyta last week."

"Then maybe . . . maybe it hasn't happened yet."

"So now you're seeing the future?"

"I don't know, Wyatt," I said, practically hissing in aggravation. "I don't *know* what's happening to me. For all I know, none of this is real. I could be strapped to a bed in a mental institution. You could be a figment of my —"

"I'm not a figment," he said. "You're not making this up. You're not strapped to a bed in a mental ward. You're here with me."

I half laughed and looked up into his wide brown eyes, thinking he was joking. But he seemed perfectly sincere. I sat back and tried to relax. Something about his steady, unflappable presence centered me.

"Let's focus on what we know," Wyatt went on. "There's a force in your house trying to call your attention to this particular scene, which appears to be from a movie. So the next logical step is to figure out what the movie is."

"I brought my laptop." I unzipped the monstrosity, pulled the computer out of its neoprene sleeve, and set it in my lap.

Wyatt leaned closer to look at the screen. I half expected him to try to snatch the computer away so he could apply his superior research skills, but he didn't.

There was a Wi-Fi network called SHEPPARD. "Password?" I asked.

He blushed slightly. "Um . . . I'll type it."

"Just tell me what it is," I said. "I'm not going to come steal your Wi-Fi when you're not home."

"It's, uh . . . 'Wyattcutiepants.' All one word. Capital *W*."

"Are you kidding?" I asked.

"My mother is a creature of habit," he said. "Every time I change it, she finds a way to get logged out and then can't remember the new password to log back in. I finally gave up around eighth grade. Anyway, can I see the search results?"

"Sure thing, cutiepants." I typed in the whole sentence and hit SEARCH. The results were assorted references to people named Henry — Henry Rollins, Henry James — and a movie called *50 First Dates*. No exact matches.

"What if you leave off the name?" he asked.

"Then we get . . ." I backspaced through *Henry* and hit SEARCH. ". . . a Beyoncé song."

"Well, that explains it," he said. "You're being haunted by Beyoncé."

"Oh, this is *ideal*," I said.

He smiled a little and then put his concentrating face back on. "What if you search for *Charice* and *Henry* — and *movie*?"

I typed it in and came up with a bunch of random unhelpful results.

"Nothing," I said. "We need to face it. This movie doesn't exist."

"What if you're right?" Wyatt said. "Maybe the killer wrote the screenplay himself."

"That wouldn't explain how it got in my house," I said.

"There are a lot of things in your house that don't seem to belong there," he said.

I didn't answer.

"You don't look convinced."

I pulled out my phone. "I left the page at home because it's so delicate, but I took a picture. Notice anything?"

Wyatt took the phone and zoomed in on the photo. "What am I looking for?"

"The letters," I said. "The lowercase *t* is always a hair above the line of the other letters."

"And the *e* is lower," he said. "So this was typed on an actual typewriter?"

I nodded. "Nobody actually uses typewriters anymore. So it's probably pretty old, right?"

"Yeah," he said, "but look — it's a photocopy. See how the corner is just a copy of a dog-eared page? Maybe the original is old, but the page you found isn't the original. Someone could have made that copy yesterday, for all we know."

"What's Namur?" I asked, typing the word into the computer. "In the vision I had, the girl thought about Namur."

Our heads nearly touched as we looked at the screen. Namur turned out to be a city in southern Belgium. I skimmed the Wikipedia entry, with Wyatt reading over my shoulder.

"Not very exciting," Wyatt said. "University . . . museum, belfry, cathedral, Del Mar Park . . ."

"Wait," I said. "Del Mar? As in . . ."

I typed *Diana Del Mar Namur Belgium*.

It was a hit.

"Diana Del Mar lived in Namur for three years," I read. "When she was a teenager."

"So?" Wyatt asked.

"So . . . Diana Del Mar lived *in my house*."

He blinked.

"Is this movie about her somehow?" I asked. I typed *Diana Del Mar Charice* and nothing came up.

"Wait, look," Wyatt said, holding up my phone. "In two different spots, someone made a mistake typing *Charice*. See how there's a letter *X*-ed out? They typed an *s* first. Try that."

It seemed like a stretch, but I typed it in: *Diana Del Mar Charise*.

"There!" Wyatt said.

The very first result was an article titled "Diana Del Mar — Screen Star to Screenwriter," from a blog called *Learning the Craft*. The author of the blog was named Paige Pollan. Her bio said she was "an aspiring 'Hollywood type' determined to do my homework before plunging into the swamp of Tinseltown."

I read the blog post:

Diana Del Mar, a beloved actress in the 1930s, turned her attention to behind-the-scenes pursuits when she found herself being rejected for roles because of her "advancing" age (35!

169

GASP!). *One of her interests was writing. Rumors swirled around town that she and none other than "Hitch" himself (the great Alfred Hitchcock, newly arrived in America following the release of* Rebecca*) were collaborating on a project. Diana was working on a screenplay and hoped to star as the character Charise. Hitchcock would direct. Soon, however, the arrangement fell through. Some speculated that Miss Del Mar would try to produce the movie on her own, but before that could happen she was found dead in an upstairs bathtub at her home in the Hollywood Hills. [Source:* Hollywood Glamour Magazine, April 1943.*]*

Dead. In an upstairs bathtub.

Yeah, that just about fit. I closed my eyes and took a deep breath.

"So they changed the spelling of the character's name," Wyatt said.

"But she doesn't say what the movie was called." My voice sounded slightly frantic. "How could she not say what it was called?"

Wyatt reached over and scrolled farther down the page to the comments. The first one, from someone called "G.A. Green," read: *Fascinating. What was the movie called?*

And Paige P. had replied: *The Final Honeymoon. It had a different working title, but I don't know what that was, sorry!*

We Googled *The Final Honeymoon,* but nothing came up. Interest in the project vanished when Diana Del Mar died. It was strange to think that even the stuff that was really important to a huge, famous movie star could disappear forever, except in dusty old copies of Hollywood tabloids.

"We need to get in touch with this Paige Pollan person and see what else she knows," Wyatt said. "This is a solid lead."

"I'm not denying that it seems significant," I said. "But how does it connect to the murders? Is the killer going to use this scene? Does the ghost somehow know that?"

"That would break the pattern," Wyatt said. "This screenplay never became an actual movie."

I breathed into my balled-up hand. "Are we ignoring the obvious answer?"

"That Diana Del Mar is the ghost?" he asked.

I nodded. "And she knows something about the killer."

"No. Let's not ignore it. Let's look into it. Maybe when you get home you could . . ."

"I could what?" I asked, even though I knew what he was going to say.

"Ask her?"

I bit down on my knuckle and stared out at the dark blue of the morning sky. "Oh, *goodie*."

"In the meantime, let's try to find out more about the movie itself. That's obviously an important part of her message to you. Even if we know who she is, we'd better find out what she wants."

"All right," I said, going back to the blog. "Fine. I'll ask the ghost what she wants. And I'll email Paige."

"Do you want anything to eat or drink?" Wyatt asked. "My mom is addicted to paying for designer water. For every four million bottles they sell they adopt an elephant or something. I'd be happy to bring you a bottle."

"No, thanks," I said. As he left, I opened a new-message window in my email.

I kept it simple: *I read your blog about Diana Del Mar and her project* The Final Honeymoon. *I have some specific questions and wondered if you'd be willing to talk to me over the phone. If so, my number is 323-555-8333. Thank you for your time.*

I hit SEND and sat back, looking around Wyatt's room and trying to picture him there. It was simple and spare, but if you looked closer, you saw some personal touches — a stack of books in the corner, a small movie poster, artfully framed.

There was more to it than there seemed to be at first glance.

Kind of like Wyatt himself.

He came back, carrying a glass of water.

I read him the email I had sent Paige Pollan, and he nodded in approval, but he was distracted.

"All right," I said. "Let me have it."

He looked perplexed. "What?"

"Whatever it is you want to tell me, but were holding back on before," I said.

He frowned, then kind of smiled. Then frowned again. "Well, last night, I . . . How do I say this? . . . I figured something out. Something that I think you'll be interested to know."

"Great." I sat back in my chair, expecting to hear him gleefully recount that Leyta Fitzgeorge actually had a long criminal history or something. "Hit me."

He looked nervous, which was unusual.

It made *me* a little nervous.

Then he spoke. "A normal, healthy adult won't have a heart attack from an isolated burst of anger."

"What?" I said, almost laughing. It was so random. . . .

And then the words sank in, and it wasn't random anymore.

"Wait," I said. *"What?"*

"Your dad." His smile was long gone. "I know what you think happened, but you're wrong. You didn't kill him."

It was like my body had turned to stone. My voice had turned to stone, too. "What do you know about my dad, Wyatt?"

"Um," he said, "I overheard Leyta last week . . . when she said his name. So I Googled him, and saw how he . . . he . . . passed away."

With every word, he seemed to be growing sorrier and sorrier that he'd brought it up. But, because he was Wyatt, he kept pushing forward.

"The morning of May sixteenth," he said. "When you guys were at the YMCA for your regular morning . . . swim."

He'd caught sight of my face. I don't know, honestly, what he saw there. I wasn't really occupying my own body at the moment. I felt like I'd been launched into outer space without warning. Or oxygen.

Unwisely, he took my silence as a cue to continue. "You had a big argument about something, and the desk clerk saw you storm out of the natatorium —"

"What is a natatorium?" I asked, my voice low.

"A room with a swimming pool." He waited to see if I'd ask anything else.

I did not.

"And after you went back in, she heard you screaming for help, and then she ran in and saw your . . ." It was like he couldn't stop. It was like he was a machine, a heartless, cold, meaningless creature whose only actual purpose is to spew information, and if he stopped, he'd short-circuit and explode. "She saw your dad. And then the ambulance came, but it was too late. It was a heart attack. And you blame yourself, and that's why you're so afraid to be angry."

I let my stare slide from his face to the floor.

"But it couldn't have been your fault," Wyatt said. "Healthy adults don't have heart attacks provoked by anger or stress. That's not a normal physiological response to —"

"*Enough.*" The word was like a concrete wall, twelve feet thick. "Enough, Wyatt. Stop."

"I'm . . . sorry," he said.

"All right," I said. "You're sorry. Great. Just do me one favor."

"Okay."

"Never speak to me again."

"But . . ."

I turned away. My eyes burned like they were fighting back a million tears, but the rage inside me was so hot that the tears vaporized. I felt pressure in my face, and electrical currents flooding my fingers with every thump of my heart.

"I'm sorry," he whispered, sounding helpless. "I thought you'd want to know."

I stood abruptly. "I should have listened to Marnie," I said. "She told me you were a stalker. But I thought, nah, maybe she misunderstood something you said or did — maybe she was exaggerating."

The light had gone out of Wyatt's eyes. He stared up at me, but he didn't answer.

"Here it is," I said. "Proof. She was right. I must be the dumbest person on the planet. I was actually starting to trust you, Wyatt. I thought we were . . . friends or something."

He didn't say a single word.

"I'm leaving," I said.

Somehow, I got out of his room and down the stairs and out the front door without losing my mind. And then somehow I made it home and ran upstairs and locked myself in my bedroom before Mom could see the look on my face.

In my room, I melted to the floor and stared at the ceiling.

And somehow — but I don't know how — I didn't die of a broken heart.

CHAPTER 23

The next couple of days passed in a dull blur. At school, I wouldn't even look at Wyatt. He followed my instructions and didn't try to talk to me, either. At home, the ghost was mercifully silent, which was good, because my nerves were down to their last gasp.

My investigation had been on hold since Sunday morning, but I knew I couldn't pretend the calm was going to last forever. Regardless of my feelings about Wyatt, I had to figure out what was going on in the house.

Thursday, as we sat at our chemistry table and studiously ignored each other, it hit me that I didn't actually *need* Wyatt's help to figure out what the ghost wanted. I could do it alone. Yeah, it might take me a little longer, and maybe I didn't have his freakishly honed detective skills, but I could do it. And then, by figuring it out and unlatching the spirit, I would also unlatch myself from Wyatt forever.

So after dinner and homework, I decided to get back on track. I turned on my computer to check my email for a reply from Paige Pollan. It had been four days since I first tried to contact her.

As the computer booted up, I summoned as much courage as I could (not much) and said, "Diana?"

There was no answer.

"Diana Del Mar," I said. "Hello?" For a moment, I thought of getting out the moldavite ring and the candles. Would those make it easier to reach her? If they had attracted her in the first place, why shouldn't I just use them now? It seemed counter-productive to ignore the most effective means of getting in touch, just because some near-stranger was feeling overly cautious. Leyta Fitzgeorge wasn't the one being awakened in the middle of the night and shoved into a bathtub.

I was about to dig the box out of my closet when the computer finished booting up. Since I was there, I might as well do a little research before opening the portal again. To be honest, I wasn't all that excited about disregarding Leyta's warning. On some level, I believed she knew what she was talking about.

I clicked on the web browser. *Explore every lead*, I thought. *Leave no stone unturned.*

So I decided to start with something easy — I Googled Paige Pollan.

That's when I realized that there would never be a reply to the email I'd sent.

Because Paige Pollan killed herself last August.

CHAPTER 24

On Friday morning, as I stood at my locker, Marnie raced toward me, a blur of green and white. She grabbed me around the neck and jumped up and down.

"Willa!" she squealed. "Willa, seriously!"

"What?" I asked, trying to peel away from her. I was exhausted from the sheer hopelessness that had descended on me after I discovered Paige's fate. I almost wished I could talk to Wyatt about it — but not badly enough to break our silence. It was lab day in Chem, so I was already planning an imaginary headache and a trip to the nurse's office to get me out of having to interact with him. Now, with Marnie shrieking and hopping around, my "imaginary" headache could easily slip into all-too-real existence.

Marnie put her hands on my shoulders and beamed at me. "It's so awesome, I don't even want to tell you. I want you to bask in the anticipation for a minute. Could you bask, please? I need to see some baskage."

"I don't know what you're talking about," I said, smoothing my cardigan where Marnie's embrace had flipped it up. "But okay, I'm basking."

"What if I said . . . I had something *amazing* to show you?" she asked, hooking an arm around my waist and leading me toward the courtyard.

"That would be . . . nice?" Her excited energy was actually starting to make me antsy.

"Feast your eyes . . . on THIS." She pulled her phone out of her pocket and handed it to me.

It was a photo of two random glamorous girls —

No, wait — it was a photo of Marnie and me. From the premiere.

I stared at myself — my luminous skin, the rosy pink of my cheeks, my large doe eyes. My hair was perfect, the red dress so elegant.

I'd never seen myself look like that before. I never even knew I *could* look like that.

And next to me, Marnie embodied retro awesomeness, from her wild sequined dress to her glasses.

"Wow us," I said quietly.

"It gets better," she said, grabbing the phone and scrolling down. "Look at the caption."

Can you say "totes adorbs," Stalkerz? Gorgeous Hollywood starlets Ramona Claiborne and Bernadette Middleton arrive at the premiere of the new Kurt Conrath flick The Never Time.

"We're . . . on . . . Starstalkerz," Marnie said. "Willa, *you and I are on Starstalkerz.*"

I'd heard of it. It was one of those gossip sites that has its own TV show and is always posting famous people's mug shots.

"No, *Ramona and Bernadette* are on Starstalkerz," I said.

"And I'm sure the website will take the photo down when they realize that Ramona and Bernadette aren't real people."

"Look at the comments!" Marnie practically shrieked. "Look — 'Bernadette is so beautiful I hate her.' Someone *hates you* because you're pretty. And this one — 'Where did Ramona get those glasses they R so kewl I want them.' Someone wants my glasses. People want to know who we are. They want to *be* us." Marnie's face was animated in a way I'd never seen. "Willa, here's what I'm thinking — we find a way to get into every party and event we can find. We always go as Bernadette and Ramona. Soon we'll be the It Girls. We'll have fan pages and thousands of followers. I mean, if we handle this right, we could get . . . like, I don't know — our own reality show!"

I scrolled back up to the photo. "But how did they even find out your name was Ramona? We decided that after we went inside, didn't we?"

Marnie gave me a saucy smile. "Well . . . I might have written a press release from a publicist about Ramona Claiborne and Bernadette Middleton, Hollywood's hottest new BFFs."

"Wait — you actually put in writing that I'm Kate Middleton's cousin?"

She grinned and shrugged.

"Marnie!"

"Oh, stop acting scandalized. What are you, a pilgrim?"

"You mean a puritan? No . . . but that's lying about a real person."

"Lying?!" She drew back, pretending to be scandalized. "On the *Internet*? No! I don't believe it! I'm pretty sure Kate

Middleton is too busy trying on tiaras to care whether some- one halfway across the world is pretending to be her distant relative. I mean, think about it. Can she prove you're *not* related?"

I ignored her crazy talk and stared at the picture. "Won't we get in trouble when they find out?"

"For heaven's sake, no," Marnie said, rolling her eyes. "This is Hollywood, Willa. I don't even know how old my own mother is. Everyone lies, and there are no consequences. It's like a magical fairyland!"

My plan for avoiding Chemistry went off without a hitch, so for seventh period I lay on a cot in the nurse's office, thinking about Marnie. After a while, the nurse left me alone, so I pulled out my phone. It took me a few different combinations of search terms, but eventually I found what I was looking for:

A photoblog called *MARNIE + WYATT = FOREVER*.

As the posts loaded on the page, one by one, I felt like I'd been spun around a hundred times and dropped down on a bal- ance beam.

Photo after photo of Wyatt and Marnie. Sitting together at a football game. Holding hands. Him giving her a piggy-back ride. Him standing behind her, resting his chin on her shoulder. Tenth-grade Marnie had a short chin-length bob and wire- frame glasses. In every photo, she was smiling brilliantly.

It was surreal, seeing them together. I felt an unpleasant twinge, and told myself it was because this was confirmation that so much of what Marnie had told me was outright lies.

Or maybe, I mused, flinching at a photo of him kissing her on the cheek, *there's more to it than that.*

The pictures spanned almost their whole sophomore school year. One from the winter formal with Marnie in a pale blue dress and Wyatt in a gray suit, posing together. A picture from Valentine's Day, showing Marnie holding a tiny teddy bear.

And then there was one of Marnie standing in the court-yard at school, holding a dozen balloons. The caption read, *Surprising Wyatt on our 6 month anniversary!*

I tucked my phone back in my purse and closed my eyes, thinking, *My life could not possibly get any more complicated.*

I was wrong about that, though. So wrong.

After all I'd been through, all the care I'd taken to stay out of trouble, in the end it was a human, not a ghost, who got me called into a parental after-school judgment session.

It was Marnie, who I thought was supposed to be my friend.

I sat at the dining room table with Jonathan and Mom. My stepfather's iPad sat on the table, and the front page of Starstalkerz stared up at us. The website, to my incredible non-delight, had added the following tidbit to the item about Marnie and me:

EDITOR'S NOTE: Whoops, Stalkerz! As many of you pointed out, this glamorpuss is NOT Bernadette Middleton, despite her claims to the contrary — in fact, we have it on good authority that her name is Willa Cresky and she's the newly imported stepdaughter of Infinity Realms *director Jonathan Walters.*

Gotta watch out for those east coast girls. Hey, she may not be royalty, but we'll give her this — she looks great in red!

That was it. Not a word about Marnie, or the fact that she was lying, too. Not a word to say that I hadn't been the one to start the story, or send out a stupid press release.

Jonathan's publicist had called him that afternoon in a red-hot fury, claiming that his new stepdaughter was a total embarrassment to his public image.

"What would make me feel better, Willa," Jonathan said now, "is hearing some explanation as to why you thought it was okay in the first place."

"I didn't," I said. "It wasn't my idea."

"But you went along with it," Mom said.

"I don't know if you understand how reputations work in the real world," Jonathan said. "Your word is your bond. When you get a reputation for not telling the truth, it can follow you forever."

I nodded. After a half hour of useless attempts to defend myself, quiet acquiescence seemed like my best chance to get out of there before my twenty-first birthday.

"We're not angry, exactly," Mom said. "Just disappointed."

But I could tell by the way Jonathan frowned that he was a little angry.

I apologized again. And then they rehashed it again. And that happened four more times and then they finally told me I could go up to my room and think about what I'd done.

As if I didn't have any other problems to think about in my spare time.

CHAPTER 25

I'd forgotten how delicate my old computer was. If you pushed the screen open too fast, or a millimeter too far, the whole display would turn a very alarming shade of muddy green. I pulled it closer and held my breath until the backlight came on again.

Then I clicked on the folder labeled DAD'S STUFF. It was only a backup, meant to be deleted after he transferred all of his files to the new computer. But I never got around to deleting it.

I clicked through, looking for the backup of his contacts list. Then I opened that and did a search for *DR*.

Dr. Pamela Tilliman, General Practitioner.

And a phone number.

It was four o'clock, which meant seven o'clock in Connecticut, which meant that Dr. Tilliman was probably long gone for the day, but I figured I could leave a message and ask her to call me back on Monday.

To my surprise, someone picked up on the first ring.

"Hello, Dr. Tilliman speaking."

"Um, hi, Dr. Tilliman," I said. "My name is Willa Cresky. My dad was a patient of yours. Paul Cresky?"

"Paul Cresky," she repeated. Her voice was deep and rich with authority. "*Oh*, Paul Cresky — yes, of course. It's been about two years since he passed away, hasn't it?"

"It'll be two years May sixteenth," I said. "I know it's late, but I was hoping I could ask you some questions."

"Well, I may not be able to answer everything," she said, "but I'll see what I can help you with."

"My dad died of a heart attack —"

She interrupted me, and I heard typing. "Hang on. I'm pulling up his chart. . . . You said you're Willa? I think I met you at the funeral. And I remember your dad used to talk about you. Didn't you guys exercise together?"

"We swam," I said, gripping a handful of my comforter in my tightly balled-up fist. "But he died. While we were swimming."

"Oh, right . . ." she said. There was an embarrassed silence.

"It's okay," I said. "I just have a question about heart attacks. Because the day my dad died — I mean, right before he died — we had a big fight."

"A fight?" she echoed.

"An argument. I mean, we weren't even yelling or anything, but we were both really angry." The sting of the memory made my throat tighten but I kept talking, unable to stop. "I left the pool, and when I changed my mind and went back, he was . . . floating. I don't know if he was dead at that point or not, but the paramedics declared him dead after they tried CPR. Everybody tried CPR. The gym even had a defibrillator, but it didn't work."

"Right," she said. "I see all that here, in the notes from the hospital. What's your question?"

I pressed the phone to my ear, my breath coming in shaking bursts. "Did I . . . um . . . kill my dad?"

"Oh, honey," she said. "No."

I waited for her to elaborate.

"That's it," she said. "That's my answer. A categorical no. Not a chance."

"But I stressed him out. I gave him a heart attack."

"Your father was exerting himself physically. And, honestly, a normal, healthy forty-four-year-old man should not have had a heart attack from that level of physical exertion. Certainly not from an argument. One where you weren't even yelling."

Wyatt had basically said the same thing.

"But then . . ." I stared at the keys on the keyboard until they all seemed to meld together. "Why did he die?"

"Hold on, let me look at something, okay?"

The line was filled with jazzy hold music. The sudden contrast almost made me laugh, in a crazy way.

A couple of minutes passed, and I was afraid Dr. Tilliman had forgotten about me. Then there was a click, and the music disappeared.

"Hello, Willa?" she asked. "Still there?"

"Yes, I'm still here." My heart was beating a thousand beats a minute.

"I just called the hospital and had the medical examiner's records emailed over," she said. "Hang on . . . 'the findings were

consistent with asymptomatic hypertrophic cardiomyopathy . . .
resulting in sudden cardiac death.'"

"I don't know what that means," I whispered.

"It's a genetic heart condition," she said. "It means that your
father lived his whole life with a mutated gene that predisposed
him for a condition known for causing sudden cardiac events,
often without any hint of a symptom prior to the event. Tell me,
Willa . . . how long had you guys been swimming that morning?"

I tried to dredge up the details, so long suppressed under an
avalanche of guilt and pain. "Maybe about fifteen minutes? We
usually swam for a half hour, but Dad stopped."

I drew in my breath sharply.

"He stopped," I said, suddenly remembering. "He said he
was suddenly really tired. He thought he'd rest for a minute and
then we could start again, but that's when we started talking
about Aiden — my boyfriend, Dad hated him — and it turned
into an argument, so I left. I went back to the locker room."

"Obviously I didn't have a chance to examine your father
myself," the doctor said, her voice gentle. "But given what you've
just said, and the findings from the autopsy, nothing you did
caused your father's death. What's more, Willa . . . nothing you
could have done would have saved him."

I stared at the computer screen, feeling a tightness in my
own chest.

"Don't take this in an alarming way, but you should probably
be screened for the condition at some point. An echocardiogram or MRI —"

"I've had those," I said. "Both of them. Everything was normal."

I remembered Mom's panic over my headaches. Was it because she knew what had really killed Dad? Then why didn't she tell me?

Maybe because I never asked. And whenever she tried to talk to me about Dad, I simply refused. I'd never been willing to talk about it.

"Well, that's good," Dr. Tilliman said. Then, after a long pause, she spoke again, with a note of curiosity in her voice. "Why did you call now? Why two years later?"

I swallowed hard. "I think I just finally wanted to know the truth."

Monday, when I set my tray down beside him, Wyatt looked at me as if I'd lit the table on fire.

Then he instinctively glanced over at the couches, where Marnie's group of friends sat without showing the slightest hint of wondering where I was.

"She's home sick today," I said. "It's safe."

"Someone might tell her," he said.

Without answering, I pulled out a chair and sat down, pushing some of his books aside to make room for myself.

"Since we're on the subject of Marnie," I said. "Can you please tell me exactly what went on with you guys?"

"You want my side of the story?" He glanced up sharply. "Does this mean you don't believe I stalked her?"

"On reflection," I said, "Marnie seems to have a complicated relationship with the truth."

He snorted. "You can say that."

"I don't understand, though," I said. "What's her deal?"

He looked unhappy. "In my estimation, Marnie's kind of pathological. She's charming, smart, and incredibly manipulative, with shockingly little concern for the feelings or well-being of other people. But hey, maybe that's just my experience."

"But why does she do those things?" I asked. "To what end?"

"To her own end," he said, shrugging. "That's the point. For the glory of Marnie."

"She was so nice to me, though," I said.

"Of course she was," he said. "She wanted you to like her. She still wants you to like her. Heck, she still wants *me* to like her, even though she's told half the school I stalked her. As much as she tries to pretend otherwise, she thrives on the approval of other people. And there's basically no limit to what she'll say to get it."

I nodded.

"I don't say this lightly," Wyatt said. "And I'd rather you didn't repeat it. Frankly, it's not my business how Marnie wants to deal with the world. She taught me a pretty valuable lesson, and for that I'm actually grateful. It's not my intention to spread rumors about her."

"Even though she spreads them about you?"

He nodded.

"So what do I do?" I asked. "Stop hanging out with her?"

"You do whatever you feel the need to do."

"Is she going to spread rumors about me, too?" As I asked the question, I realized the whole Bernadette Middleton drama wasn't too far off the mark from rumor-spreading. "Actually, scratch that. I think I know the answer."

Wyatt gave me an understanding look.

I sat back in my chair. Then I looked at Wyatt and took a huge breath. "And . . . also . . . you were right," I said, studying my sandwich on the lunch tray. "About my dad. I talked to his doctor. He had a genetic heart condition."

"Genetic?" Wyatt looked alarmed. "Then you should probably be screened for it."

"It turns out I have been. Thanks for your concern, though." Then I tried to smile apologetically, but I'm pretty sure it came out as a pained grimace. "And I'm sorry for what I said at your house."

"No," he said. "I'm sorry. You were wrong about a lot of things, but you were right that I had no business looking into your personal affairs."

"We were both wrong," I said. "Do two wrongs make a right?"

"Maybe in Marnie's world." He gave me an ironic smile. "So . . . anything to update?"

"Um, yeah," I said. There was a pretty major update. I told Wyatt how I'd discovered Paige's death online.

"Hold on." Wyatt stared at me with his eyebrows raised. "You sat down and led with Marnie, rather than this huge revelation?"

"Because I knew that once I told you about Paige, we wouldn't be talking about anything else," I replied.

"Good point." He nodded. "So did you look up the details of her death?"

"No," I said. "I just . . . ran out of energy. I mean, I've been *begging* the ghost of Diana Del Mar to throw me a bone — not literally — and she's gone. I mean, what's the point?"

"The point?" Wyatt looked genuinely confused. "The point is to find out the *truth*."

I'd forgotten how comforting it was to have someone around who believed you. Who was willing to help. I felt a grateful smile fighting its way to my lips.

But as my eyes met Wyatt's, the cafeteria and everything in it faded to a white oblivion.

I can't stop staring at the rectangle of light. For the first couple of days, it represented so many things — hope, my chance of escape. Now there's only the abject terror that courses through my veins when he lifts the door and walks down the steps.

He's here, demanding that we go back over the scene, over and over, even though I know my lines by heart. Right up to the part where the script cuts off, without telling how it ends.

But I know how it ends — I've seen the movie. It ends with me plunging backward through a glass coffee table. Dead.

He approaches me, and I try not to flinch — one of my strategies is to make him think of me like a friend, not a victim. Like we have a rapport. To humanize myself.

It might even be working.

"Brought you something, Lor," he says. "Can you lean forward? Like that, thanks."

He reaches around my neck and fastens a thin gold chain, then looks down at it, frowning.

"What is it?" I ask, trying to see. "Thank you."

I smile, giving him as trusting a gaze as I can summon, but the look in his eyes chills the warmth from my smile.

"It's nothing," he says coldly. "A cheap imitation. It's totally disposable."

Then he walks away.

CHAPTER 26

Hey," Wyatt said. "Look at me. Take a breath. You're here. You're okay."

I blinked, hearing his voice and obeying his words without questioning them.

"You had another episode," he said.

"Yeah," I breathed. "No kidding. He . . . he called her *Lor*."

"Lorelei." Wyatt's mouth was set in a grim line as he automatically flipped open the notebook and started making notes. "Any new information?"

I shook my head. "No, no . . . But . . . there was something weird about the necklace. I think it might have been different this time."

After school, Mom had to run to the mall, so I made her drop me off at home first. As I opened the front door, I heard a low rumbling sound. I didn't think anything of it — for a second at least. There was always construction going on in the neighborhood, people pulling down old houses to build new ones, or replacing parts of their houses so they wouldn't slide down the hillside in an earthquake.

But this particular rumbling was coming from *inside* the house.

I set my backpack on the entry table and turned around.

The rumbling became a roar, and I looked up the stairs just as a wall of water came rushing down toward me. It was like someone had taken the contents of the pool and dumped them from the second floor.

Everything went into slow motion.

I had just enough time to scream before the wave smashed into me, knocking me down. For a second, I had that feeling you get at the beach when a big wave unexpectedly pulls you under, and you can't tell which way is up.

Reed came racing out of Jonathan's office and down the stairs.

"Willa!" he cried. "What happened? Did you fall? Why are you wet?"

I couldn't speak. I looked around and saw that, aside from me — as wet as a drowned rat — and the wet patch of rug I had landed on, the foyer looked completely ordinary.

"Um," I said, as he reached down to help me up, "it's kind of hard to explain."

He watched me patiently, and I realized that the way I'd phrased that implied I was still going to try to explain. Which I wasn't.

Time to retreat.

"I have some stuff going on right now," I said, looking up at him, trying to make my face apologetic. "My life has a lot of different . . . aspects. I don't quite know how to say it, actually. It's probably better if I don't."

"Yeah," he said. His shoulders drooped slightly. "I know what you're trying to say."

"You do?" I asked.

He nodded, then reached out and took my hand. "What happened between us . . . now's not the right time. Maybe in a year or two. But there are too many factors in play at the moment."

He thought I was breaking things off between us? Or was he breaking things off with me? I expected to feel a pang of heartache, but I felt strangely okay. Maybe the fact that a ghost had just sent a tidal wave of water over me distracted me from the memory of Reed's kiss.

Reed frowned. "But that doesn't explain why you're wet. Or why you screamed."

Well, now that I didn't have to worry about impressing him, I was free to come up with an explanation that made me sound like a lunatic.

"I fell in the fountain," I said.

His eyebrows went up.

"And then I screamed because . . . sometimes it feels good to scream, you know? I didn't know you were here. Sorry if I alarmed you."

My words probably confused him even more, rather than clearing things up, but he nodded slowly.

"Do you need a towel?" he asked.

"Nah," I said. "I'll go change."

I gave him the world's awkwardest smile, took my bag from the table, and sailed up the stairs with my head held high, like this was all part of a typical Monday afternoon.

As I stood in my bathroom, combing out my wet hair, I ran back through what had just happened. I was surprised to realize that I felt not the least bit sad. In fact, I felt strangely relieved.

Was it possible that I didn't like Reed as much as I assumed I should? Getting the attention of a guy who could easily be cast as the dashing romantic hero in a movie wasn't the kind of thing you could throw off lightly.

And yet, here I was, throwing it off pretty lightly.

There was no explanation for my reaction.

Well, I thought, *maybe there's someone else you like more than Reed.*

I spent the rest of the afternoon following obscure leads online, trying to figure out why the ghost of Diana Del Mar would feel the need to soak me (yet again), and how she could be connected to the murders – if that's even what the visions were supposed to be telling me. But something major was missing, just like Wyatt had said. By dinnertime, I built up so much frustrated, nervous energy that I knew I had to burn some off or I'd be up all night. So after we finished eating, I changed into my swimsuit and went down to the den, where Mom was sitting on the couch reading.

"Can I go swimming?" The words were a question, but I knew the tone of my voice implied an *or else* situation.

"Of course," she said. "Do you want me to sit outside with you?"

"No," I said. "I'm good. You can spy on me through the windows if you feel the urge."

The brilliant underwater light sharply defined the tiled floor of the pool, each tiny square casting its own little shadow. I took a good look around for dead bodies and then started to swim.

I pulled myself toward the deep end with long, powerful strokes. I thought it might feel different to be in the water, after talking to Dr. Tilliman. But it was pretty much the same as always. I suppose a rational person would consider my father's death reason enough to stay out of pools for the rest of her life. Not to mention the last terrifying thing that had happened to me in this very pool. Further evidence of how twisted I was, I guess. I couldn't stay away. I was drawn to the water.

Maybe it's human nature to be drawn to the things that have hurt us the most.

I swam until I was hot and panting, so tired that I could have curled up on the tile and fallen asleep.

At least the whole thing had gone off without incident.

Until.

Until I climbed the steps and wrapped myself in a striped towel. And noticed something — no, *two* somethings — a pair of small puddles on the tile closest to the pool. When I angled my head, I saw them for what they really were . . .

Footprints.

Whoever had left them had been standing at the edge, looking out over the pool . . . looking at me.

The prints led away. I followed their trail and found myself standing in front of the guest cottage, where they went up the steps and across the small porch. Then they stopped.

I put my hand on the knob.

"Willa?"

I spun around to see Jonathan walking out of the house, at a pace that was a hair too fast to be casual.

"Hey, sorry," he said, coming closer. "We never talked about the guesthouse, I guess. We don't go in there, um . . . ever. The wiring's very old and I haven't had a chance to have somebody come and look at it yet."

"Okay," I said. Not like I'd really wanted to go in.

"Great. Thanks for understanding." Then he stood with his hands on his hips for a moment, looking around.

It dawned on me after a few seconds that he wasn't going back inside until I did, so I stepped down off the porch and walked toward the main house, with Jonathan following a couple of feet behind me.

"Sorry if I startled you," he said. "I was doing dishes, and I saw you out the window."

"You didn't startle me," I said. I turned to look over my shoulder and saw that — as some part of me had totally expected — the footprints had vanished.

"All right, well . . . the dishwasher calls." He made a left into the kitchen, seeming highly relieved to get away from me.

Mom glanced up from her book as I passed the den. "What was that about?"

"Jonathan came outside because he thought I was going into the guesthouse," I said.

"Oh." She frowned. "Nobody goes in there."

I nodded and started for the stairs, thinking, *Somebody does*.

CHAPTER 27

What's going on with you?" Marnie asked the next morning. We were sitting on the floor in front of my locker, finishing up some homework before the first bell.

"Huh?" I tore my attention from the Trig assignment and glanced over at her.

"You've been acting weird lately," she said. "Distant. Like you've got other stuff going on."

"Oh, no, Marnie," I said. "I wouldn't dream of having a life outside of our time together."

She picked up on my sarcasm and shot me an annoyed glance. Then she glanced at my work sheet and copied the answer I'd just written onto her own paper.

"Wait a second," I said, moving my notebook out of her view. "How long have you been cheating off me?"

She ignored the question. "Kas said you ate lunch with Wyatt yesterday."

"Yeah? Well, I did."

Neither of us spoke for a minute.

"Do you have a problem with that?" I asked.

"A problem? No . . ." she said. "I expected more from you, that's all. I mean, I warned you about him —"

"Marnie," I said, careful to keep my voice even, "I think a lot of what you said about Wyatt was lies."

"Lies?" She laughed humorlessly. "Okay, sure."

Not exactly a denial, was it?

I sighed and faced her squarely. I guess if we were going to do this, now was as good a time as any. "I saw the photos; I looked up the blog. You guys were clearly an actual couple."

She didn't get angry. She gave me a blank smile. "When did I ever say we weren't?"

I gaped at her for a second. "At your house, after the premiere."

She shook her head. "Hm-mm. I don't think so. You must have misunderstood me. You can be . . . a little obtuse sometimes. No offense."

"No," I said. "I didn't misunderstand. You said he thought you were going out and it was really awkward for you. But you guys did go out."

"Of course we did!" she said, exasperated. "We were, like, the It Couple. Why do you think we had a blog?"

Okay. Deep breath. This was veering from uncomfortable to downright bizarre.

"And the balloons," I said, even though I knew I should stop. "You said he came to your house with balloons, but *you* were the one who gave them to *him*."

There was a moment when our eyes met and there was a laser connection between us, an unmistakable hyperloop of the serious, actual truth. And we both felt it.

But Marnie recovered and sat back, shaking her head. "I took a chance on you, Willa. When no one else in the entire school would talk to you, I invited you to sit with me. I introduced you to my friends. I even took you to an important Hollywood event, where you proceeded to lie to journalists about —"

"Okay, no," I said. "Stop. Don't even finish that sentence, please. We both know who invented Bernadette Middleton and sent that press release."

"I thought we were friends," she said, fixing a wide-eyed stare at me. "What are you accusing me of?"

I realized, all at once, that she actually didn't get it. And then I realized that there was no point in continuing our conversation.

"Look," she went on, "I realize now that you have a thing for Wyatt. Maybe you're . . . I don't know, threatened by me or something? But believe me, you're welcome to him. He's all yours. I'm sorry you got so many wrong ideas. I was only trying to look out for you."

Staring at her, I felt almost nothing. No anger. No desire to make her admit her lying ways. Only a tiny hint of regret for the loss of the person I thought she had been.

Wyatt was right — Marnie was pathological. But she couldn't be held accountable. She was a force of nature. A runaway train.

I knew I had a choice now. I could either accept it, and her, or I could spend a ton of energy agonizing over the situation.

Spending tons of energy agonizing over things was pretty much my specialty, after all.

I shrugged. "All right," I said. "Apology accepted."

Her eyes sparkled and she shot me a brilliant, empty smile. "I knew I liked you. Hey, what do you have for number twenty-two?"

I tilted my work sheet so she could see the answer.

When the bell rang, she got to her feet. "So . . . I guess you'll probably want to find somewhere else to stay this weekend."

Oh, right. I forgot about that. "Of course," I said, my stomach sinking at the thought of ruining my mother's honeymoon.

"Cool." She nodded. "I have big plans anyway. I mean, a thing I'm doing later this week. And then I might have really big news. I just might be too busy to . . . you know, babysit you."

Okay, ouch. But I forced myself to ignore the barb. I knew she was being deliberately mysterious, trying to bait me into grilling her. "What kind of big news?" I asked.

"Can't tell you. Top secret." She pantomimed zipping her lip. "Anyway, you and Wyatt do whatever —"

"It's not like that," I said.

"Suuuure," she said, in her driest voice. "You talk about him all the time and hang out with him and look up pictures of him online because you hate him so much, right?"

Her musical laugh filled the hallway.

"The world's full of skeptics. I know — I'm one myself." She gave me an odd smile. "Just watch out for Wyatt. He's no gentleman, see?"

Then she walked off, leaving me speechless.

203

"You look different," Wyatt said.

"Free?" I asked, setting my tray on the lunch table.

"No." He studied me. "Annoyed."

"It's been an interesting morning." I started to sit down.

"Wait, don't get settled here," Wyatt said, running a hand through his hair. "I have to tell you something. I was thinking we could go out to the courtyard."

"But it's raining," I said.

"Even better," he said. "More tables to choose from."

"Why can't we ever sit and talk like two normal people?"

He gazed at me evenly. "Because if someone hears what I'm about to say, I could go to jail."

We ended up in a corner of the courtyard, sheltered by a slight overhang. The rain cooled the air, the clouds blocked the sun, and we sat side by side, shivering. I crossed my arms and buried my hands in my dark green Langhorn-issued cardigan, resisting the urge to huddle close to Wyatt for warmth.

"C-can you h-hurry?" I asked. "Before we f-freeze to death?"

"No one had seen Paige Pollan for four days before she was found," Wyatt said, glancing down at his notebook for confirmation. "Her school assumed she was home sick, and her mother was in Vegas — she worked weekends as a blackjack dealer and sometimes just stayed the whole week there. She had no idea her daughter was missing. But when they found the body, the coroner estimated she'd been dead for less than twenty-four hours — not four days."

I breathed on my hands and then tucked them inside my sleeves. "So she skipped school, hung out at home for a few days, and then killed herself?"

He shook his head. "She had a goldfish. It was dead when the police found her. People who are planning to kill themselves — I mean, people who don't do it in a moment of passion — do it because they think the world will be better without them. They don't let their pets die just because they feel depressed."

I didn't know exactly what Wyatt was hinting at, but I was pretty sure I wasn't going to like it. "Maybe the fish died accidentally — goldfish are pretty delicate, right?"

"All that," he said, "I could rationalize away. If it were only that. But then I found this."

He handed me his notebook, where he'd written out a paragraph.

I'M SORRY. I HAVE BEEN VERY LONELY AND STRUGGLED WITH A LOT OF THINGS. NO ONE UNDERSTANDS THE FEELINGS I'VE HAD. NO ONE IS ON MY SIDE. IT'S LIKE I'M COMPLETELY ALONE. I REALIZE THIS IS THE COWARDLY WAY OUT BUT I CAN'T STOP MYSELF FROM BEING A COWARD. MY WHOLE LIFE IS LIKE A BAD DREAM.

THE KIND OF DREAM YOU DON'T WAKE
UP FROM.

PAIGE

I read the words over and over until they swam in front of my eyes.

"It's her suicide note," Wyatt said, a mite unnecessarily.

The kind of dream you don't wake up from.

Suddenly I didn't even feel the cold. "Paige saw the script," I said. "Somehow she knew that line."

"It makes sense, in a way," Wyatt said. "We know she was a fan of Diana Del Mar."

"But that line," I said. "What are the odds?"

"The odds of any of this happening are astronomically slim," he said. "I don't think we should worry about odds anymore."

I turned to him. "You said you found that. How is that possible? I want the truth about where you get your information."

"Right. That's why I brought you out here." He cleared his throat nervously. "My dad's a crime-scene consultant for the LAPD. Sometimes I take his security pass and access evidence storage. And occasionally I look at investigation information online."

"You . . . *what*? Is that even legal?"

Wyatt sat back uncomfortably. "Not by the remotest stretch of the imagination."

"Does your dad know about this?"

Wyatt shook his head, his lips pursed.

"How do you get in?" I asked.

He took a second to answer. "I know the guy who controls the access."

"You know the guy who controls the access . . . ?" I said. "Wait, do you mean you *bribe* the guy who controls the access?"

Wyatt sighed deeply. "He knows I'm not going to abuse the information I find. Listen, it's not immoral — I'm not even sure it's unethical. It's just illegal. Don't judge me, I don't want to hear it."

I shook my head, shocked. Perfect, precise, by-the-book Wyatt, breaking into the police archives and accessing information illegally.

Okay, it was pretty scandalous, but it was also kind of . . . audacious and cool.

Imagine that.

"That's why you have to write everything down in your book," I said.

He nodded. "When I go there, I leave my phone at the desk, and I can't photocopy anything because it would show up on my dad's records. So I copy it all out by hand."

"Wow," I said, trying to picture it. "And your dad has no idea?"

"None." Now Wyatt looked extremely unhappy. "If he found out, he'd . . . I don't even know what he'd do. Can we go back to talking about Paige, please?"

"Sure," I said. "She obviously knew about the movie, right? Is it so hard to believe that she would use the line in her suicide note? If she liked Diana Del Mar enough . . ."

"She must have liked her a whole lot," Wyatt said. "Diana

Del Mar was found dead after taking sleeping pills and falling asleep in a full bathtub. Paige Pollan died the exact same way."

"Like . . . in tribute?" I shivered, not because of the cold.

Wyatt frowned and didn't answer.

"It's not right," I said. "I know there's something we're not connecting."

"But we'll keep working on it." He looked at me, his expression somber. "Remember when you asked me when I'd be done, and I told you I felt like a piece was missing?"

"Yeah," I said. "Of course."

"Well . . . I don't feel that way anymore. I feel like we found the missing piece. We just need to figure out how it fits into the puzzle."

Mom spent the afternoon rushing around the house, packing for Palm Springs as if they were going on a three-month trek to Siberia and not a three-day trip to a city two hours away from home.

I racked my brain for a way to tell her that I'd been uninvited from Marnie's house, but the right moment never seemed to arrive.

So instead, I came up with a foolproof plan, which was: Don't tell her.

After all, I was seventeen years old, practically an adult. Plenty of people my age stay home alone all the time. And I wouldn't even be truly alone — I had the ghost, right?

I was in my room trying to catch up on English Lit reading when there was a light knock on my door.

"Willa?" Mom said.

"Yeah, come in."

She carried in a small empty suitcase. "Did you pack yet? I thought you might want to use this."

Oh, right. As far as she knew, I was going somewhere. "Thanks," I said, taking it and setting it on the floor next to the bed. "Are you excited?"

She smiled, shrugging. "I guess. I feel bad for leaving you. Maybe we should have done a familymoon."

"First of all," I said, "*familymoon* is a totally disturbing word, and an even more disturbing concept. Second of all, go have fun. Relax. Stop worrying about me for a couple of days."

"I'm a mother," she said. "I know it's a cliché, but I'll never stop worrying about you."

I made a face. "Do I seem that helpless?"

"Oh, Willa, of course not." Mom reached over and rubbed my back, like she used to when I was a little girl. "You're the opposite of helpless. You've been growing so much lately. But . . . they say when you become a mother, part of your heart walks around outside your body."

"That would be me, huh?" I asked. "The mobile segment of one of your bodily organs?"

She shrugged. "I'm not going to apologize for loving you more than anything else in the world."

I leaned my head on her shoulder. "You really think I'm growing?"

"Oh, yes. Don't you feel it? Since we got here, you've developed this . . . I don't know, this aura of confidence."

"That's totally ironic," I said, "because the stuff that's happened to me here is so non-confidence-aura-making."

"You've had a hard time at school?" Mom asked, sounding slightly heartbroken.

I didn't answer.

"But, honey, don't you see? Even if it's tough now, those are the things that are making you stronger. Facing difficult circumstances. Getting through them. And look, you have Marnie — and you're friendly with Reed — and you're coming out of your shell a little."

I was incredibly glad that we were sitting next to each other so she couldn't see how red my face turned when she mentioned Reed.

She sat up and gave her hair a little shake. "I'm *proud* of you. And I'm sure your father would be, too."

Tears stung my eyes. "Stop. You're going to make me cry."

"I'm sorry. I don't mean to be such a drama queen."

"We're both drama queens," I said. "Or hadn't you noticed?"

She stared out the window. "I guess you're right. Poor Jonathan, having to live with us."

"Poor Jonathan? What about poor you? And poor me? Why is Jonathan the only one whose suffering is considered legitimate?"

Mom sighed. "That's not what I meant —"

"I'm tired of feeling bad about everything," I said. "And you should be tired of it, too."

Mom shrugged. "I feel selfish. I wanted to marry Jonathan — you didn't get a say in that. And then you got dragged out here, also without a say. And now that I'm here, honestly, I don't even know what to do with myself all day."

I looked at Mom, who was staring at the floor. "Really?" I asked her softly.

"Yeah," she said. "And I know I should go back to work, but what if I can't get a job? What if I'm not good enough?"

"Are you kidding?" I asked. "Of course you're good enough. You think the people here are so special? They're normal people. You're probably smarter than ninety-nine percent of them."

Her left cheek dimpled, the way it always did when she was trying not to smile.

"Start applying," I said. "You'll get something right away. Or you can have Jonathan call in some favors."

She laughed. "I couldn't do that."

"Mom," I said. "He married you. He puts up with your nutso daughter. You think he won't make a few phone calls, if it would make you happy?"

She sighed. "I just wish I knew how long it would take for me to feel like myself again." Suddenly, she grabbed her head with both hands. "Like this! I mean, how did I end up *blond*? I swear, Willa, sometimes I look in the mirror and it's like I don't even recognize the person looking back at me."

I rested my head on her shoulder. "I recognize you."

She smiled through her tears and rubbed my upper arm before pulling me into a giant Mom-hug. "You're one of a kind."

"That's probably for the best," I said.

She kissed me on the forehead and then stood up. "Oh, look, your sink is running. How strange. Is the faucet acting up?"

"No," I said. "I don't think so. I'll keep an eye on it."

"Dinner'll be ready in about an hour, okay? I made spaghetti." She went into the bathroom, shut off the faucet, hugged me again, and left, closing the door gently behind her.

I lay back on my bed and stared at the ceiling for a while, feeling oddly at peace.

Later that night, as I brushed my teeth, my whole body suddenly felt warm and clammy, and my head began to ache. I took this as a not-so-great sign.

I closed my door and climbed into bed. Even though I was already hot, I didn't push the blanket off. I wanted protective layers between myself and whatever the night had in store for me.

As I reached over and switched off my bedside lamp, I heard a short, sharp shattering sound.

I forced my eyes shut so tightly that they ached immediately.

I'm ignoring you, Diana, I thought. *La la la, I can't hear you.*

Except of course I could.

Through the darkness came another sound:

Squeak, squeak, squeak.

I sat up and walked over to the bathroom, gave the door a tiny shove, and reached in to switch on the light.

Nothing happened.

Pushing the door open a few inches farther revealed what must have been the source of the first sound — a lightbulb in a thousand pieces on the floor.

That didn't explain (a) why the lights hadn't come on at all, because there were two bulbs, and (b) the source of the second sound, which was now poking me in the brain with a fiery-hot knife.

SQUEEEEEEEEEEAK.

Could it be a mouse? But it seemed to come from up high. Then my eyes went to the lone lightbulb that remained in the fixture over the vanity.

Ever so slowly, making the faintest *squeak, squeak, squeak,* the bulb was spinning. Before I could dash forward to catch it, it came free and plunged to the counter below, shattering.

The ghost was there. Right now. With me.

In a panic, I backed away, staring in horror into the darkened room.

"What?" I asked, my voice trembling. "What do you want, Diana?"

Another crash. The towel bar fell, leaving two patches of torn plaster in its place.

Then the bathtub faucet and shower both turned on at once.

Was it going to destroy the whole bathroom?

Feeling utterly helpless, I sank to the floor, ducking my head and squeezing my eyes shut. Like a little kid making herself as small as possible.

"Please," I said. *"What do you want?"*

The faucets turned off. The room fell quiet.

I opened my eyes and glanced around.

In my bedroom, on the wall opposite the bathroom, in huge black letters, was written:

WRONG

Behind me, the sink faucet turned on again.

Suddenly, the word *wrong* was appearing on every inch of the wall, and floor, and ceiling of my room. *WRONG WRONG WRONG WRONG WRONG.*

The closet door burst open. Thousands of rose petals flew out, swirling in midair.

I watched for a moment, speechless, and turned to run for the door.

Then I saw my bed.

The sheets and blankets had been completely stripped off. My pillow was shredded, its stuffing strewn everywhere.

Drawn on the mattress, in black, was a giant question mark.

"What?" I said. *"What?"*

I spun in a slow circle, taking in the chaos around me. The flower petals churned silently overhead.

"Wrong . . . *question*?" I asked.

And in a whoosh, everything disappeared. The rose petals were gone. The walls were wordless once again. I heard the faucet shut off.

"Wrong question," I whispered, looking down at the pillow stuffing that littered the floor.

Not *what do you want*, but . . .

Maybe there was a reason Diana Del Mar wasn't replying to my questions.

"Who?" I asked. "Who are you?"

I swallowed hard and waited for my answer.

More writing appeared, once again covering every available square foot of wall space in the room:

I AM AN ASPIRING HOLLYWOOD TYPE
DETERMINED TO DO MY HOMEWORK
BEFORE PLUNGING INTO THE SWAMP
OF TINSELTOWN I AM AN ASPIRING
HOLLYWOOD TYPE DETERMINED TO
DO MY HOMEWORK BEFORE PLUNGING
INTO THE SWAMP OF TINSELTOWN
I AM AN ASPIRING HOLLYWOOD TYPE
DETERMINED TO DO MY HOMEWORK
BEFORE PLUNGING INTO THE SWAMP
OF TINSELTOWN I AM AN ASPIRING
HOLLYWOOD TYPE DETERMINED TO
DO MY HOMEWORK BEFORE PLUNGING
INTO THE SWAMP OF TINSELTOWN

I closed my eyes and sat down on the bed.
And then I said, "Hi, Paige."

CHAPTER 20

The next morning, after cleaning up the mess Paige had made and sneaking around the house to find replacement lightbulbs, I couldn't wait to get out of Mom's car to find Wyatt and tell him about everything that had happened.

But my mother was practically wringing out a hankie at the idea of being away from me for a whole weekend.

I tried to extract myself from her clingy embrace. "You're going to be gone for seventy-two hours," I said. "And Monday afternoon, when you come to pick me up, I'll come trotting out that gate like always."

"I wouldn't describe your movement as trotting," Mom said, not letting go of my hand, "even on the best of days."

"A joke!" I said. "Why, that's *wonderful*, Mother, what *smashing* progress. So listen, you have my phone number, and I have yours, but don't call me. This is your honeymoon, remember?"

She frowned. "Not even to say good night?"

"You can text," I said. "You get two texts a day. How about that?"

Mom sighed.

I gave her a hug. "Have fun," I said. "And remember, a honeymoon doesn't involve actually mooning people."

"I'll bear that in mind."

"Can't have you getting arrested." I kissed her on the cheek, then slid out of the car and hurried to the gate.

Behind me, I heard her call out, through the open window: "Be sure to say thank you to Marnie's parents!"

I spun around and saluted, which in my humble opinion was a very effective way to get out of actually lying to her.

Marnie was absent again. Not that she and I had any relevance to one another anymore, I guess. But it was nice to walk over to Wyatt's table at lunch without her eagle eyes watching me.

"It's Paige," I said as soon as I sat down. I hadn't been able to find Wyatt that morning, and my news came bursting out. "The ghost in my house is Paige Pollan."

"What?" Wyatt looked up from his laptop in shocked disbelief. "How do you know?"

"Trust me," I said. "She made it very clear."

"Then . . . then . . . this changes a lot of things," he said. "We need to kick-start our investigation. We need to figure out what Paige's death could possibly have to do with your house. This weekend."

I shook my head. "We can start on Monday. My mom and stepdad are out of town, and if Paige burns the house down when I'm not even supposed to be home, there's going to be a lot of explaining to do."

Wyatt looked perplexed. "It would be better if she burned the house down *next* week?"

I nodded. "Much."

"We don't have to mess with the actual ghost at all," he said. "I was thinking more along the lines of trying to talk to kids from Paige's high school, or going back over the police report from her death. . . ."

"Oh," I said. "Then knock yourself out."

"What about you?" he asked. "Aren't you going to help?"

"Sure I will," I said. "I'll be home with the fire extinguisher at the ready."

He rolled his eyes.

"Listen," I said. "If there's one thing I've learned, it's that when Paige has something to say, she's going to find a way to say it. At some point she's going to let us know what the next steps are. I can't afford to go looking for trouble this weekend."

"We're not looking for trouble," he said, sounding a little defensive. "We're looking for answers."

"The answers we get are always troublesome," I said. "Do whatever you want, but I can't play until next week, okay?"

Wyatt pushed his laptop a couple of inches farther away from himself, which I took as a sign that he agreed with me, even if he didn't like it.

We ate in silence for a couple of minutes, and then Wyatt flipped his notebook open. "Why would Paige Pollan's ghost be at your house? Yes, she was a fan of Diana Del Mar," he mused. "But enough of one to be drawn to her house when she died?"

"That's not even half of it," I said. "I mean, the script, the lines she writes on the walls, 'Henry' . . . that all ties back to Leyta Fitzgeorge, and the murder investigation."

"Only Paige wasn't murdered," Wyatt said. "She committed suicide."

"Well, maybe she was the murder*er*," I said, feeling a sudden chill of fear.

"But there have been two more murders since she died," he said.

I relaxed.

"Although . . ." Wyatt thumbed back through the pages. "Maybe the *ghost* is murdering people now."

I threw a sweet potato fry at him. "Do you *mind*?"

He looked up at me, shaking his head. "Don't you want to figure out the truth?"

"Wyatt, I'm staying home *alone* this weekend," I said. "If you put that kind of thought in my head, and then Paige gets excited and decides to give me a little haunted-house performance, I will *die* of fright. I promise that I'll give it everything I have on Monday. But I can't do this today."

He made a face, but he shut the notebook and slipped it into his bag.

"Let's try something else," I said. "Like talking about something other than murders and ghosts and dead people."

He folded his arms on the table and rested his chin on them. "I don't know about anything else."

"You don't like music?" I asked.

He shrugged. "Well, yeah. I mostly listen to country —"

"No," I said. "Stop. You do not."

"What's wrong with country music?" He sat up. "Marnie got me into it."

"That's awesome," I said. "If I buy you a giant belt buckle, will you promise to wear it?"

He gave me a withering glare. "Never."

"Wyatt the cowboy," I said. "Like Wyatt Earp!"

"He wasn't a cowboy," Wyatt said. "He was a sheriff."

"All right, so we'll get you a big, shiny star."

"Willa," Wyatt said, a hint of warning in his voice. But there was a tiny smile on his lips. Then his eyes narrowed. "Why are you in such a good mood?"

"I'm not sure," I said.

"Because Marnie's not here?"

I shook my head. It had never been about Marnie. It had never been about Wyatt, either. Or Mom. Or my dad. Or Reed, or any one thing, really. Not even the ghost. Those things were like individual curtains blocking back the light in a very dark room.

But suddenly I was pushing them all aside. And each situation was letting in a tiny bit of light.

"I just think things are looking up," I said. "Is that insane? To expect that you're going to be . . . like . . . okay?"

"That's not insane at all," Wyatt said. "That's what we're all aiming for, right?"

I nodded, smiling. "What about books? Do you like to read?"

"Of course I like to read," he said.

"Let me guess," I said. "Obscure Russian philosophers?"

"I'm more into Tom Clancy. Military stuff. Strategy, politics. What do you read, *Us Weekly*?"

I sniffed haughtily. "Not my taste."

"Oh, sorry," he said, raising an eyebrow. "You probably prefer the British tabloids, *Bernadette Middleton*."

"Could you not?" I groaned. "That was *all* Marnie's doing."

"Yeah, it felt like Marnie. It had her stamp on it." He looked down at his half-finished sandwich. "But . . . you, um, you did look like a movie star in that picture."

"Stop mocking me," I said, blushing.

"I'm serious. You were totally believable. You looked fresh faced and —"

"Fresh faced?" I repeated. "Weirdest compliment ever."

He shot me an affectedly arrogant look. "Maybe I'm not trying to compliment you. Maybe it's an observation."

"All right, Sherlock Holmes. Thanks for your analysis."

"Fine." He sat up straight and looked at me. "You looked *beautiful* in that picture."

Oh.

I blinked and glanced down at the table, collecting my thoughts and feelings, which were scattered all over the place.

"Hey," I finally said, nudging him with the side of my shoulder.

When I looked back up, Wyatt was looking at me. Our eyes met, and I felt a *zing!* of energy move through me.

"Yes?" he said softly.

"Thanks."

"Don't mention it." He looked back down at his lunch and picked up an apple slice. "Be careful. Your face might stick like that."

Stick like what? I wondered.

And then I realized I was smiling.

Wyatt dropped me off after school. But first, we stopped at the grocery store, where I stocked up on the kind of food Mom never allowed in the house — frozen pizza bites and macaroni and fake cheese, a whole box of those little chocolate cupcakes with icing squigglies on top, and a two-liter bottle of Hawaiian Punch. I might be dead of malnutrition by Monday, but at least I'd spend my last weekend in carb-induced nirvana.

The house was blissfully calm and still, with no sign of Paige. I began to hope this might be the start of one of her quiet periods, leaving me with a week or two of semi-normalcy. Maybe all she'd wanted was for someone to know she was here.

After arming the alarm system, I curled up in front of the TV with a two-pack of cupcakes and found a marathon of *Pageant Tots*. Four hours later, feeling like I could use a good brain-scrubbing, I went to the library to look over Jonathan's DVD collection.

It occupied about sixty linear feet of shelf space and contained basically every movie I'd ever heard of, organized in alphabetical order.

The arrangement was so perfect that it was totally obvious when a movie had been removed. There were a few spots where movies were missing — *Vertical Limit* leaned on *Very Bad Things*. *Heat and Dust* rested on *Heaven*.

I began to get a strange feeling in the deepest pit of my stomach.

I drifted to the *B*'s.

Birdman of Alcatraz. Then a space. Then *Birdy*. In the *K*'s, I found *A Kiss Before Dying*. Then it skipped to *Kiss the Girls*.

Okay, no.

No, no, no, no.

Calm yourself, Willa. Just because the missing movies fit perfectly with the four movies that the Hollywood Killer used as his inspiration doesn't mean . . . well, anything.

Right? I couldn't even be totally sure that those were the missing films.

Then, off to the side, I saw a small three-ring binder with a label on its spine that read *DVD Inventory*. I grabbed it, flipping to the *B*'s. My heart flip-flopped as I read down the list, to *#B31 Birdman of Alcatraz*, and then read the next listing: *#B32 The Birds*.

#H14 Heathers. #K29 Kiss of Death. #V9 Vertigo.

I took a step back, trying to tell myself not to make something out of nothing. So Jonathan owned all four movies that the murders were based on. So what? Lots of people owned them. They were popular, critically acclaimed movies.

So they all just happened to be missing from their spots.

So what?

With every *so what*, my stomach twisted more tightly around itself.

Be reasonable. Maybe Jonathan pulled them all when he heard about the murders. Maybe he wanted to watch the scenes that inspired the killer, because he was curious. Maybe he was looking for connections and clues.

It was a little morbid, but then — who was I to judge?

In the pocket of my jeans, my phone vibrated with an incoming text.

It was from Mom — *Good night sweetie, love you. Tell Marnie hello and thanks! Great day here, tomorrow we're going to lay by the pool ALL DAY.*

As happy as I was that my mother was having a great time, my carefree night was beyond ruined by my discovery of the missing movies. I went back to the den and turned off the TV, and then, feeling oppressed by the sudden silence and darkness, I headed for my room.

I burrowed under the covers, for once actually wishing Paige would find some way to tell me she was there.

Turns out the price of freedom is being alone.

CHAPTER 29

Paige never showed, and the night of uninterrupted sleep did a lot to calm my mind. In the light of the morning, the simple explanation seemed like the most likely one: that Jonathan owned the DVDs and got curious about the movies when he heard about the murders. Everyone in LA was obsessed with the Hollywood Killer.

Besides, if Jonathan were a murderer, would he be that obvious about it?

I put on a pair of yoga pants and a long-sleeved T-shirt, basically a half step up from wearing pajamas, and I was downstairs eating a cupcake for breakfast when my phone buzzed.

Mom had texted: *Good morning!*

I ignored it for the time being, figuring it would seem more believable if I waited until later in the morning to reply. If I was sleeping over at a friend's house, no way would I be up by 8:30.

After my nutritionally impaired breakfast, I decided to do something I'd been putting off for weeks. I dug through my closet and found the shoe box containing my moldavite ring and the Walter Sawamura book. All I needed was something silver.

I'd been waiting for the right moment to grab a little spoon or something from the sideboard in the dining room, but then I realized that I had something silver of my own — even better, something I didn't particularly want to keep around.

I poked through my small jewelry box for the pair of silver hoop earrings Aiden had given me for my fifteenth birthday. Just looking at them made me feel a little quiver of sadness.

At some point, I should probably let Aiden know that I didn't hate him for what he'd done. That I actually understood why he'd done it. I even picked up my phone and started to write a text – *Hi, remember me? Just wanted to say sorry for crushing your soul for so long and then blaming you for needing to make a change. I get it now.* But then I chickened out.

I put the earrings in the box, wrapped the whole thing with duct tape, and went to look for something to bury it with.

I'd never been inside the garage, but it was neat and well organized, and I had no problem finding a shovel. I was on my way back out, with the shoe box tucked under my arm and the shovel in my hand, when the door opened to reveal Reed.

He gasped when he saw me, and for my part, I shrieked and dropped the shoe box with a *thunk*.

"Willa!" he said, letting out a startled burst of laughter. "I didn't expect to see you in here."

After a few days of not seeing him, I'd forgotten how cute he was, with his sun-kissed skin and perfectly mussed hair.

I bent to scoop the box off the floor and then held up the shovel. "I just came for this. What are you doing here?"

"It's Saturday," he said. "I came to get the Porsche for her weekly bath."

Mom and Jonathan had been planning to take the Porsche to Palm Springs but switched at the last minute to the SUV, in case they discovered the burning need to buy some giant antique chair or something. So the sleek little car sat inside the quiet garage like a well-behaved horse.

"Did he even drive it this week?" I asked.

Reed sat in the driver's seat long enough to turn on the ignition. Then he climbed out while the engine rumbled and purred. "All the more reason it needs to get out on the road for a few minutes. You can't let a car sit too long. It'll dry-rot."

I nodded, as if I knew anything about cars.

Reed stepped closer to the Porsche and rubbed at an invisible speck on the paint.

Seeing him like this — in black board shorts and a faded yellow T-shirt, as handsome as a movie star, I couldn't help but think about our kiss. About how crazy I was for letting him slip between my fingers.

I wondered if he ever thought about kissing me. And then I told myself that there was no way on earth.

"How've you been lately?" he asked.

"Um, good," I said. "Surprisingly good."

"I saw the picture of you and your friend at the premiere." He shook his head. "That was wild."

"Mom and Jonathan definitely thought so," I said, unable to hide the dark note in my voice.

"Willa . . . are you sure you're all right?"

I was surprised by the question. "Yeah. I am."

"You don't seem like yourself." He smiled disarmingly. "You don't usually grumble."

Maybe you don't know me very well, I thought.

Before I knew what was happening, Reed stepped toward me, then leaned down and placed a gentle kiss on my lips.

The opportunity to be kissed by someone who kisses like Reed isn't the kind of thing a girl takes lightly. I felt a familiar flutter in my stomach, tingly weakness in my arms and legs. I kissed him back, relishing the delicate pressure of his hands on my back as he pulled me closer.

He drew away for a moment and looked down at me, his eyes a question.

When I didn't say anything, he leaned in and touched his lips to mine again. With every second that passed, I felt reality melting away. Who needed to think about murders and missing movies and haunted houses? It was so easy to get lost in his warmth and his delicious scent and the sensation of his fingers moving lightly through my hair. . . .

In the pocket of my yoga pants, my phone buzzed.

I jumped, startled back to the present.

Reed stared at me for a beat, looking equally dazed. His voice was soft and throaty. "There's something about you that makes me forget to care that your stepfather is my boss."

The word *stepfather* further obliterated the mood for me. I gave him as polite a smile as I could manage and looked at the floor. There was a small puddle of standing water a couple of feet away, reflecting the sunlight.

His gaze dropped to his hands. "Sorry," he said. "I guess I'm no gentleman."

How do you respond to *that*?

Reed cleared his throat. "Can I tell you something?"

"Yeah," I said. "Of course."

"My parents were killed in a plane crash when I was fifteen," he said.

Pronouncements like that should come with a warning label. I felt like I'd been punched in the gut. "My God, Reed, I'm so sorry. I had no idea."

"It's all right," he said. "I know you know what it's like to lose a parent, so . . ."

"I do," I said, feeling like I was being tumbled end over end. "It's . . . it's terrible."

He chewed on his bottom lip. "I lived with my grandfather while I finished school. He moved here from Denver to take care of me, but he was in pretty poor health. So he passed away, too, shortly after I graduated from Langhorn."

I didn't say a word.

"I never had any brothers or sisters, and my dad wasn't close with his siblings, so I was basically on my own. I couldn't afford college, so I went looking for work in the industry. I interviewed with Jonathan for this job, and somehow, miraculously, I got it, even though I had zero qualifications. Jonathan's been like the big brother I never had. He looks out for me. He's tough, but it's because he wants me to learn and do well. He's meticulous and exacting, but it just makes me work harder. He's my role model. I can't even tell you how much his good opinion means to me."

"Wow," I said, considering Jonathan in a new light. After all, he'd married a widow with a teenage daughter. He did everything he could to make me feel at home. He kept trying to be cordial to me, even when there was a huge chasm between us. I felt guilty for my hostility toward him, and guiltier still that I'd suspected him of being a murderer last night.

"I feel connected to him," Reed went on. "Like he's my family now. And, Willa . . . I feel the same thing when I look at you. Only not *exactly* like family." He gave me a shy smile that lit his eyes up like stars. "Because that would be weird."

"Uh, yeah," I said, managing to smile.

"So . . . what if we don't try to sneak around?" Reed asked. "What if we just ask Jonathan if it's all right?"

Making things more official? Telling Jonathan? I'd gotten pretty comfy with the idea that Reed and I would never be a thing. (Then again, I'd gotten comfy with the idea that I wasn't going to be kissing him anymore, and look what happened to *that* plan.)

I was more than flattered by his romantic interest in me — who wouldn't be? But I couldn't shake the feeling that, on some level, we didn't connect. That even though we obviously liked each other, he didn't know who I really was. He didn't get me.

Like Wyatt does, I thought. And then I stood there, stunned by my own thoughts.

"Reed . . . I'm not sure," I said. "I don't know."

My phone buzzed again.

"Sorry, I'm blowing up over here," I said, in a lame attempt to lighten the mood. I reached into my pocket and switched the phone to vibrate. "Who knew I was so popular?"

Reed nodded. "Anyway, I should get going. And you should get . . . digging?" He glanced at the shovel with one eyebrow raised.

I forced myself to look somber. "Dead bird on the patio. I figured it deserves a proper burial."

Confusion flashed across his face, which I could totally understand. Burying a dead bird in a shoe box was more of an activity for the under-ten set.

I wondered if it might cause him to rethink his interest in me. And whether that was a good or bad thing.

Reed climbed into the Porsche, and I watched him drive out of the garage. I gave him a quick wave before starting through the house into the backyard.

I left the shoe box inside while I went to dig a hole down by the citrus trees. I'd never seen Mom or Jonathan go anywhere near that part of the yard, so there was hardly any chance that the box would be discovered.

It was a warm day, and I was coated with sweat almost instantly. Plus, digging a hole a foot deep was a lot harder than I thought it would be. You don't just slide the shovel into the soft soil — the dirt here was packed like stone.

I got the first six inches dug and then, panting from the effort and heat, decided to come back and finish later, when the sun wasn't so high overhead. When had it turned to summer? I leaned the shovel against a lemon tree and went inside to shower and put on shorts and a T-shirt. I put the shoe box back in my closet, where Mom wouldn't happen across it.

Speaking of my mother, by the time I finished showering, it was time to text her back, but I couldn't find my phone. I walked down to the kitchen and found it sitting on the counter. I chugged a glass of water and absently checked my texts.

There were eight new ones.

I frowned and sat down at the kitchen table, scrolling through them.

There was one from Wyatt — *Going to the place to look at the stuff wink wink* — that made me laugh. His next one was a little strange, though. *Have you heard from Marnie today by any chance?*

Then there was another one from Mom: *Jonathan accidentally packed your laptop. Do you have his with you at Marnie's?*

And then one from an unknown number with a 213 area code: *This is Kelly Delaine, Marnie's mom. Have you seen her? We are so worried.*

Wyatt: *Marnie hasn't been home since yesterday morning.*

I was glad I was sitting down, because my breath was shallow and quick. I dreaded continuing down the list.

From the 213 number again, Marnie's mom: *Sorry to bother you. Please call when you can. Very concerned.*

Another text from Mom: *Reed will be getting in touch to pick up Jonathan's computer, okay? Text me when you wake up.*

From Wyatt: *Marnie is missing and the police think it may be the serial killer. I'm home now, call when you can.*

My phone rang in my hand, surprising me so much that I dropped it. It hit the table with a clatter. I managed to pick it up.

"Hello?" I said, my voice shaking.

"Willa?" It was an unfamiliar female voice.

"Yes?"

"This is Kelly Delaine calling." Her voice was breathless, verging on panicked. "I'm sorry to bother you — I didn't know if you'd seen my texts. I just wanted to know if you'd heard from Marnie at all. Or if you were aware of any plans she might have had for yesterday or today."

"Um . . . no," I said. "I'm really sorry. I haven't seen her since Thursday."

Her mother exhaled in this long, slow, hopeless way that sent a spike of fear straight through my heart. Then she thanked me and hung up, and I sat in the kitchen shaking — actually shivering like a scared person in a movie.

With trembling fingers, I called Wyatt.

"Hey," he said, his voice low and serious.

"I just talked to Mrs. Delaine."

"Marnie never came home," he said. "It turns out she's been sneaking out to auditions. Her parents had no idea."

"Auditions? Like, to be an actress?" I asked, shaking my head. "She never said a word about that to me."

Although she did talk once about how much she detested actors. And going by Marnie's logic, that basically meant she was dying to be one.

"Do the police really think it could be . . . ?" I couldn't even finish the thought. No matter how strange things got between me and Marnie, I couldn't bear the idea of something happening to her.

I swallowed.

"Yeah," Wyatt said quietly.

"She never even *hinted* at it," I said, then had a flash of memory. "Well, wait. The last time I talked to her, she said she might have big news, whatever that means. Maybe she thought she was going to get a role in something?"

"What kind of role?" he asked.

"Let me think," I said, closing my eyes.

What was it Marnie had said to me, during that conversation? Something odd. Uncharacteristic. Almost like she was quoting a movie or something.

I pictured her staring intently down at me from behind her cat-eye frames.

"He's no gentleman, see?" she'd said.

Still holding the phone, I ran into the den and perched in front of the computer. Quickly, I typed those words into the search bar. There were no results — until I deleted the word *he*.

"Detour," I said.

"What?" Wyatt asked.

"On Tuesday, Marnie quoted a line from a movie called *Detour*. Maybe she was memorizing the script for her audition." I scanned the screen.

"We should tell someone," Wyatt said. "We should — Dad?"

"What?" I asked.

"Hang on, Willa."

The sound was muffled, like he'd set the phone down, and then there were loud voices and lots of thudding footsteps.

"Wyatt?" I asked, gripping the phone tightly. "Are you okay?"

"Kind of," he said, sounding rushed. "But I can't talk right now."

"What? Why not?"

"Because I'm getting arrested."

Then he hung up.

CHAPTER 30

I stared at my phone, paralyzed. This was too much to process. Wyatt arrested, Marnie missing . . . ?

I needed to call Mom. I would have to confess that I'd lied about staying with the Delaines, but honestly I wasn't even afraid of that. I just wanted her home so I wouldn't be alone. It was irrational to think that the murderer would come after me now, but fear isn't the most rational force in the universe, is it?

The low-battery warning popped up on my phone, and I got up to take it to the charging cord that was always plugged in by the entrance to the kitchen.

The charger was gone — Mom or Jonathan must have packed it. But I noticed for the first time a little white envelope leaning against the back door. I slipped open the door and grabbed it. The logo in the corner said *Pool Pros Inc.*, and someone had scrawled, *Jonathan, I found your stepdaughter's necklace in the filter.*

My necklace . . . ?

With my heart in my throat, I dumped the contents of the envelope into my open palm.

It was a thin silver chain, with a solid silver charm.

A rose.

I stepped back.

This was the necklace from my visions.

I buried my face in my hands, my whole body tingling with dismay. My first instinct was to call Wyatt — but then I realized that he was probably on his way to jail.

Think, Willa, think.

This was the necklace I'd seen in my visions — but only in three of them. Brianna's, Faith's, and . . . and the one we couldn't identify, with the roses on the table.

The one where the victim had taken the necklace off and put it in her pocket, so it might fall out and be discovered.

And it *had* fallen out. And it had been discovered . . .

In our pool.

I got a flash of the ghostly body floating serenely overhead that first night, while I kicked and struggled at the bottom of the pool.

"Oh, God," I whispered. "It was Paige, it was Paige, it was Paige."

The phone buzzed in my hand. The battery bar was red, and I just had a chance to see a text from Mom before it died altogether:

Jonathan's going to meet Reed halfway. He feels bad making Reed do a 4 hour round trip.

I had another charger up in my bedroom. I turned to leave the kitchen, but stopped in my tracks when I saw the hallway.

The walls were covered in writing, words that were familiar to me by now . . .

THIS IS THE KIND OF DREAM YOU DON'T WAKE UP FROM, HENRY

Written over and over and over.

"I get it, Paige," I said. "I understand."

I peered toward the foyer and saw that the words were there, too. They seemed to cover every surface in the house.

I spun back to look around the kitchen, only to see that these walls weren't the exception — except, instead of the line about Henry, they were covered with the number 818 — *818 818 818 818 818 818 818* —

As I stared around the room, the screen of Jonathan's laptop flashed to the front page of Paige's now-forgotten blog. Then it began to scroll downward.

Finally, it stopped on the very post that Wyatt and I had read, the one about Diana Del Mar.

I studied the page.

"What?" I asked out loud. "What am I looking for?"

The screen scrolled down by itself, revealing the comments — well, the single comment. I looked at the commenter's name — G.A. Green — and then copied and pasted it into the search bar.

Nothing.

I sat back, thinking, and then clicked on the hard drive icon. I was crossing all sorts of boundaries, breaking all sorts of rules, but I didn't care. I was too close now.

I browsed the names of Jonathan's folders and even poked through some of the contents, but nothing jumped out at me. I was about to quit, but then I clicked on a folder labeled *Development Notes*, revealing a single file called *Special Projects Status Report*.

My heart flip-flopped.

The document consisted of a simple chart with six rows of information.

I scanned down the first column: *Scales, Fisher, Green, Bernard, Frowe,* and *Lovelock*.

An uneasy vibration began to thrum somewhere inside me. I knew those names from somewhere.

The second, third, and fourth columns contained simple two-letter pairs, four-digit numbers, and then a letter/number combination.

The top line, *Scales*, read *BL, 0517, B32*.

My focus shrank to a pinprick as I read down the list, as fast as I could make myself. I couldn't stop, because if I stopped I would lose my mind.

>*Fisher: FF, 0609, K29.*
>
>*Green: PP, 0818,* and a blank column.
>
>*Bernard: LJ, 1031, H14*
>
>*Frowe: TR, 0318,V9.*

Before I made it to the end, I clicked the mouse to close the document. I couldn't bear to look at it any longer.

"Oh, God," I whispered.

BL was Brianna Logan. *FF* — Faith Fernandes. *LJ* — Lorelei Juliano. *TR* — Tori Rosen. The four-digit numbers were the dates they went missing — the dates of their "auditions." And the letter-number combinations were the locations of each film in Jonathan's DVD inventory.

That was when it hit me — the memory of where I'd heard the names Scales, Fisher, Bernard, and Frowe before: in the articles I'd read about the murders. They were the names of the bogus talent agencies that the girls had written in their calendars.

So my stepfather, who owned all of the movies that had inspired the killings, also had weird, almost hidden files pertaining to each of the victims.

And Paige Pollan was one of them. 818, the number she'd been trying to tell me all along, wasn't part of a phone number — it was a date. *Her* date. August 18. Green must have been the name Jonathan used when he booked her "audition." He'd hand-picked her off the Internet after finding her blog post about Diana's movie.

I hung my head, a wave of nausea passing over me. Paige must have thought she was so lucky, to be discovered by a talent agent.

And all along, she'd been one of the Hollywood Killer's victims. Only for some reason, no one had made the connection. Probably because her death was ruled a suicide. There was even a note . . . but that was a scene in its own way, wasn't it? It was an homage to Diana's death.

More pieces fell into place. The script page, the vision . . . Paige was calling my attention to Diana Del Mar's movie. A movie that had never been made — not by a real director, anyway.

But the Hollywood Killer had given it a try. After all . . . where better to find a forgotten Diana Del Mar script than in

Diana's own house? And who would have better access than the man who lived in the house?

Don't jump to conclusions, I scolded myself. *All of this information could have been collected from the news. Maybe Jonathan is interested in the murders the way Wyatt is. And Wyatt isn't the murderer.*

For a moment, I froze and listened, sure I could hear footsteps coming down the hall toward me. Then I realized that it had been the sound of my own heart, thudding against my chest. Nausea came over me in a wave, and I leaned back in the chair, staring at the dark wood beams on the ceiling.

This isn't happening.

There had to be another explanation. There *had* to be.

But there was one way to know for sure.

My heart in my throat, I opened the file again — following a hunch I prayed was wrong.

But it wasn't wrong.

The row at the very bottom of the chart was labeled *Lovelock*.

And the columns that followed it read *MD, 0424, D20.*

Marnie Delaine. Yesterday's date. Then I got a sickening, poisonously bad feeling in the pit of my stomach.

I rose out of the chair and walked down the hall to the library. To the shelf full of movies that started with *D*.

There it was — an empty space, about twenty discs in. Right between *Deterrence* and *Devil in a Blue Dress.*

The perfect place for a movie called *Detour.*

I turned to walk out of the room, but before I made it three steps, everything went white.

I can't stop crying.

"Tori," he says, and I can tell he's running out of patience. "Tori, listen to me. You're supposed to be an actress. How can you expect to have any kind of career if you can't control your emotions?"

I try to tell him I don't care about acting anymore. I just want to go home.

But I know he won't let me. He gets frustrated and turns away, muttering angrily to himself.

I gaze at the line of razor-thin light high in the corner of the room. I don't remember how I got here — he drugged me, after we met at the abandoned building he'd claimed was his office. But now I know the room as well as my own bedroom. I've been here for days, with nothing to do but sit and look around . . . and cry.

I should stop crying. Not because it makes me a bad actress, but because it makes him mad. Still, he can't hate me that much, can he? He gave me a present — a necklace. It's gold, with a little half-moon charm hanging down from it —

242

CHAPTER 31

"W illa?"

The touch on my arm tore me out of the vision. I realized I was on the floor in the hallway, and Reed was standing over me.

"What happened?" he asked, frowning. "I kept calling your name, but you look so dazed."

"I fell," I said, wincing as I stood up. Judging by my aching tailbone, it must have been a pretty hard landing.

Reed insisted on helping me to the kitchen and getting me a glass of water. I thanked him, but I was too distracted and upset to make conversation.

All I could think was the granite-hard truth: *Jonathan is a murderer. My stepfather is the Hollywood Killer.*

I had this horrible feeling that I was being watched and forced myself to turn around. When I looked out the window, I almost fell over.

The pool was filled with brilliant red liquid, swirling so dark and thick that you couldn't see past the surface.

I balled up my fists, thinking, *It's not real. The pool isn't full of blood.*

It was Paige, sending another sign. Of course she'd be sending the warnings fast and furious, now that I knew her killer lived in the house with me.

"Willa? You sure you're okay?"

The voice snapped me out of my reverie, and I turned to see Reed standing a few feet away, watching me with concern.

"I didn't mean to come in the house without knocking. . . ." He spoke carefully, self-consciously. "But you didn't answer the door, and the alarm wasn't set. It seems like something's wrong."

"No," I said, though my voice sounded like it had been run through a cheese grater. "I'm . . . fine."

I glanced back at the pool water. Now it was perfect, pale aqua. Reed spoke again, but I didn't quite hear his words.

"What?" I said. "Sorry. I'm a little . . . out of it."

"I said I won't keep you, but now I'm wondering if I should stay for a little while. Do you think you might have a concussion?"

"I'm fine," I said blankly.

"I'm sure you are." He shot me a smile and took Jonathan's laptop off the kitchen counter. "Any big plans for your parent-free weekend?"

I glanced at him without smiling. I didn't feel like pretending to be normal or okay. "No," I said. "Not really."

"I'll just go, then. Seems like you want to be alone." Reed's cheerful expression faltered and he headed for the door.

I started up the stairs, but as I approached the second floor, I became aware of a static quality in the light behind me.

When I glanced down, Reed was looking up at me from the doorway, biting his lip. "This is going to sound odd, but were you by any chance . . . looking at some of Jonathan's files?"

"What?" I asked.

Balancing the laptop on his left forearm, Reed turned it toward me.

The *Development Notes* folder was still open.

"Oh, um, yeah," I said. "I didn't realize right away that it wasn't my computer. I clicked on the files without really looking."

He glanced at the screen. "Oh. Okay, then."

I went back down to the foyer. "But . . . I found something kind of strange."

"Strange?" His eyes cut sharply up to meet mine. "How do you mean?"

I had to tell him, even if he wouldn't believe me. "Um . . . Brianna Logan," I said. "She was the Hollywood Killer's first victim. And the agency name the police found in her calendar was Scales. Do you remember reading that in the news?"

"Possibly." He blinked. "I'm not sure. What are you trying to say?"

"Um," I said. "Nothing, really. Just that I found this chart . . ."

He leaned back against the doorframe, looking up at me with concern in his eyes. "I do know that Jonathan has been working with his agent to try to get the film rights for the story. I mean, so is everyone else in town. But that's what you found, I'm sure."

I nodded.

Reed didn't seem willing to let it go. "He wasn't even here when the last girl disappeared. He was in Connecticut."

Suddenly, he frowned.

"Although he came back for one day," he said. "At the beginning of the week. But I'm sure there's no connection."

Except he didn't sound sure. He sounded distinctly unsure. And he was acting really unhappy and flustered all of a sudden.

"Reed . . ." I said.

He shook his head. "Listen, it's nothing. I'll figure it out, okay? I mean, it has to be nothing."

I nodded.

Looking at me, Reed visibly relaxed, even cracked a smile. "What are we even *talking* about? This is crazy. Jonathan couldn't be a . . . I'd better get going. I'll talk to you next week, okay?"

He shut the door, and I walked to the bottom step and sank down, my head in my hands.

Who just accuses their stepfather of murder, without even asking him about it?

A crazy person, that's who.

I sat like that for probably fifteen minutes, utterly at a loss as to what I should do or even think. Forget the computer file. Forget the ghost. Did I really believe my mother had fallen in love with a serial killer? Some vague sense of dissatisfaction, of an unanswered question, lingered at the back of my mind.

Finally, I stood up and padded slowly to my bedroom. I was tempted to crawl back under my covers right then and there, even though it was the middle of the day. I was worn out from the morning — the week — the month — my life. I was so tired.

Then I heard a sound from downstairs.

CHAPTER 32

I crept to the top of the stairs and listened with every bit of attention I could scrape together in my panicking mind.

A sound — a footstep? Or my heart again?

I closed my eyes and listened so hard it hurt.

No, I wasn't imagining it. A footstep. Downstairs.

There was someone in the house.

"Reed?" I called. Maybe he'd forgotten something and come back inside.

But there was no answer.

My cell phone was downstairs, and the battery was dead anyway. I tried to recall what time Mom had texted about Jonathan driving back from Palm Springs.

Something moved in my field of view, practically giving me a heart attack. Looking down, I saw a thin stream of water moving forward like a snake, trailing ahead toward the end of the hall, almost as if the floor slanted downhill – which, of course, it didn't.

I glanced back down the stairs, and as I did, the thought came automatically: *Don't be crazy, Willa.*

But you know what? This wasn't crazy. This was me trusting my instincts.

The water reached the end of the hall and seeped under the door to Jonathan's office. I went on tiptoe, staying as close to the wall as I could, praying I wouldn't step on any creaky floorboards.

Then, shattering the quiet, there came a cough from downstairs.

And a dragging sound, like someone was moving furniture around.

I kept going. With every agonizing step, I was sure I was going to give myself away. Somehow I made it to Jonathan's office and opened the door.

When I saw the room, I gasped.

The whole room was covered in the same two words, repeated over and over:

GET OUT GET OUT GET OUT GET OUT GET OUT

The rose petals led to an open window. I deviated from the path just long enough to pick up the phone and hear the thick silence of a dead phone connection.

Someone had cut the line.

I no longer had the luxury of agonizing over whether I was overreacting.

I hurried to the window. The drop was at least sixteen feet, but there was a trellis bolted to the exterior wall below the window — where the jasmine bloomed so fragrantly at night. I didn't have time to worry about whether it could support my weight. I swung my leg over and struggled to grip the tiny holes

with my toes. By the time I got to the ground, my bare feet were full of splinters and cramped from holding on so tightly — but at least I was out.

I crept around the side of the house, pausing to peer into the front yard. Unfortunately, there was no way to get through the front gate without coming into easy view through the huge den window. If Jonathan was still in the house, I could run for it — but if he saw me, and chased me, he would almost certainly overtake me.

I saw the front door start to open and darted back to the rear of the house, where he wasn't bothering to keep watch.

He didn't have to. Because he knew, like I did, that the only way into and out of the property was through the front gate. The fences at the sides of the house were eight feet tall, with metal spikes on top and nothing to use as a foothold. Behind the citrus trees in the back, the hillside dropped off steeply into the ravine, littered with cactuses that had spines the size of sewing needles. Even if I made it down there, I wouldn't make it more than five or ten feet — and then I'd be a sitting duck.

Why hadn't I grabbed a pair of shoes?

He would have heard you. He would have known what you were planning to do.

I had to find someplace to hide — someplace where he wouldn't look right away. The guest cottage sat silently, facing the pool, an impartial observer.

I looked down, and in front of me, a single rose petal fluttered to the tile. A few feet away, another one appeared. I followed the sparse path around the side of the guest cottage, where there were two windows hidden from view of the main house. If I broke one, would Jonathan hear the impact of a rock on the glass?

As I looked at the window, it swung open.

I overturned an old bucket that someone had stashed back there and used it to reach the window and crawl inside. I pulled the bucket in after me, then closed the window and locked it.

I looked around. The main room was small, with a kitchenette off to one side. The walls were cheap wood paneling, and the carpet beneath my feet was chocolate brown and mashed flat, sprinkled with dust and small white flecks fallen from the decaying popcorn ceiling. It felt strangely oily against my bare skin.

At some point in its history, this had been a cute, functional little guesthouse, but now it was a creepy, smelly hole of a place, packed with old furniture — a ragged, damp-looking sofa, a huge wood cabinet with a little rounded glass TV screen in it, a coffee table with crooked spindly wooden legs . . . Every imaginable surface was covered in junk, mostly cardboard boxes and bulging plastic trash bags.

The windows were all covered in brown paper, each one rimmed by a brilliant square of sunlight seeping in from behind the paper's curled-up edges.

To my left was a door that led into a bathroom. Next to it was a set of shutter-like accordion doors — a closet?

As I stared at them, they opened with a creak.

Honestly, I don't even know why I was surprised. Did I say a creepy, smelly hole of a place? Obviously, I meant a creepy, smelly, *haunted* hole of a place.

I walked over to the closet. Bonus — there were shoes in there, a lot of them. Fancy, high-heeled, vintage-y looking shoes, old enough to have belonged to Diana Del Mar — not the kind of thing you'd normally wear to hike through a ravine, but certainly better than nothing.

But when I tried to slide my foot inside one, I realized that Jonathan was right — movie stars did have tiny feet. I held one up and looked at the number on the sole. Size five and a half. I couldn't even force the toes of my size-eight foot inside. It was a mathematical and physical impossibility.

Outside, a shadow passed in front of the papered-over door.

I knew he couldn't see me, but the sight still turned my blood to ice.

I was standing motionless when a sound in the closet caught my attention. I looked over just as all of the clothes slipped off their hangers to the floor. Then the two dozen or so hangers began to swing, all at different speeds, making a horrible scraping sound on the ancient wood bar.

"Quiet!" I hissed, darting over to the closet. I was about to pull them all down — I might be trapped in here, but at least I could keep Paige from telegraphing my exact location to a murderer.

My plan was interrupted when I saw the hinge.

There was a hidden door disguised in the wood paneling of the closet wall.

When I gave it a push, it opened easily, revealing a small, dark space. I reached my hand inside and found a light switch, flipping it on.

A flight of stairs led down into absolute darkness.

A biting scent floated up and invaded my nose. I turned away, my nostrils stinging, and remembered what Leyta Fitzgeorge had asked me — what seemed like a weird question at the time — whether I ever smelled the strong smell of vinegar.

I did now.

Gently closing the door behind me, I crept down the steps, which opened into a room roughly the same size as the room upstairs.

On the far wall was a small pull-down movie screen, like the kind you use in classrooms with an overhead projector. A small olive-green leather sofa faced the screen, and a rolling cart directly behind the sofa held an old-fashioned film projector.

This must have been Diana Del Mar's workroom. I remembered Paige's blog entry about her — how she had wanted to make movies. In this room, Diana didn't have to be a smiling starlet or box office poison. She got to be who she really wanted to be — a filmmaker.

Close to me there was a large table that looked like some ancient version of a computer, with a screen in the back, raised up like a monitor. On the flat part of the table was an array of buttons and control dials. There were also six big, flat turntable pieces. Two of the turntables held a film reel each, and the film wound through the spools on the machine from one to the other, connecting them.

It must have been an editing machine — the kind they used before everything was edited on computers.

Next to the table was a small rolling cart, with a metal rack that stood about five feet high. Curling pieces of film hung from the rack's thin metal hooks like snakeskins.

I walked toward the desk on the side wall. It was sturdy, constructed of heavy steel. On it were a typewriter, a telephone, and a few piles of paper. There was a tray marked IN and one marked FILE and another one marked READ. I reached toward the typewriter and tapped out a series of letters on the dusty keys: *q w e r t y*

The *e* on the page was slightly lower than the rest of the letters, the *t* slightly raised.

This exact typewriter had been used by Diana Del Mar, more than seventy years ago — to write the script Paige had presented to me in the bathtub.

I picked up the phone to check for a signal, but the line was dead — it probably had been for decades.

In the corner of the room, there was a simple door, painted the same drab color as the walls. I tried the handle, but it was locked.

As I turned back to the stairs, the lights cut out.

I stood in perfect, horrific darkness for about three seconds, and then with a groan, the editing machine came to life behind me. The film reels began to spin, and a movie scene appeared on the screen.

It was a man and woman sitting at a dinner table set lavishly with flickering candles and a huge vase of roses. The woman was played by Diana Del Mar herself — there was no mistaking her radiant, heart-shaped face and her shining eyes. The man was played by an actor I didn't recognize, a handsome man with dark hair.

There was no sound, but you could feel the tension between them. The camera slowly moved in on Diana as she took a sip of her wine. Then it cut to the man, watching her carefully. Diana was speaking. They conversed for a minute, and then the man spoke a single angry line.

The shot cut to Diana. She stared into her wine glass and said something quietly. And then her mouth moved in the shape of the words I'd know anywhere —

This is the kind of dream you don't wake up from, Henry.

I'd known it was coming, but it still stopped me cold.

This was a scene from Diana's movie. The one Paige had written about in her blog. I searched my memory for the film's title. *The Final Honeymoon.*

On a shelf next to the table was a stack of empty film cans — the ones that had held the reels that were loaded on the editing table. I picked one up and looked at the label on its top.

It read: THE DINNER PARTY (WORKING TITLE ONLY)

I'd heard that name before . . . but where?

Then it hit me. From Reed. It was one of the movies he'd listed as his favorites. But it wasn't even the real name of the movie. It was only a working title, one that even Paige hadn't known.

Which meant . . . Reed had been down here. He'd seen this movie. He'd heard that line.

Suddenly, there was a jump in the action on the film. Diana's character was standing up from the table, holding her wine glass. The camera was close on her dazed eyes. The glass slipped from her hand. She stumbled, trying to walk away from her chair, and made it almost all the way out of the dining room before collapsing to the ground. The man watched her with a small smile.

It was a murder scene. She was dying. Henry had poisoned her.

It was the scene I had seen references to in my vision. The one Paige had been meant to perform. It was supposed to be Paige's murder, only something had changed — this wasn't how Paige had died.

The film stopped with a jerk and rewound itself, then started playing, so I had to watch Diana recite that line again: *This is the kind of dream you don't wake up from, Henry.*

It made me think of Marnie's line, that she'd used so proudly. *He's no gentleman, see?*

And just thinking that gave me an uncomfortable twinge. Like the one I'd had on the stairs earlier. That feeling of overlooking something important. Of a piece not fitting in the puzzle.

Weirdly, I thought of Reed. And it occurred to me . . . Why hadn't he been surprised to see me? I mean, yes, he was surprised to find me carrying an alleged dead bird in a shoe box. But he shouldn't have expected me to be at home. As far as anyone but Marnie, Wyatt, and I knew, I was at Marnie's for the weekend.

Then my heart seemed to slow to a stop, as I remembered his words in the garage that morning.

I guess I'm no gentleman.

It was too similar to Marnie's words: *He's no gentleman, see?*

Had Reed been watching *Detour*?

Maybe Reed knew I wasn't at Marnie's because he knew Marnie wasn't there, either.

I glanced back at the frame frozen on the editing machine, Diana Del Mar's face in a stricken expression of regret and sorrow.

Reed called this one of his favorite movies.

What if those weren't Jonathan's files I'd found on the computer?

What if they were Reed's?

And with that thought, the pieces came smashing together with a deafening, horrifying impact.

Reed was an insane psychotic killer. . . .

He'd killed all those girls.

And now he was after me.

CHAPTER 33

I paced Diana's office. Reed's priorities would be to keep me from getting to a phone or computer and to keep me from escaping out the front gate. Eventually, he'd realize I had to be in the guest cottage and find a way to force me out.

Keeping me from calling for help was easy enough. He had my cell phone. The landline was useless. And now he had the only computer in the house, too.

I felt faint and flushed. Now that I knew his secret, there was no way he would let me live. Which meant I had to either find a way out . . . or be his next victim. I could scream and hope someone heard, but by the time anyone came to help, Reed would have found me.

There was no way out. I was trapped.

I made my way back upstairs to the main floor of the guest cottage, looking for something to use as a weapon. My best chance for escape would be to knock Reed unconscious and then run for my life. A baseball bat could work, or even a broken chair leg.

In the end, the best I could find was the metal base of an old lamp. I dropped the bucket out the window and began to climb out. As I left, I looked at the closet in the corner of the room.

And that's when I remembered . . .

My father's old laptop was in my bedroom closet.

Reed didn't even know it existed.

I scanned the yard for a full sixty seconds before scrambling to the trellis and climbing back up. I had to leave my lamp behind, but there would be other blunt objects inside the main house.

Once I had silently hauled myself through the window, I dropped into an army crawl and began dragging myself slowly toward my room. Passing by the stairwell, I saw Reed sitting on the step just outside the open front door. He looked composed and relaxed — but there was tension in his posture, and I knew he was keeping close watch on the yard.

I held my breath and kept going. Finally I made it to my bedroom door, which was closed. As quickly as I could, I eased up off my elbows and turned the knob, grasping it with both hands to keep the catch from snapping back after I turned it.

And then I was in the room, closing the door behind me. It slid shut with only the slightest whisper of sound. I reached up and turned the lock — but it wasn't the kind of lock that would keep someone out. Not if they really wanted to get in.

I ran to the closet and grabbed the old laptop — and a pair of running shoes. I locked myself in the bathroom, to buy some extra time in case Reed figured out where I was. I carried the computer in, set it on the counter, and plugged it in.

The screen slowly lit up.

Then, to my horror, it made that *DA-DAAAAAHHH!* boot-up sound. I nearly peed my pants in surprise.

It took an eternity for the home screen to load, but there was still no sign of Reed.

I was safe . . . for the moment.

I loaded up the web browser. I'd deleted all of my social network accounts months ago, so unfortunately, I couldn't log into Facebook and post *HELP HE'S TRYING TO KILL ME!* to a concerned group of people who would be able to find me right away.

I searched for *contact police online*, but the results were useless — a bunch of people complaining about not being able to contact the police online. There were a few police departments' CONTACT US! forms, which I figured would get me rescued in about a week and a half, if Reed would be kind enough to postpone his serial killing for a while.

I decided to send an email blast to all my contacts, something like *SEND THE POLICE TO MY HOUSE ASAP!* I opened a new blank message, selected every name in my address book, and in the subject I typed, *SEND POLICE IMMEDIATELY 2121 SUNBIRD LANE HOLLYWOOD.*

I was about to hit SEND, when I decided to add to the body of the email: *NOT A JOKE ALONE WITH REED THORNTON HOLLYWOOD KILLER PLEASE HELP — WILLA.*

I moved the mouse to the SEND button . . .

And clicked it.

I sat back, watching the little wheel spin — not surprising, considering all the addresses it had to send to —

And then the lights went off.

Reed had cut the power.

Oh, no.

The laptop ran on a battery, so the screen stayed lit. But the spinning wheel stopped. An error message popped up onscreen: *Error sending message. No wireless connection detected.*

A few seconds later, I heard the approaching clunks of distant footsteps coming up the stairs. After a slight pause and the rattling of the stupid, useless lock on the door, he entered my bedroom.

Oh, no, no, no.

"Hey, Willa." Reed's voice had a hollow cheerfulness to it. "It's me. Are you all right?"

"Um," I said. "I'm not feeling very well. I'd kind of like to be alone."

"Is it from your fall?" he asked. "Why don't you come on out and I can drive you to an urgent care place? You should probably get looked at."

"No, it's nothing like that." I raked a hand through my hair. "It's kind of embarrassing. Just a stomach thing. I actually called my mom before. She should be here any second. You can go."

He paused, and for a second I thought I might have fooled him.

There was a soft impact on the door, and I cowered away before realizing that he was leaning against it. "Just out of curiosity," he said, "what exactly are you typing in there?"

My whole body began to shake. "I already emailed my mom and Jonathan! They'll be calling the police any second!"

"You're bluffing," Reed said in a light, pleasant tone. "I know you're upset, and I think we should talk. Why don't you come on out?"

"If you run now, you can get away," I said. "Before the police get here!"

He shook the door, a sound that made me nearly pass out from fear.

"It's important that you know that I've been through this before," he said, all the diplomacy gone from his voice. "And I always win."

I felt a tightening at the base of my throat.

"I can take the door down if I have to," he said. "But that's going to make me unhappy. And if I'm unhappy . . . I can promise *you're* going to be even unhappier."

A sob came from someplace deep down in my body, near my heart. My teeth gritted and my eyes squeezed themselves shut and I forced it back down.

I couldn't lose control.

"Now," Reed said, and his voice was perfectly even and pleasant. "Which one of us is going to open the door?"

"What are you going to do to me?" I asked.

"That's no concern of yours," he said. "Open the door, Willa."

"You killed those girls . . . all of them." As I spoke, using my own words for cover, I knelt and opened the cabinet under the sink. I reached around in the dark until my hand hit a piece of sharp metal — the towel bar that Paige had so kindly pulled out of the wall. "I don't understand why you're doing this, Reed. You'll get caught. There's no way they won't connect you to the other murders if you kill me."

"If I decide I want your perspective, I'll ask for it," he said. "Open the door."

My hand trembled so badly that it fell away from the lock twice before I could twist it. I had time to think, *Is this the worst mistake of my life?*

As Reed opened the door, I raised the towel bar and swung it at him, and made contact with the side of his head — hard.

He howled and doubled over.

I rushed past him, scrambling down the stairs so fast I thought I might miss a step and go tumbling head over heels.

"WILLA!" Reed yelled, his voice thick with rage.

I didn't stop to look back. I ran straight for the front door and reached up to turn the dead bolt.

Only I couldn't. This was an old-fashioned lock, where you need a key to get through it from either side. You could get locked in just as easily as you could get locked out. I'd never thought about it before, because we always left the key in it.

But now it was gone.

I turned and ran for the double doors to the backyard. I had shoes on now — I could climb over the fence and escape through the ravine.

Reed thundered through the hall as I sprinted across the tile toward the gate down into the citrus orchard.

While I ran, I tried letting out a blood-curdling scream — but screaming used up energy I needed to outrun someone who was stronger and faster than me.

The shaky rock steps leading down to the first terrace wobbled beneath my feet, and I nearly lost my balance. The next terrace was a six-foot drop, so I ran along the edge, toward the stairs on the far side.

I should have jumped.

Reed did.

By the time I got to the stairs, he was already down at my level, only a few yards away. His face and hair were bloody, his eyes lit up with fury.

There wasn't time to run.

I had to stay and fight.

I raised the towel bar and went to hit him with it again, but he caught my wrist in midair and wrenched my arm behind my back, yanking the towel bar away and tossing it down the hill.

I tried to scream, but he pulled me back against his chest and clapped his hand over my mouth. A bitter, awful scent flooded my nostrils and burned my throat, and I realized he was holding a wet rag over the lower half of my face. I tried to fight him off, but already my arms and legs were quickly growing heavy. I ended up clawing weakly at his wrist with my free hand, drooping back toward him like a rag doll.

He released my arm and then gently lowered me to the ground, the cloth still resting on my face.

The worst part was that he didn't even have to hold on to me — all I could do was lie there on the ground, inhaling pungent fumes. It was my last chance to fight, but I didn't even have the strength to try.

Behind the rag, I opened my mouth to try to shout, but the sound that escaped was like the mewl of a scared kitten.

Reed leaned over me, a smile on his blood-spattered lips. "You've been a bad girl, Willa," he whispered. "A very bad girl."

Then I closed my eyes.

CHAPTER 34

*D*rip . . . *drip* . . . *drip* . . .

A headache drilled into my skull. My back felt tight, my stomach queasy, and my lungs like someone had gone over them with sandpaper.

I couldn't move.

I opened my eyes.

I was in the den, propped up in a chair that had been wrapped in a black plastic trash bag. The floor below me was covered with more trash bags. My hands were pulled behind me and taped together, and my legs were taped together at the ankle, and then taped to the crosswise supports of the chair.

My head felt hot, and my scalp itched. Was I . . . was I wearing a wig?

When I tried to call out, my voice was muffled. A piece of tape held my mouth closed. If I tried to move my lips, it pulled at my skin painfully.

Someone was whistling.

Reed came into the room. It took me a second to understand

what I was seeing — he wore a tuxedo, and his face was clean, with no sign of any injury or blood.

"I know what you're thinking." He leaned against the side of the bookshelves. *"I thought I clocked that guy in the head with a piece of rusted metal.* But making movies is all about the illusion, Willa. A little makeup goes a long way. Want to see?"

No, I was pretty sure I didn't want to see. But he disappeared and came back a moment later with a hand mirror.

"For instance, look at yourself," he said, coming closer. "You're lovelier than ever. If I hadn't left my phone at home — they can track your movements by your phone, you know — I'd take a picture."

I flinched and closed my eyes, but the foreign sensation of the wig on my head made me desperate to know what he'd done to me.

When I saw my reflection, I gasped.

The girl in the mirror had flawless wavy golden hair, a perfectly smooth ivory complexion, and sleepy eyes with thick lashes that looked about a half-inch long. I couldn't tell you what her lips looked like, though, because there was a piece of blue masking tape over her mouth.

"To be truthful, when I first met you . . ." He leaned down closer to me, his voice softening. "I didn't picture you like this. I thought you were pretty, but not leading-lady pretty. No offense."

His words made me feel like throwing up. Even with my eyes shut, I could still hear his breathing — a relaxed *in-out-in-out,* only a foot away.

"But then you changed. You got stronger. And then, after that picture of you surfaced on the Internet, I saw you as more than just a little girl. See, it's about vision. Vision and keeping an open mind. Trusting your instincts. Attention to detail."

I sensed him moving behind me, but I couldn't tell where he was. So when I felt him take hold of my wrists, I whimpered into the tape.

"I'd like to cut you free, but I can't trust you anymore, Willa. You really messed things up." He sighed. "I can't believe I chose yet another girl who decided to mess things up. The last time I tried this scene it went so badly I had to pull the plug."

I realized he was talking about Paige.

"But don't you worry — that's not going to happen. You're nothing like . . . that girl. We'll get through this, and it'll be wonderful — my best effort yet." Knowing he was behind me sent a wave of terrified shivers down my entire back.

I let my head fall until my chin touched my chest.

"No!" he snapped. "No crying! You'll wreck your eye makeup."

Being ordered not to cry by the serial killer who's about to kill you isn't all that effective. I felt the lump rise in my throat in spite of his warning.

Reed grabbed my jaw and tilted my head back so I had no choice but to look up into his eyes. *I said no crying.*

I blinked furiously, trying to suppress my tears.

"Good," he said. "Now you hang tight for a few minutes. I'm almost finished setting the scene. Then we'll get you into your wardrobe and start rehearsals."

Left alone, I focused on trying to free my hands or legs. But Reed returned before I'd made any actual progress.

"Time to go to set," he said. "First you need to get into costume."

He held up a dress — the same cherry-red dress I had worn to the premiere.

"Like it?" he asked. "I borrowed it from a mutual friend."

From Marnie . . . where is he keeping Marnie? My heart sank. Had he already killed her?

"I'm going to cut your arms loose first, then your legs, and you're going to change. Don't worry, I won't look. But don't bother trying anything, understand?"

I nodded. Where would I go, with my ankles still tied together?

When I'd finished, he clucked approvingly and grabbed my wrists, quickly wrapping a zip tie around them. "It's not the most accurate dress for the film," he said, "but I rather like it on you. Sit, please."

I sat back down in the chair.

He went around behind me, tilted the chair back, and then dragged it, the plastic wrap, and me toward the dining room, talking as he went. "It's important to be flexible, Willa. To be willing to interpret things. What's important is the big picture, not the petty details."

I stared at the table.

It was set for a romantic dinner. A vase of roses was placed off to one side, and all the chairs had been removed except the ones on the opposite ends. There were white porcelain plates and ivory cloth napkins, gold flatware and crystal goblets filled with wine.

Straight out of *The Dinner Party.*

This was my scene.

My death scene.

CHAPTER 35

Reed set my chair at one end of the table. On the plate in front of me were four pages from a screenplay, laid out side by side.

"You'll be playing Charice." He tapped her name. "A beautiful but wicked young woman who enticed Henry into marriage and then proceeded to make him the most miserable man on the planet."

I couldn't focus at all. The words on the pages might as well have been written in a foreign language.

Reed crouched down next to me. "Willa. I'm going to take the tape off. But you have to promise me you won't scream."

I was desperate to be able to breathe through my mouth again . . . but I didn't honestly know if that was a promise I could keep. It was like my whole life boiled down to a two-item to-do list: *Try to get away* and *scream*.

But I nodded.

"It wouldn't do any good, anyway," he said. "No one is going to save you. No one is going to find you — not until Jonathan and Joanna get home Monday. As soon as we finish up here, I'll text Jonathan to tell him I'm on my way, drive the computer out to Palm Springs, and then come back to LA." He raised his eyebrows playfully. "Gonna be a busy weekend for me. Would you believe I double-booked myself?"

I breathed in sharply. So Marnie was still alive.

And Reed was still planning to drive all the way to Palm Springs. He'd left his phone at home, so he didn't know that Jonathan was actually planning to meet him halfway — my stepfather had probably texted him to suggest it. And if Jonathan didn't get a text back from Reed, then there was a chance he would keep driving and make it all the way back to the house.

And Reed had no idea.

I felt a dim surge of hope.

"Listen," he went on. "I'm an artist. What I'm going for is the integrity of the scene. So I don't want to have to force you to cooperate . . . but I will, if you make me. Do you understand? If I hurt you, it will be *your* fault. You'll only have yourself to blame."

He reached up and gently peeled the tape off of my face. The feeling of being able to stretch my jaw and breathe through my mouth was an overwhelming relief. And somehow I managed to contain my screams. It wouldn't do any good to make him angry now.

"Let me touch up your makeup," he said, retrieving a tackle box from the sideboard. With a practiced hand, he dabbed a wedge-shaped sponge in pancake foundation and spread it lightly over my chin and lips. Then he fluffed powder over my whole face. After that, he picked up a lip pencil. "Open your mouth a little."

I felt nauseated. I couldn't believe we had kissed. That I had enjoyed his kisses. Now his gentle touch — as if he had the right to touch me at all — made me want to scrub my skin off.

"Good girl." He wiped at the lip liner with the side of his thumb. "Now pout."

I closed my eyes and puckered up. I could feel him apply the lipstick with short, dragging strokes.

"Smudge your lips together," he said.

I obeyed.

"All right, now we're going to run lines. I'll be playing Henry." He set the makeup kit back on the sideboard.

The sideboard.

There are knives in the sideboard.

Obviously, I couldn't do a thing until he cut my hands free. And my legs. But he'd have to, eventually. When Charice died, she was walking away from the table. I couldn't do that if I was bound to the chair.

If I could get a knife . . .

I would have only one chance. If I failed, he'd probably be so angry that he'd kill me before we finished the scene . . . like Paige? Is that what he'd done to Paige?

I forced myself to stop stealing glances at the sideboard.

Reed went around to the other side of the table and sat down, all business. "The thing to remember about this scene is that even though she married him for his money, she's grown to love him, in her own way. But Henry's feelings for her have vanished. At this point, he's stringing her along — but Charice doesn't know that. She thinks he still loves her. So there's this pathetic element of hope in her performance."

I remembered Diana Del Mar's shining, begging eyes from the footage I'd seen.

"All right." He cleared his throat, then picked up his wine glass and leaned toward me. "My dear, this is a night to celebrate our past."

In less than an instant, he'd morphed from a crazed, twitchy serial killer to a calm, suave guy. I stared in confusion.

He raised an eyebrow.

Remembering myself, I looked down at the script. Then I looked back up. "I'm supposed to be pouring wine."

"That's blocking," he said impatiently. "That will come after we're comfortable with the dialogue. You need to *feel* the scene before you try to act it."

"Oh," I said. "Sorry."

"My dear, this is a night to celebrate our past."

I forced myself to focus on the words. "And — and our future, I hope."

He chuckled softly and sat back. "I remember the night we met. In New York. You were leaving that nightclub. . . ."

"Chico's," I read.

"You dropped your handbag, and by the time I picked it up, you were already in a taxi. My father told me to forget it — that there couldn't be anything of value inside such a cheap, ugly little thing."

The conviction with which he said the lines made me feel

like he was somehow talking about me — that *I* was the cheap, ugly little thing.

"I remember." My voice trembled and I fumbled the words as I read. "But my grandmother's sapphire bracelet was in that bag."

"So I told the old man to go to Halifax, found your address, and hopped in a cab to follow you home."

"It's a good thing you did, too," I read. "Marge didn't have the taxi fare."

"Madge."

That line wasn't in the script. I looked up at him. "What?"

"Not 'Marge' — Madge. Attention to detail, Willa."

"Right, right, sorry," I said. "Um . . . Marge didn't have the taxi fare."

"*Madge*, Willa."

I was trembling all over.

"Don't cry," he said. "Don't you dare cry. It's a five-letter word. Say it — *Madge*."

"Madge," I whispered. "Madge didn't have the taxi fare."

"Madge was never good for anything." He picked up his wine glass and swirled it. "She was a hanger-on, a second-rate back-row chorus girl."

"We used to have fun, though. She was nice, in her own way."

"If I hadn't shown up, you two would have spent the night in debtors' prison."

"I suppose so."

"When I handed you your bag . . . the look in your eyes . . . I'd never seen anything like it. I'd never seen someone who looked so alive, from the inside out."

The script said, *Charice smiles into her wine glass, pleased.*

I looked down at the table. No way was I going to be able to force a smile.

Reed leaned forward, getting into the dialogue. "On our honeymoon, in Namur . . . those were the happiest days of my life. I felt that I'd plucked a jewel from the night sky, and there you were — all mine."

"I remember Namur," I read. "The little boy who sold apples next to the hotel, and that old woman who kept offering to tell our fortunes."

"Yes," he said.

"I wonder what she would have seen. I wish I had known."

"You do?" He set his wine glass down. "I don't. I'm glad I didn't know. At least I had some happiness before I figured out who you really were — why you'd married me."

"Oh, no, Henry —"

His voice sank to a growl. "Days of happiness — followed by years of misery. The peculiar misery of a man whose wife sees him as a sucker. Someone to steal from, lie to. A plain old mark to be cheated and cheated until he has nothing left to surrender."

"But that's not true. I cared about you from the beginning. I loved you."

Reed closed his eyes. A small, rueful smile came over his lips. "You may love me now, Charice, but I'm afraid you never did back then. If you had . . . why, life would have been so beautiful. Such a dream."

"It can be one now," I said. "The way I feel about you now . . ."

He looked up at me, and I met his eyes. I didn't need the script. I knew this line by heart.

"This is the kind of dream you don't wake up from, Henry."

There was a long, heavy pause.

"Maybe for you it is, my darling. Maybe for you."

The script said, *Charice hears everything that's missing from his voice — mercy, hope, and most of all, love. She fights to keep tears from her eyes.*

The next line was Reed's. "I suppose we oughtn't to continue this charade any longer. I've lost my appetite anyway."

"Please stay, Henry. Please let's give it another try. I'm so different now. We're both so different."

"No, my dear. It's no good trying to keep a thing alive once it's gone. One last toast? Raise your glass to what we might have been. In another world, another life."

Reed raised his glass.

"It says I raise mine," I said. "But I can't."

"No, of course not," he said, snapping out of character. "We'll get to that after we run the lines a few more times. All in all, I'd say you did okay. I think we can work together and get a performance to be proud of."

Charice raising her wine glass was the last thing on the page — on any of the pages I had.

The footage flickered in my memory — Diana standing and turning away from the table, her wine glass slipping from her hand, her slow descent to the floor as she realized what was happening. She had tried to grab hold of a little table. There was no little table in this room. So what if I tried to grab hold of the sideboard instead? What if I could reach the knife?

But what if we were only going to run that part of the scene once — and what if the poison Reed used to kill his victims was already in my body at that point?

Something inside me turned to stone.

If I had to die, at least I could try to take Reed out with me.

"So what did Paige do wrong?" I asked.

Reed snapped to attention. "What do you know about Paige?"

"Nothing."

"Paige Pollan could have been a great actress." He practically spat the words out. "But she couldn't take direction."

"So what did you do to her?" I swallowed hard. "She never finished the scene. You . . . you drowned her, didn't you?"

Reed's stare was perfectly emotionless. "She deserved it."

"You did it *here*?" A horrible thought occurred to me. "Did you bring them all here?"

Was Marnie somewhere on the property at that very moment? I thought of the locked door in the corner of the screening room.

He frowned slightly, in a way that answered my question. "Whenever Jonathan went out of town, I would come here and explore. It's a great house, you know. There's an unfinished cellar off the chauffeur's quarters that leads all the way to the guest house. That's how I found Diana's studio. How I found her movie." He sat back, and his voice turned cold. "Paige refused to learn her lines. She kept messing up. I could tell she was doing it on purpose, trying to buy herself some time. *You* wouldn't do that, would you, Willa?"

I shook my head.

"Finally I'd had enough. It was my third time — I knew how things were supposed to go. She was being difficult just for the sake of making me angry. So I gave her something, took her out to the pool, and then I . . . took care of her."

"You drowned her . . . in Jonathan's pool. And then moved her back to her apartment and made it look like a suicide."

Reed smiled a ghastly, demonic grin. "Yes. But I took my time with it. I made sure she knew that she'd made me angry."

A coating of cold fire spread over my skin.

"You made me angry, too, Willa. So I'd advise you to be as well behaved as you can for the rest of our time together. Because I can say with complete certainty that you'd prefer the easy way over the hard way."

Part of me couldn't even catch my breath. The other part of me was finally soaking in the idea that this was really happening.

I was caught by a psychotic serial killer.

If I couldn't find a way out of this, I probably had two hours left to live.

And now he was telling me in fairly clear terms that I had two choices: one, cooperate, and make my death relatively easy. Two, fight back . . . and risk dying horribly.

It was as though Reed could tell what I was thinking.

"Want to know how I did it?" he asked, leaning forward. "I waited until the pills made her sleepy. Then I took her out and pushed her into the pool. She managed to get herself to the edge. And then I peeled her hands off the side and pushed her back out into the water. She was so tired she couldn't swim anymore, so she tried to float . . . and I took the pool skimmer and pushed her down. But only for a few seconds. Then I let her float back up and try to catch her breath. Then I pushed her down again."

As he spoke, my lungs burned and my stomach went sour. I felt as though I was there with Paige, being pushed underwater. I remembered the feeling, from my first night here, of not being able to surface. My whole chest ached – and my heart ached, now that I had a sense of the fear and pain she'd experienced in her last moments.

No wonder she was an angry ghost.

But where was Paige now — when I needed her? Why wasn't she here, helping me? She'd been so eager for me to uncover her killer's identity . . . but what if that was all she'd wanted?

I'd thought having a ghost in the house was scary. But that didn't compare with the paralyzing fear of her having abandoned me.

Reed stood up and walked toward me. In my panic, I struggled in my chair and bumped the table, nearly knocking over the wine glass at my place setting.

Reed caught it before it could fall. He turned my chair to face him and crouched down to whisper softly, only inches from my ear.

"It took ages, Willa," he breathed. "And she fought and fought . . . she tried so hard. Even though she knew the entire time that she would never win."

Tears filled my eyes, but I didn't blink. I was afraid blinking would cause them to spill over and smear my makeup.

I have to be good. I have to do what he says.

Even if he was going to kill me anyway, I had to do what he said.

"You're not like her, though," he said. "You'll behave, won't you?"

I nodded.

"Say it out loud."

I moved my lips in the shape of the words, but no sound came out.

"I'll behave," he said. "Say it."

"I'll behave," I repeated.

He touched my cheek with the palm of his hand. "I know you will. Now, shall we run our lines again?"

CHAPTER 36

After we'd been through the scene about four times, Reed came over and cut my hands free. He wanted to get started on the blocking.

We were getting close to the final performance.

"Try swirling the wine in the glass," he said. "Like you're lost in thought."

I'd never drunk anything from a wine glass before, so it felt awkward in my hand. Apparently I was doing it wrong, because he smacked the table impatiently.

"If you're not even going to *try* —"

"I am trying!" I protested. "I've never done this before."

He took a deep breath. "I'm sorry, Willa. It must be frustrating. I have to remember . . . a director is like a coach."

"Is that what this is about for you?" I asked. "Being a director?"

"It's about creating moments," he said. "Crafting them."

"But . . . I thought making movies was about making things that people will enjoy."

He shook his head. "That's commercialism. I'm not interested in crass efforts to appeal to the lowest common denominator. I want to make something powerful. Something with impact. Something that conveys my vision absolutely — even if nobody else ever sees it. Something I can . . . *control*. So much of life is out of our control, and it just makes me feel so . . . insignificant."

"That's why you leave the people you kill out for other people to find? To be significant?"

Reed looked at me, a coldly superior gleam in his eye. "Because I know it makes their lives that much more interesting. It gives them something to aspire to."

"You mean you like the attention," I said.

He scowled. "I don't care about the attention."

I wasn't eager to draw his anger, so I sat back without replying.

"Now," he said. "Let's go through this one more time. I'll try to be more patient."

We ran the lines again. This time, when I picked up the glass to swirl it, he picked up his own and showed me how to move my wrist to keep the liquid moving inside.

When we got to the end — almost the end — he sat back. "Very good."

My back was tired from sitting up so straight, and my butt was numb from being in the chair for hours on end. Outside, the day had darkened into twilight. How many hours had passed while I was unconscious?

"I think we might be ready." He smiled at me — a smile that under any other circumstances could have been described as warm, maybe even caring.

"Ready?" I asked. "No, I need more time to —"

"Hush," he said, and just like that, the smile was gone. He got up and went to the kitchen. When he came back, he had a glass of water and two small white pills in his hand. "Here. Take these."

I stared at the little pills. "What are they?"

"Just something to help you relax. Remember, Charice is drinking the poison throughout the entire dinner. She's getting dreamier and dreamier. These won't kill you ... but they'll make it easier to stay in character. Don't worry, Willa — this is only a dress rehearsal, not the real thing."

"Is this what you gave Paige?" My voice was a pitiful little squeak.

"Yes. But you don't have to be like Paige. She chose an ugly, meaningless death. You don't have to do that. You can accept your fate and fade out beautifully, like Charice."

Without putting up a fight, he meant.

I stared at his hand. Suddenly, he grabbed my face and pinched my nostrils. When my mouth opened to gasp for air, he pushed the pills to the back of my tongue. Then he held my mouth shut.

"Swallow," he said.

I couldn't breathe. I struggled, trying to shake his hands off my face.

"Swallow, and I'll let you breathe."

So I swallowed. The pills left a bitter taste on the back of my tongue.

"Have some water," he said, handing me the cup.

I took a few sips, and he took the cup away. Then he pulled my hands back and taped them together, securing them to the chair.

"All right, Willa," he said. "Hang out for a little while and try to relax. I have to go check on something."

He left the room.

Marnie, I thought. *He's checking on Marnie.*

At first, I struggled to get free. Then, when that didn't work, I sat back and stared at the table, trying to think of a new plan.

Gradually, my breathing grew slow and steady. The room, bathed in low light from the chandelier, seemed to glow.

"Hello." Reed's voice came from behind me. My pulse picked up a little — but the glow on the room didn't diminish.

How long had he been away — twenty minutes? Thirty?

"Hi," I said. My voice sounded almost as light and pleasant as his did.

He reached back and cut my hands free. "Are you ready to get started?"

Thoughts buzzed through my brain like lazy bumblebees. I had a vague recollection that getting started wasn't the best option, but I didn't have any better ideas. "Okay."

I was rewarded with a soft smile of approval. "Good girl, Willa."

Before I knew what was happening, he had reached his arms around my neck. I felt the cool, quick touch of a chain against the skin of my throat.

"My mother's rose necklace," he said. "I guess you could call it a souvenir. I use it to remember my girls by. I had misplaced it . . . but you found it for me, didn't you? That was kind. It's very special to me."

I stared numbly ahead, not looking up at him.

He went back and sat down on the other side of the table. "Do you remember the lines?"

"I — I think so."

There was a sound behind me.

Reed jumped to his feet, as light and quick as a cat. He pointed at me. "Stay there. If you call out, I'll make you sorry."

A key was turning in the front door. Someone was coming in.

But Reed didn't walk toward the foyer. He ducked into the kitchen.

"Hello . . . ? Willa, are you home?"

It was Jonathan.

"Who's here? Why isn't the alarm on?"

I was afraid to speak. Reed had said he would make me sorry.

Jonathan came into the dining room. He whipped his head around, trying to take in the table, set for a romantic dinner, and my outfit. "Willa, what's going on? Are you drinking *wine*?"

"Call the police," I said softly. "You need to go. Reed's here."

"*Reed* is here? And you're drinking wine together? What are you talking about, the police? Is — is that a wig?"

"It's from a movie," I said.

Jonathan stared at me — and then his energy shifted.

He understood.

I had a feeling like a fog was lifting. Emotions came through the fog, sharp needles of fear. "Be careful!" I hissed. "He knows you're here!"

Jonathan turned to look around, but it was too late. There was a flash of movement behind him.

"Watch out!" I cried.

As Jonathan pivoted in place, Reed raised a heavy ceramic figurine and brought it down on his head.

Jonathan dropped to the ground.

Reed stood over him, panting heavily. Then he looked at me, his eyes rimmed with red and his nostrils flared. *"I told you to be quiet."*

I couldn't think of a reply. I'd snapped out of the dreamy haze into a state of stark terror.

Moving quickly, Reed taped my arms and legs to the chair and then stuck another piece of tape over my mouth, muttering about how he would have to fix my makeup later. Then he grabbed Jonathan by the arms and dragged him out of sight.

I stared, petrified, as my stepfather's feet vanished around the corner. A minute later, the dragging sound stopped, replaced by a new sound: running water.

Reed was filling the bathtub in the downstairs bathroom.

Oh, God. He was going to drown Jonathan. I got an image in my head of my mother arriving home to find both her husband and her daughter dead. And I couldn't do a thing about it. I hung my head as hopelessness descended over me.

In defeat, I raised my eyes to look around the dining room. *This is what the room where I will die looks like on the night that I will die.*

Suddenly, everything in my messed-up life seemed precious and amazing, shining and brilliant. I wept in my heart that I'd never have the chance to say good-bye to my mother.

And I'd never have another chance to talk to Wyatt.

I wondered what Paige had been thinking as she fought for her life, struggling to surface, only to be cruelly pushed back under. Who was she fighting for? Because I understood on a fundamental level that any will I had left would have to be drawn from the love I felt for other people — for my mom. For Wyatt.

If I found the strength to resist, it would be for their sake. Fighting for them suddenly seemed more important than fighting for myself.

Something cold and wet brushed against my face, and I opened my eyes.

A rose petal lay on my plate.

It was a sign from Paige. She was here.

My eyes, fluttering around the room, landed on the sideboard.

The knives. If I could get to them, somehow . . .

That's crazy, Willa. He'll torture you.

Yeah, maybe so, but . . . what was the alternative, to do exactly what he wanted me to do? Just *let* him kill me?

Suddenly, I felt a fire inside me. It was a familiar sensation — and my automatic response was to push it back, suppress it. Not let it affect me.

But then, for the briefest moment, I tried not suppressing it.

I let myself feel the true horror and shock of what was happening. I let myself envision Reed's cold eyes staring across the table at me. The sound of his voice commanding me to play a willing part in my own murder.

The fire spread. First, it spread to my heart. Then to my head. Then through the rest of me.

And I found that I was sitting there, practically panting.

With rage.

How dare he? I thought. *How dare he do this to people?*

The tub was still running. If Reed was in the bathroom, he wouldn't be able to hear me moving.

He'd done a much shabbier job taping my wrists together this time, and with only a small amount of concentrated effort, I was able to get my hands free. Then I leaned over and untaped my legs. I got to the sideboard, pulled opened the center drawer, and shoved the lid off the flat box.

The light from the candles flickered off the knife blade.

I grabbed it and slid the drawer shut.

From the bathroom came a grunt of effort, and then a loud splash.

I'd need to surprise him, catch him off guard. So I slipped back in my seat, setting the knife under the right side of my skirt. Then I quickly leaned over and bound my legs back to the chair, reached my hands behind me, and rewrapped my wrists with the tape.

About two seconds after I finished, Reed walked in, his tuxedo wet from the bathtub. He looked winded and upset.

"What are you looking at?" he snarled. I shifted my gaze to my plate.

He was a hundred times more dangerous now because things were going badly.

But I could be dangerous, too.

He bent over and ripped the tape from my legs, then tore the piece off my wrists and mouth, making me wince as the adhesive pulled at my skin.

"What are you doing to Jonathan?" I asked. "Did you kill him?"

Reed grunted. "It's not your concern."

"I thought you said he was like family to you."

He ignored me. "Let's get started. I'm tired of waiting."

"Is my lipstick okay?" I asked.

"You're stalling, Willa. It won't help." He gave me an exasperated look, then turned for the makeup kit. "But I might as well —"

His back was toward me.

GO. GO. GO.

I reached under my skirt and grabbed the knife. Then I propelled myself out of the chair, toward Reed's back.

He heard me and began to turn around.

But I was already on him. I plunged the knife into his side. He gasped and let out a primal roar.

I gave him a hard shove, and he tumbled backward. Then I ran out of the room, toward the front door. All I had to do was make it to the road and pray somebody was driving by — and that they'd be willing to stop.

What I hadn't counted on was that, over the course of the evening, my legs had fallen asleep. As I moved, blood rushed back through the veins, essentially turning my legs into unusable stumps. Even though Reed was injured, I wouldn't be able to outrun him all the way to the gate. I staggered across the foyer, threw the door open, and screamed at the top of my lungs as I crumpled onto the porch.

Then I started crawling, determined to drag myself to the road if I had to.

But Reed grabbed me by the back of my dress and pulled me back inside the house. He slammed the door closed, struggling to get me into a choke hold with his left arm. In his right hand, he held the bloody knife.

He was breathless with fury. *"Huge . . . mistake . . . Willa . . ."*

The feeling was coming back into my legs now. I kicked backward and threw him off balance. He tried to grab me by the hair, but only succeeded in pulling the wig off my head. I raced for the stairs, scrabbling up on all fours. He was right behind me. I made it to the top barely two steps ahead of him. I could lock myself in Jonathan's office and climb out the window again. . . .

I ran to the end of the hall and tried to shove the door open.

There was a low, gurgling laugh from behind me.

"Yeah, it's locked," Reed said. "I locked it. I locked them all, actually."

I turned to face him. He hadn't bothered to follow me down the hall. He stood at the top of the stairs. Blood ran from the wound in his side, staining his white shirt ruby red.

"You think you're clever, don't you?" he said. "But you've got nowhere to go, sister."

I glanced at the banister. How far was the drop to the first floor?

"Go ahead," he said. "Break your legs. See if I care."

Oh, God.

He stood rooted smugly in place, clutching the knife as if he knew a thing or two about knives. "You're going to pay for this, Willa. Your poor mama's going to cry her eyes out when she sees you."

I was distracted momentarily by something else glinting in the light, besides the knife blade . . .

Water.

A trail of wet footprints on the floor, between Reed and myself.

Paige?

"Stay back," I said. "I'm warning you."

He laughed flatly. "Big, tough Willa. Haven't you noticed that I keep winning? Didn't I tell you that I *always* win?"

I couldn't let him corner me. I was still woozy from the pills and not moving very fast, but I'd rather be a moving target than a sitting duck. He was hurt, too.

I drew in a breath and charged toward him. As I got closer, I ducked and flattened myself against the wall.

But I didn't make it. He used his whole body to shove me to the ground. I fell back and hit my head on the sharp edge of the baseboard, so hard I saw stars. Then I scooted as far away as I could, which wasn't very far.

Reed loomed above me, holding the knife. "Want to know what I'm going to cut first?"

On the ceiling above him, black words bubbled into existence.

Just three short words:

"Wait, Reed . . . please." I held my hands up in surrender. "I just have one question."

He smirked. "What?"

I took a deep breath. "Do you believe in ghosts?"

His smirk turned to a confused sneer. "Do I —"

There was an explosion of blue light between us.

Reed cried out in surprise, giving me a moment to dash out of his reach. I turned back and looked at him —

At him, and at Paige.

Her ghost stood in the center of the hallway, a girl made of light.

Reed stared up at her in terror. "What . . . *what are you?*"

Paige looked over at me. In her gaze I saw sympathy, understanding, sorrow . . . but also anger. Resolve. Strength.

She turned back to Reed, who was basically reduced to blubbering.

"What is this?" he asked. "What's going on?"

Paige smiled and took a step toward him. She spoke in a voice of hollow whispers. *"This is the kind of dream you don't wake up from, Henry."*

When he tried to move out of her way, his foot landed on one of the wet footprints and slipped.

He tumbled backward down the stairs.

And then there was stillness.

CHAPTER 37

I crawled to the banister and saw Reed lying unconscious —
maybe dead — on the floor of the foyer below.

I glanced up at Paige.

She gave me a look of satisfaction . . . but also full of regret
and wistfulness.

And then she disappeared.

I raced down the stairs, past Reed's body, and into the guest
bathroom.

The faucet was still running. The bathwater was pink with
blood from Jonathan's wounded head. The water level had just
reached his mouth. I shut the water off and then hauled him
over the edge so he was lying down on the floor. I turned his head
to the side, and a bunch of water streamed out of his mouth. But
he still didn't wake up.

Oh, God, what if he *never* woke up?

I could *not* sit there and watch him not breathe and not open
his eyes and not be alive anymore.

It would break everything that was left of me.

"No, no, no," I said. "No, you are NOT going to die tonight!"

Desperately, I racked my memory for the first aid I'd learned back in ninth grade. I wrestled him into a sitting position and drew my balled-up fists into the soft space beneath the center of his ribs. As I did it, I felt emotions rush through me, raw and unprocessed, and for a moment I closed my eyes and went back to that morning at the YMCA trying to save my father.

Live, I remembered thinking. *Live, Dad. Live.*

Now I thought, *Live, Jonathan.*

Please live.

Suddenly, his body began to convulse with a series of racking coughs. I ran out of strength to hold on to him, so I laid him down on his side and watched and waited as he came back to life.

He drew in a huge gasp of air, and his eyelids blinked heavily.

"Willa," he croaked.

I was too overcome with relief even to speak.

"Are you all right?" he asked. "You're bleeding."

"So are you."

He started looking around frantically. "Where is he? We need to get out —"

I was already moving toward the door. "I'll be right back. I have to get help."

"Where are you going?" he asked, trying to sit up.

"It's okay. Don't move. Wait here."

I got up and walked over to where Reed lay in the foyer. I thought about checking for a pulse, but decided that could wait.

I kicked the knife so it slid under the heavy cabinet by the door and went to the dining room for the roll of tape Reed had used on me all night.

I hesitated before grabbing his hands — what if my touch woke him? What if he was only dazed?

I had a feeling that, if he sprang to life, he would have more than enough fight left to finish me off.

"Is he . . . dead?"

I jumped at the sound of Jonathan's voice. He was slowly staggering toward us.

"I don't know," I said, and my whole body began to tremble. I honestly didn't know whether to hope the answer was yes or no.

"Be careful," he said. "Here . . . I'll sit on him. Start with his feet, okay?"

I nodded as Jonathan painfully lowered himself onto Reed's chest.

I wound the tape around his ankles about fifty times.

"Now his hands," I said.

"We need to call 9-1-1," Jonathan said.

"This first," I said. "Here, watch out."

Jonathan stiffly climbed off Reed, and together we flipped him over. Jonathan grabbed his wrists and held them tight while I circled them with the tape.

"Hold him down," I said. "I guess I'll see if he's alive."

I lay my two fingers flat against his neck, under his right ear. I couldn't shake the feeling that he was going to jump up and attack me.

294

But he didn't.

"Is there a pulse?" Jonathan asked.

I felt the faint, slow beat of Reed's blood under my fingers, and my entire body went cold.

"Yeah," I whispered. I wanted to cry, but I couldn't. My eyes felt swollen and painful.

"My phone's ruined," Jonathan said, taking it out of his sopping-wet pocket. "Do you have yours?"

"No," I said. "Reed took it. And the landline is dead. I'll go outside and flag down a car in a minute, but first . . . I need the code to get into the garage."

"Wait . . . are you okay to walk?" he asked.

I nodded, even though it wasn't totally true. "What's the code?"

"It's four fours. Why?"

I didn't answer. I left the front door open and staggered over to the garage. Every step hurt, and my head ached from being slammed into the wall. Lights seemed surrounded by halos, and I saw two of everything.

But I managed to type in 4-4-4-4, and the door opened with a rumble. I flipped on the lights and walked over to the corner, where I'd seen the puddle of water that morning.

There was a door in the side wall, behind an old bike. It wasn't even disguised — it just looked like it hadn't been used in eons.

The chauffeur's quarters. That's where he'd been keeping them, rehearsing with them. Preparing them for their deaths. He had easy access, since he could come and go into and out of the garage as much as he pleased. And it was far enough from the house that no one would hear the girls crying and screaming for help.

I shoved the bike away and pulled the door open.

Stairs.

From the bottom of the stairs came a soft, muffled sound.

"Willa?" Jonathan stood, slightly swaying, in the open garage door. "What are you doing?"

"Marnie?" I called.

The muffled sound stopped, and turned into a muted shriek.

"We're getting help," I said. "Sorry I can't come down for you right this second, I . . ."

I was so dizzy I could hardly walk. Jonathan slumped against the garage wall like he might collapse at any moment.

"Who's down there?" he asked.

"His next victim," I said. "Besides me, I mean. Her name is Marnie."

The devastated look that came over Jonathan's face just about broke my heart.

"Could you go down and tell her she's safe?" I said. "I'm going to get help."

He nodded and slowly began to descend the steps while I shuffled to the gate. When I pulled it open, I saw headlights approaching from around the corner. They blurred in my vision until they were four bright diamonds of light.

I raised my arms and stepped out into the middle of the street, thinking, *Wouldn't it be just my luck to survive all that and then get run over by some loser checking his text messages?*

But the car slowed as it neared me, and then stopped. The driver's side door opened, and after a few seconds, a woman about my mom's age got out.

"Could you please — Hey, are you all right?" she asked. "Good God, what happened?"

"Please," I said. "Call 9-1-1."

Then I sat down in the middle of the street and passed out.

"Her name is Willa. She's my stepdaughter. We were attacked in our house by . . . an intruder." I heard Jonathan speaking before I forced my eyes open. I was propped up in his arms, on the ground, just inside the gate. He glanced down at me and relief crossed his face. "Hey, try to stay awake, all right?"

"All right," I said. "I'm okay. I think I was just overwhelmed."

Jonathan managed a weak smile. "You're well within your rights on that count. The police are coming. And an ambulance."

"I don't need an ambulance," I said.

"Nice try," he said. "You're bleeding from the head. And you're woozy. Your eyes are bloodshot. Did he give you something?"

I thought of the white pills and nodded.

"Do you know what it was?"

I shook my head. Somebody had covered me with a jacket. "What about you?" I asked. "He hit you, too. And you almost drowned."

"Don't worry about me. I'm all right. My mother always said I have a thick skull."

By now there was a small crowd of people around us. And

there were a bunch of people in the garage, too — they must have been helping Marnie.

Sirens wailed in the distance. Somewhere in the ravine, a pack of coyotes started howling along with them.

Jonathan kept glancing up at the people around us, and then back down at me. "Are you *really* okay? Did he hurt you? I can't believe . . . all this time, it was . . . Reed. In our house. In our garage."

I blinked back my tears. I couldn't believe it, either.

Jonathan ran his hand over my hair in an awkward, reassuring gesture. "Your mom's on her way back. She's going straight to the hospital. Willa, I'm so sorry you had to go through that."

At the thought of seeing my mother and being wrapped in her arms, I couldn't hold back my tears any longer. All of the emotions I'd tried to ignore all night — fear, humiliation, anger — burst forth in a tidal wave. I started to cry huge, ugly-cry sobs.

Jonathan hugged me closer, rocking back and forth. "It's okay," he said. "We're safe now, Willa. You saved us."

CHAPTER 38

When my mother got to the hospital, she came barreling into the room. But she wasn't hysterical, as I had expected her to be. She was strangely calm as she spoke to the doctors and nurses and police. She seemed so strong.

She hugged me and kissed my forehead and cheeks about a thousand times, and then she took hold of my hand and didn't let go.

I had a concussion and a cracked rib and we were waiting for the results of my blood tests, since nobody knew exactly what was in the little pills Reed gave me. But I was feeling okay — all things considered.

Hey, I wasn't dead — that was something, right?

After the initial flurry of activity, the room was deserted, just me and Mom.

"Don't you want to go see Jonathan?" I asked. "I'll be okay for a few minutes."

"He's fine," she said. "I talked to him before."

"But maybe you should —"

"Willa," she said softly. "He's worried about you. He wants me to stay here. I'm not leaving you, sweetie. Not tonight."

And she didn't. When I woke up in the morning, she was curled up in the faux-leather visitor's chair, her hand still wrapped around mine. She told me the doctor had been by to let her know the white pills Reed had given me were sedatives, designed to make me sleepy and weak. They would be completely out of my system within a few days.

And Reed was in police custody. He would live, but he might be paralyzed. I nodded, trying to take everything in.

I thought about the house, and wondered if Paige's ghost was gone now. If she was at peace. I hoped she was.

I was sitting up and having some orange juice when a knock came on the door. Mom and I looked up and saw Wyatt Sheppard standing there.

"How did you get past security?" Mom asked, a little alarmed.

Wyatt turned bright red.

"It's cool, Mom," I said. "He has connections. This is my friend Wyatt."

This explanation didn't entirely satisfy my mother, but she nodded anyway and shook his hand. Then she stood up and kissed me on the cheek. "I'll go check on Jonathan."

When she was gone, Wyatt took a step into the room. I sat up straighter, my pulse speeding up — a fact made embarrassingly obvious by the beeping monitor next to my hospital bed.

"I . . ." he said softly. "I don't know what to say."

"Wow," I said. "That's a first."

He didn't even come close to laughing. His lips were turned down at the corners. Not a trace of his usual smirk. And his voice was low and strained. "Did he hurt you?"

"Not badly," I said. "I mean, I don't want to go through it again, but I'll live."

"Willa," he said. "Don't talk to me that way."

I looked at him in surprise. "What way?"

"Like this isn't serious. I — I feel very serious about this. About you." He took a deep breath. "When I heard what happened, I felt like . . . like I'd been ripped in half. I wanted to find that guy and tear his head off."

"There's no need for that now," I said, managing a little smile in spite of the stinging tears in my eyes. "He's going to jail. Forever."

Suddenly, I remembered thinking of Wyatt in what I'd feared would be my last moments.

"What about you?" I asked as Wyatt took a step closer to my bed. "You got arrested, right? What happened?"

Sinking into Mom's vacated chair, he breathed into his hands and shook his head, like he didn't know where to begin. He told me the story of the police showing up at his house, how he'd been taken to the station and fingerprinted, and then how his dad had stepped in and called in a mess of favors to keep Wyatt from being charged with trespassing — or worse.

So Wyatt wasn't going to jail. He was, however, grounded. He didn't even ask his parents how long the grounding would last. He figured it would let up around graduation.

But given the circumstances, his parents had allowed him this one trip to the hospital.

"Given what circumstances?" I asked.

"Given that I . . . I begged," he said. "I told them that my best friend was almost murdered by a serial killer, and if they didn't let me come see you —" His voice broke, and he looked toward the bright window, blinking furiously.

"Stop," I said. "It's okay."

My best friend, he'd said.

"I'm glad you came," I said. "I wanted to see you."

And Wyatt reached over carefully and put his warm hand on top of mine. I laced my fingers through his and we sat there like that until Mom came back.

I was discharged from the hospital two days later, but the house was still an active crime scene, so we couldn't go back yet. Jonathan booked a suite in a hotel and started making plans to sell the house. As far as he and Mom were concerned, we couldn't be rid of it fast enough.

My feelings were a little more complicated.

So much bad happened there, I wrote in my journal. *But it wasn't the house's fault. In a way it seems like the house was a victim, too. Maybe it hated its own role. Maybe the house is what gave Paige the strength to resist. Maybe somehow the spirit of Diana Del Mar was fighting alongside me the whole time I was fighting back.*

Or maybe I'm

I stopped and held the pen away from the paper before I could write the word *crazy*.

I didn't think that anymore, so it was time to stop saying it.

Over the following week, we talked to the police endlessly. I explained in as much detail as I could without including any ghosty parts. Luckily, the story still made sense — how I'd started to get a weird feeling about Reed that day. How I found Diana's workroom and recognized the name of the movie. How Reed and I fought our way to the top of the stairs, and then he slipped in a puddle of his own blood and fell. Everything checked out, and the police didn't seem suspicious.

Besides, I was a pretty decent teller of half truths at this point in my life.

We were bombarded with requests for interviews and quotes. Some producer friend of Jonathan's even wanted to buy the movie rights. But Mom took charge and deflected them all. She talked to the lawyers, the media, even Jonathan's agents. She handled it all like it was second nature to her. Jonathan was pretty impressed.

I, personally, would never have expected anything less.

Reporters dug into Reed's past and cobbled together a portrait of a serial killer — smooth, confident, charming, but alienated. Bad-tempered, with a record of lashing out in school. The victim of an inferiority complex made worse by the loss of his parents and his time with a grandfather who was described by their neighbors as "mean as a snake."

It was so strange to try to remember how I felt about Reed back before I learned what he really was.

I could recall the slow gentleness of his manner, his soft smile, his placid eyes. It was like he'd been two people. Himself, and not himself. And what would have happened if I'd never found out the truth? We might have gone on taking walks and having casual, flirtatious encounters in the kitchen. Sneaking kisses . . . Part of me even wondered if, without the Bernadette Middleton debacle, he never would have looked at me as a potential victim.

When you thought about it that way, I guess you could say Marnie kind of did me a favor.

I'd have to face Reed again at the trial. I can't say I was in love with the idea, but I wasn't scared.

It takes a lot to scare me, I've discovered.

CHAPTER 39

When I went back to school two weeks later, everyone on campus seemed to regard me like a stolen relic from some ancient tomb — worth catching a glimpse of, but not worth venturing too near.

Marnie practically glowed from all the attention, though from time to time I caught phantomlike flashes of fear in her eyes. She and I were bound by something deep, something I could read in her expression whenever she looked at me. I had saved her life. But I could tell that she didn't want to talk to me, or be near me, or generally have anything at all to do with me.

Which was fine — I was done judging Marnie. Everyone copes in their own way. Not just with almost being murdered, but with being alive. With having parents who die, or ignore you. Maybe someday she'd learn that the truth, however uncomfortable it may be, is worth looking for.

Or maybe she wouldn't.

Wyatt stayed by my side every possible moment — before school, during lunch, and after school, when he was allowed to drop me off at the hotel before heading back to another evening of being grounded.

At the end of my first week back, the police finally gave us the all clear to pack up our things. Jonathan hired a professional moving service to take care of it all. By Sunday afternoon, there would be no trace of us left in the grand old mansion.

When I climbed into Wyatt's car on Friday afternoon, I turned to him. "Can you be late getting home?"

"Not a chance," he said, then thought for a second and added, "How late?"

"Like twenty minutes?"

He shrugged. "What are they going to do — ground me until I graduate from college?"

"Great," I said, fastening my seat belt. "Take me to Sunbird Lane, please."

I have to admit, I kind of loved making that *Sploh!* expression appear on his face.

Before he could protest, I repeated myself. "Twenty-one-twenty-one Sunbird Lane? Do you need directions?"

He frowned, pulling out onto Crescent Heights and turning right toward the canyon. "Does your mother know you're going back there?"

The skin on my palms began to prickle. "If I say no, will you still take me?"

"Of course," he said.

A happy tremor went through me, which was a nice distraction from the anxiety starting to build in my stomach at the thought of being back on the property. Sentimental journal ramblings aside, this was the house where I was tormented and almost psycho-killed by a psycho killer.

I laughed nervously, twisting a lock of hair around my finger.

"What?" Wyatt asked.

"I was just thinking . . . like, the *least* creepy thing about this house is that it's haunted."

He slowed the car. "Willa, are you sure —"

"I'm sure," I said. "Please keep driving."

When we got to the house, there were a few photographers lingering around. But they kept their distance as Wyatt punched the gate code and drove inside.

One of them shouted, "Are you Willa?"

And Wyatt yelled back, "No, she's Kate Middleton's cousin Bernadette!"

Stepping into the foyer wasn't as bad as I thought it would be. All the blood was gone, of course. The dining room had been neatly put back together, as if nothing had ever happened in there. There were no huge sheets of plastic or toolboxes full of makeup. No props from the scene that was supposed to end with my death.

I took a long, shuddering breath and stared up at the second floor.

"You all right?" Wyatt asked softly.

"It feels so sad," I said. "The house feels so lonely."

"Don't be lonely," he said. "I'm here."

But that wasn't quite what I meant. I meant that the house herself — of course it was a she — was lonely. Melancholy, like she'd been abandoned.

Don't worry, I told her in my head. *Some weird person is going to buy you and move in and invite tons of people over so they can show off that they live in a house where a serial killer carried out his psycho schemes. Honestly, the person will probably be a jerk, but you won't know any better. You're just a house.*

You'll be fine.

We walked in silence up to my room, and my pulse picked up at the sight of my open bathroom door — now *there* was a room I never needed to set foot into again.

"What exactly are we doing here?" Wyatt asked. He spoke in hushed library tones.

"I'll explain in a minute," I said, going into my closet. I reached down, behind the half-empty laundry basket, and pulled out the pink shoe box. I looked at Wyatt. "Fancy a trip to the backyard?"

He shrugged.

We walked past the pool, which was beginning to look a little green from the weeks of neglect — it almost seemed to me like the pool was the house's face, and she felt sick about what had happened.

I walked over to where the shovel still stood leaning against the trunk of a lemon tree, a few feet from my initial unsuccessful digging efforts.

It dawned on Wyatt, then, why we were there — to finally follow Leyta Fitzgeorge's instructions and bury the shoe box.

"I have to do this before we leave," I said. "This stuff belongs here."

"What if somebody digs it up?" he asked.

"They won't," I said, picking up the shovel and starting to dig. In the shady afternoon, it was much easier. And when I started to get winded, Wyatt took the shovel and dug the rest.

We knelt on the ground next to the hole and gently lowered in the box. It felt like burying more than a book and a couple pieces of jewelry (and a bag of salt). It felt weirdly like we were burying Paige, too. And maybe all the other restless spirits who'd swarmed around me for years. And the rest of the Hollywood Killer's victims.

I wished I could bury the rose necklace, too. But I had to content myself with the idea that, after the trial, it would be as good as buried in the police evidence storage. It didn't really matter.

I knew in my heart that Paige was at peace.

Maybe she was hanging out with my dad and they were talking about how aggravating I could be.

Wyatt cleared his throat, and our eyes met.

"Are you going to say something?" he asked.

"I'm not sure," I said. "It sort of feels like I shouldn't, actually."

He nodded, then stood up and got the shovel. I sat and watched the dirt cover the pink surface of the cardboard until it was gone. Then, when the hole was level with the ground again, Wyatt patted the sandy soil smooth and tossed the extra into the ravine.

"And that's that," he said, helping me to my feet.

I carried the shovel back up to the patio but didn't bother taking it into the garage — I left it leaning against the back wall of the guesthouse, next to the overturned bucket that had helped save my life. I didn't want the movers packing it and taking it with us.

I glanced at my phone. I'd texted Mom to say Wyatt and I were stopping for a quick coffee, but somehow we'd been at the house for almost an hour. Wyatt was way later than I'd told him he would be.

"Ready to go?" I asked. "I'm afraid I'll get you in trouble."

"Don't worry about that," he said. "Honestly, if you asked me to rob a bank with you, my dad would probably be cool with it. He's a little in awe of you."

"And of you, too, right?"

He looked taken aback. "What did I do?"

"You did . . . a lot."

"Name something specific," he scoffed.

"Things don't have to be specific to be important," I said. "You were part of everything."

We were standing by the back rail, a few yards away from the pool, looking down at the ravine and the city beyond it.

I felt a chill of loss. I'd found a piece of myself in this house, and now, leaving it, I felt as if I was leaving a piece of myself behind. This would be my last chance to be there. To say good-bye.

"Want to sit for a couple of minutes?" Wyatt asked.

I nodded, my eyes suddenly full of tears.

I sat on one of the wicker love seats and waited for Wyatt to sit in the chair across from me.

But he didn't.

He sat down right next to me and reached for my hand.

"Willa . . ." he said softly.

"What?" I asked.

"You almost *died*," he said, and on the last word, his voice collapsed into itself.

"That's what people keep telling me."

He shook his head in frustration. "Before everything happened, I'd been planning to tell you something. And now I don't know when I should tell you. Or if I should. Ever."

I looked up and watched a pinprick of an airplane making its way over the city, toward the airport. "You should," I said.

As I waited for him to speak, I felt like different parts of me had turned into delicate silk kites that were all floating off in different directions. Weightless.

But instead of answering, Wyatt leaned forward, took my face in his hands, and kissed me softly.

All the pieces of me came back together in a warm, happy rush.

My heart raced, and my skin felt awake under his touch.

Proof that I'm still alive, I thought.

Then we looked at each other. I could have stared into his soft, wry brown eyes for a hundred years.

"I just didn't know there were people like you," he whispered.

The weird thing is, I didn't know there were people like me, either.

I'd thought I was a girl who didn't belong anywhere. And now, even though I was the same person, I wasn't that girl anymore. I felt like I belonged — like I had the *right* to belong — anywhere I went.

"Wyatt," I whispered back. "Are you *sure* you want to do this?"

"Yes," he said, without so much as a millisecond of hesitation.

"The only thing is" — I pulled back — "I'm kind of broken."

Wyatt's hand tightened around mine. "I don't think you're broken. I like you just the way you are."

My face flushed, and I leaned into his chest.

"No," he said, and I could feel the *thump-thump-thump* of his heart under his crisp white school shirt. "No, I . . . I *love* you just the way you are."

I nodded, even though he hadn't asked me anything. "Me, too," I said. "I love you the way you are, too."

I thought about how hard it had been for me, in the beginning, to be around someone who wouldn't settle for a thin veneer of lies — someone who wanted either the real me or nothing at all. And as my hand traced a line down his sleeve, I thought about how I could never again settle for anyone who didn't push me to tell the truth. To face the truth. To live it.

Even when it hurt.

The breeze picked up, and Wyatt wrapped his arm around me. Our bodies fit together like we'd been designed to sit leaning into one another. Missing pieces of a puzzle, two halves of a clue in a mystery.

I rested my head on his shoulder and closed my eyes, and I felt the soft canyon wind weave through my hair.

ACKNOWLEDGMENTS

With every Acknowledgments I write (and every annual soul-searching about how to actually spell "Acknowledgments"), I am again reminded that being an author is a journey, not a destination. And it's a journey that one can't take alone. So while the people in my life might be getting sick of being thanked by me, I'm just going to keep doing it. (At least until the megalomania sets in.)

Thank you to my husband and my daughter for being the absolute best and most important things that ever happened to me. To my little sister, Ali, for being wonderful. And much love to Dad, Mom, Helen, Juli, George, Duygu, Kevin, Jillian, Robert, Rebekah, Zack, Onur Ata, Jeff, Vicky, and Aunt B.

Thank you to Chelsea DeVincent and the rest of the Soapboxies, who are like a second family to me. And to our amazing extended circle of friends. And to those rowdy lads.

Thank you to Matthew Elblonk (working with you just gets weirder and funnier every year), and to everyone at DeFiore and Company, who I have to assume spend a lot of time and energy keeping Matt in line. And thank you to Holly

Chen and Maddie Elblonk, because from what I have been hearing for years on end, you are both fantastic, and it's time you got your names in a book.

Thank you to my editor, Aimee Friedman, for brutally offing, like, twelve invasive minor characters and otherwise providing such consistently awesome editorial support and input. And making it fun. AND pretending I don't occasionally make one wish to bash one's head against one's desk.

Thank you to the team at Scholastic: David Levithan, Charisse Meloto, Stephanie Smith, Bess Braswell, Emily Morrow, Emily Heddleson, Antonio Gonzalez, Yaffa Jaskoll, Elizabeth Krych, Alix Inchausti, Jody Revenson, Jennifer Ung, Rachel Schwartz, and Larry Decker. You guys are amazing.

Thank you and thank you and thank you to the parents, booksellers, bloggers, teachers, administrators, librarians, and media specialists who make it possible for people to read my books.

And lastly, thank you to my incredible readers. You are, as individuals as well as collectively, the cat's pajamas.

ABOUT THE AUTHOR

Katie Alender is the acclaimed author of several novels for young adults, including *Bad Girls Don't Die*; *From Bad to Cursed*; and *Marie Antoinette, Serial Killer*. A graduate of the Florida State University Film School, Katie now lives in Los Angeles with her husband and their daughter. She enjoys reading, sewing, and watching movies. To find out more about Katie, visit katiealender.com.